Karen Woods was born and raised in Manchester, where she still lives. Karen left school without any formal qualifications and obtained her inspiration from attending an adult literacy course. Since then she's written twenty novels as well as adapting some of them for the stage. Karen works in education and is passionate about introducing people of all ages to the power of storytelling.

TEASE

KAREN WOODS

Harper
North

HarperNorth
111 Piccadilly,
Manchester, M1 2HY

A division of
HarperCollins*Publishers*
1 London Bridge Street
London SE1 9GF

www.harpercollins.co.uk

HarperCollins*Publishers*
1st Floor, Watermarque Building, Ringsend Road
Dublin 4, Ireland

First published by HarperNorth in 2022

1 3 5 7 9 10 8 6 4 2

Copyright © Karen Woods 2022

Karen Woods asserts the moral right to
be identified as the author of this work

A catalogue record for this book
is available from the British Library

ISBN: 978-0-00-846172-0

MIX
Paper from
responsible sources
FSC™ C007454

This book is produced from independently certified FSC™ paper
to ensure responsible forest management.

For more information visit: www.harpercollins.co.uk/green

For my brother, Darren Woods (Woody)
and in memory of my son, Dale.

Woody, my brother, my friend, my angel.
Miss you forever our kid.

Dale, good night God bless my son.

Prologue

Blinded by the lights, the girl stood in the glare – unable to see who was out there, who was watching. But she could sense – almost smell – their hunger and anticipation. They wanted her and, as the music began to pulse, they were going to get her.

The girl began to move, to let the music flow through her. And as she stepped out to dance, perhaps it was for the best that she didn't know it would be the last time.

Chapter One

'Oh, Mother, give it a bleeding rest, will you? I've heard it all before and my mind is made up. Get off my case and leave me alone, for Christ's sake; sit down and relax.' Karla Bradshaw stood looking at her reflection in the oval mirror on the wall and twirled her long chestnut-brown hair around her index finger as she studied her make-up. Her mother was always going on about her choice of men. 'He's married, and so what? Tell me something I don't already know. For crying out loud, wind your neck in and breathe, woman. You're going to give yourself a heart attack if you carry on shouting like this.'

Mary Bradshaw had told her daughter, time and time again, about the married man she was messing about with, and she hated that Karla never listened to a word she said. It scared her, made her blood boil, but her words always fell on deaf ears. Mary had to make sure she was being heard loud and clear this time, before the shit hit the fan. She coughed to clear her throat as she rested her clenched fist

1

against her waist. 'It will end in tears. Mark my words, young lady, you'll be crying again and wishing you'd never laid eyes on that lying, conniving bastard. You're probably not the only one he's sleeping with, either. Men like him have no shame. Any hole and they will fill it. Trust me, I know. I've met his sort a hundred times before.'

Karla snapped, her words fired out like bullets from a loaded gun. 'For once, Mother, can't you be happy for me? Jordan loves me and I love him, so take a pill and relax. You always put doom and gloom into any relationship I have. Nobody will ever be good enough for me in your eyes. Just let it lie. It's none of your damn business.'

Mary scowled and gritted her teeth tightly. She'd knock her bleeding block off if her daughter thought she could keep talking to her like this. Street talk it was, common as muck. It was as bad as the yobs she heard when she was walking past the shops on the estate. Mary Bradshaw was as hard as nails, but she prided herself on her standards. This was a woman who'd had to fight for everything in her life, and being weak was never an option for her. If you fell down, you picked yourself back up and put a smile on your face. Never show failure, never admit you're weak – that was her motto. A single parent, working two jobs and never with money to spare to make the changes she wanted in her life, she had lived from hand to mouth most of the time, not a pot to piss in. But she always had hope. She was down at the bingo hall whenever she had a few pounds left at the end of the week, hoping her luck would change. But so far, it never had.

Mary studied Karla and edged closer to her, inhaling her sweet perfume, the scent of lies and deceit sprayed all over her. It was a present from her daughter's lover, she knew that much. One of many gifts buying her affection, and more. Karla was beautiful, with enchanting blue eyes and, yes, she had a great rack on her, Mary had to give her that. But she knew looking like she did could lead her daughter into trouble. Mary pointed her finger at her now, making sure Karla heard every word she had to say. 'Do I have to remind you about the last man you told me you loved?' She raised her eyebrows, her head tilted to the side slightly, her nose crinkled. 'He left you barefoot and pregnant at fifteen, and it was me who had to pick up the bastard pieces when it all fell apart. Not anybody else.' Her eyes were steely as she continued, 'Imagine if I wasn't around to look after your Elsa. Your life would have been in tatters by now, messed up. I'm the one who was there when that baby was crying all night long, not anybody else. Where was her father then, eh? The one you told me loved you and would always be in your life? Yeah, don't waste your breath, because we both know the answer.'

Karla looked her mother straight in the eye. This was a low blow. 'Do you have to bring the past up, Mother? Elsa is eighteen now – we've raised her to adulthood without her needing to know. There's a reason why we decided Elsa shouldn't know her dad, a reason why it says "father unknown" on her birth certificate, a reason why I thought we agreed never to mention his name under this roof. I got through it, didn't I? I made a mistake, yes, but come on, you've not exactly got a clean slate, have you?'

Mary could feel her temper was pumping. She'd done what she had to do when her daughter was growing up and she wasn't proud of some things, but that was then and this was now. She was older and wiser. Lessons learned. Maybe Karla reminded Mary of herself in her glory days – but it didn't mean she wanted her daughter repeating her own mistakes. You could tell Mary had been a stunner in her day. Her dark-raven hair was now filled with silver threads and, while her eyes looked tired, there was a strength in them – a strength you only got by going through hell and walking out the other side. Mary snapped. 'Don't you bleeding dare compare my life to yours. I wasn't a gold-digger like you are. I didn't sleep with married men, for a start. As soon as a bloke flashes the cash, your knickers are down and you're on your back. Have some respect for yourself, woman, even if you haven't got any for me.'

Karla placed her hands on her hips. 'Lovely words, Mother. How can you talk about your own daughter like that? What I'm doing is called "living". You might want to try it yourself and get off my back. I'm taking every chance I get, just like everyone else who has any sense.' She held her head to the side, her voice cocky, though she knew she was dicing with death. 'What, should I sit in this front room every night knitting a jumper or something? Or maybe I should become a coach potato, watching the soaps on TV, watching everybody else's lives, like you do. You need to concentrate on your own shit instead of mine. You've got fuck all else to do all day except gossip about other people's business.'

Mary let out a laboured breath. She had to calm down, otherwise she'd lose the plot. 'You should be more careful about the company you keep, that's all I'm saying. Jordan

Maylett is a womaniser, and you know that without me
telling you. You know the rumours, just like everyone
around here does. So, don't you dare try and tell me the
man is a keeper. He's a wanker. A dirty, no-good bastard
who is married, to top it all. The lowest of the low.'

Karla's eyes widened. 'Yes, and so were half the men you
bedded in your day. So what if they weren't married? Not
one of them were decent. Let me think,' she stroked the
corner of her mouth. 'We had "Uncle" Henry, "Uncle" John
and, last but by no means least, "Uncle"-fucking-Mark. The
list is endless. And, if my memory serves me rightly, not one
of them treated you with an ounce of respect. Mark left you
half dead, kicked you to within an inch of your life, so don't
you dare start dictating to me how I should live my life.
Jordan is married for now, but that will change. He's getting
a divorce. He loves me, Mother. We will be together no
matter what, so save your breath and get used to it because
he's going nowhere.'

Mary closed her eyes; the memory of Mark, and too many
other men like him, was still there. The beatings that she'd
suffered, the abuse in her younger years. She opened her
eyes wide and dismissed the comment. 'I'll believe it when I
see it. Just don't come crying to me when it all goes tits up.
And it will, you know. It's just a matter of time. They all say
their marriage is over and their wives don't understand
them. I just can't believe you've fallen for all his bullshit. You
think you know it all, when really you know fuck all. Go on,
crack on doing what you're doing and see if I care.'

Karla was lucky Mary hadn't got right up in her face.
Usually for this kind of backchat she would have gone nose

to nose with her. But Mary wasn't finished yet. She had to have the final word. She held her head up high and had one last pop. 'And what's more, the man is a pimp. He has them young girls dancing in the clubs, and God knows what else he gets up to with them. I can smell a rat a mile away and he's got "love-rat" written all over him. Perhaps I should go and see his wife, see if she knows he's divorcing her. I bet she hasn't got a bleeding clue he's messing around with you.' Mary smiled, relieved she'd found something to stop her daughter in her tracks.

Silenced, Karla pulled her candy-pink lip-gloss from her jacket pocket and turned back to the mirror. What was the point of defending her lover? Her mother was never going to give him the time of day. Best to shut up and let her think she'd won. She'd never have the nerve to tell Jordan's missus.

Mary marched about the living room pretending to clean up. The house was her pride and joy; bright and homely. Mary had worked hard for all she had, even if most of it was paid for on the never-never. Keeping up with payments was an art form. Well, when she wasn't ignoring the demands. Letters were always piled high in her letterbox, bold red type shouting about the money she owed. But they couldn't have what she didn't have in her purse, could they? That's what she kept telling herself, anyway. The money from her cleaning jobs always ran out before the bills dropped on the mat.

A quick rub around her pouting heart-shaped lips with the lip-gloss and Karla yanked her cream leather bomber jacket from the back of the chair. Mary could tell she was eager to get out of this war zone.

6

'I'm not sure if I'm coming home tonight, so lock the front door. Tell Elsa I've left her a tenner on the bedside cabinet to grab a pizza or something later.'

Mary blanked her and carried on with her chores. Only once Karla had left the front room did Mary let herself sink down on the sofa. She held her head in her hands – tough love was tough on both sides. Karla might think she was being vindictive, but she had to look out for her daughter in the only way she knew how. This was a car crash waiting to happen, she knew it, and she couldn't stand by in silence.

Chapter Two

Karla stood outside the garden gate with her mobile phone held firmly to her ear. There was shouting in the distance, kids chasing each other. Karla was agitated as she walked one way then the other. Her mother had really got to her tonight. Her stress level was through the roof.

'Where are you? I've been waiting outside for ages now. I've had to come out of the house because that mother of mine is pecking my head. I swear she makes my blood boil. I don't know what her problem is with you, but she never lets up for one single minute.'

Karla's silver heels clipped along the pavement as she continued talking. There was a strong north wind tonight and the winter months were well and truly kicking in. She wasn't dressed for the weather, either. A black mini skirt and a milky-pink sparkling vest top that you could see her lacy bra through. Dressed like a slapper she was, according to her mother. The Manchester estate where she lived had a reputation, to say the least. Ask anyone: they'd say most of the residents here were on benefits or drugs. Harpurhey was well known for its crime rate and was forever on the news. The dregs of society lived here, or so the media said. But Karla saw another side to the place. Grafters, hopefuls, and maybe a few folk who'd worked out there was one rule for the rich and another for the poor. A motorbike skidded past Karla and she shouted at the rider, 'Will you piss off out of my way?'

The cheeky young lad smirked at her and came past again. 'Show us your tits and I'll leave you alone,' he chuckled.

Karla ignored him and carried on talking on the phone. 'I'm not getting a taxi, Jordan. You said you were picking me up. I've got no money on me, anyway.' She had a face like thunder as she listened to the voice on the other end. 'God, can't you just leave what you're are doing, and come and get me? I'm perished here and I'm not made of money!' That was an understatement. She had no income, let alone a bank balance. Right now Karla was skint, pot-less, on the bones of her arse. Any money she had, she'd blagged, borrowed or swiped from her mother or her lover. Her Universal Credit for this month was long gone. She ended the call and marched along the pavement. It didn't look like she was getting picked up. Instead she headed towards the bus stop, angry but head held high.

Across town, Jordan stood at a bar, one arm resting on it. His head was moving to and fro as he listened to the beat kicking in, baseline pumping through the speakers. The tight-fitting t-shirts he always wore showed off his toned body. The guy was a unit, a tank. The women loved his look, and he loved their adoration. He was never shy of letting them touch his toned abs. 'Poser', some called him, but so what if he loved himself? He didn't spend all those hours in the gym for no one to appreciate the results.

Passion was where he could be found most hours of the day. He loved the club he owned and often watched the lap-dancers practise their moves a bit more closely than he should have. Taking a professional interest, he claimed. This business was his bread and butter, and he was always on the look-out for new workers. Pretty girls, young girls, desperate ones who were down on their luck: he cast his net wide. He had to stay sharp to keep his edge over the competition. Club wars, as he called the simmering feuds that criss-crossed the city, were never far from his mind. Right now there was big beef with Lenny Jackson who ran a chain of clubs in the city centre, and he could never take his eye off the ball because he knew the moment his guard was down Lenny and his boys would strike – get him raided, plant some dodgy gear or burn his club down – whatever it took to take everything he had.

He and Lenny had history, and neither of them would ever back down. They both knew they would fight to the death, if needed. Jordan knew Lenny would think his girls were fair game too. His eyes flicked to the left where one of his best earners, Jenny, was practising her new dance. His eyes covered every inch of her toned, young body. He knew this girl was going to be golden from the first second he set eyes on her. She'd done well for herself over the last few months and, in her own words, she owed Jordan her life. Without him, she would have been still living on the streets, selling her body, anything to keep her head above water. He knew what some people said about him, that he made his dirty money from innocent girls, but he figured most of the girls knew what they were letting themselves in for. For them he was a saviour, not a demon. But there was always a price to pay.

Jordan kept all the girls who worked at the club on a tight leash. He approved every new recruit, and made sure the punters got what they paid for. He had a sixth sense for the special girls, the dancers who would make him the most money. He always kept it secret where he got these girls from, but practically every other week another girl joined his team, they seemed to come from nowhere. Some would dance once or twice then never show up again – while others had what it took to rise to the top.

At the age of forty-three, Jordan had done more than alright for himself. He was smashing it, he told himself, never short of cash or company. He shot a quick glance down at his Rolex. It was nearly opening time, and as usual he was making sure his ship was in order before the punters started to arrive. It was a big night tonight. Three stag parties were due in. Jordan knew more than anyone that he had to keep focused tonight and make sure his girls were safe. Once these men had a few beers down their necks they wanted to get up close with the girls, touch their young firm flesh. To the men, it was all part of the night out, their guilty pleasure the Mrs back home would never find out about. What happened on tour, stayed on tour. But

Jordan had a line he wouldn't let anyone cross. Not without paying for it.

Karla stormed in through the double doors behind him and quickly straightened her windswept hair. She was fuming.

'Bleeding hell, look at the state of me now. I don't know why you just couldn't have come and got me. It's horrible getting the bus. It's full of weirdos and scruffs.'

Jordan rolled his eyes.

'I told you, I've got a lot on tonight. Stop stressing. Go and make sure the girls are nearly ready. I want them top-notch tonight. Tell Gina to do something with that hair, too, and make sure her hairy legs are shaved. Imagine how I felt when an old geezer pulled me up the other day claiming my girls were sub-standard. Make sure they're looking their best. Do you hear me? No excuses, otherwise they'll be out the fucking door.'

'I will do, but get me a drink first. I've had my mam on about you again. Saying you're a player.'

Jordan shook his head: more drama that he didn't need in his life. 'Tell her to fuck off. She doesn't even know me. She's a bitter old cow and I'll put her in her place if she carries on slagging me off.'

Karla froze. This was her mother he was talking about and, even though she'd seen her arse with Mary, *she* was the only one allowed to complain about her. She rolled her shoulders back. 'It's the rumours, isn't it? There's no smoke without fire, she said.'

'Oh, don't start going on about that again. I've told you before, if you believe the gossips then you can do one. I can't be arsed with a paranoid bird. I run a club. There will always be girls around here. Lots of them. Some of them chat shit, and you know it.'

Karla folded her arms tightly in front of her and sighed. 'I never said I believed the rumours, did I, smart-arse? If I did, do you think I would still be standing here?'

He smiled and showed off his pearly white teeth. 'So, shut up whining then and let's get these girls ready instead of moaning.'

Karla flicked her hair over her shoulder and went behind the bar. 'I'll get my own drink, then, shall I?'

Jordan watched her from the corner of his eye and smirked. He had her where he wanted her, and he knew it. She was going nowhere. Jenny was still on stage, twisting her body around the pole and Jordan's eyes were back on her. He cupped his hands around his mouth and shouted over at her. 'More pussy shots, Jenny. If these men wanted a normal dancer, they'd be at home watching bloody *Strictly*. Tempt them, seduce them, make each of them think they're the only man you can see.'

Jenny nodded her head and kept her legs straight as her body folded in two. There it was: the money shot, the crowd pleaser. Jordan nodded slowly.

Karla clicked her fingers in his ear. 'Oi, what's the plan for later? I've told my mam I'm not coming home, so we can go to that nice hotel again if you want. You can spoil me.'

Jordan frowned. She was doing his head in again and she'd only been here a few minutes. 'Stop planning my night for me. I don't know what I'm doing yet. You know how things happen in this place. I'll have to be near to sort shit out, if it kicks off. Anyway, Pam is moaning about me staying out all the time. I need to start going home a bit more. I don't want to ruffle her feathers any more than I have to. She can fuck a lot of stuff up for me if she gets wind about you. Trust me, the woman is a crank when she gets started. So, be thankful she doesn't know anything. Let's keep it like that, eh?'

Karla's eyes were wide now, raging. 'So what if she finds out about us? You're getting a divorce, aren't you? You don't have to answer to her anymore. Tell her to piss off.'

Jordan smashed his clenched fist on the bar and the glasses shook. He meant business. 'She's still my wife. I've got to keep her sweet until I've sorted things out. She'll take me to the fucking cleaners otherwise. I'll lose it all. Is that what you want?'

Karla was bright red and stuttered, 'So, hurry up then and sort it out. I'm sick of having her in the picture. File the bleeding papers and let's move on. We've made plans, or are you forgetting?'

Jordan bit down on his bottom lip and turned his head away from Karla before his temper blew. She was being a brat.

Karla wiggled out from behind the bar and stood next to Jordan. Her long, slender fingers stroked slowly across the stubble on his chin. 'I want you to myself, babes. I can't help it if I love you, can I?'

His nostrils flared. 'Help me get the show on the road tonight, then. I don't need any more stress this evening. I've told you, my life is complicated. Be patient with me. Remember, good things come to those who wait.'

Karla necked her drink in one and slammed her empty glass on the bar. 'I'm gone. Stop worrying: my lips are sealed.'

He watched her glide along the floor towards the stage. She was pushing her luck, this one. She was not somebody he planned on having in his life for much longer. Too needy, always wanting more. No, she was getting the elbow as soon as something better came along.

Karla stood watching Jenny with envy in her eyes. She was gorgeous, a sexy body, a hit with all the men. Jealousy, the green-eyed monster, reared its head. 'Right, stop prancing about out here. Go and get ready. Jordan says you need to up your game tonight and look your best. You've been slacking lately and he's on the verge of carting you.'

Jenny was gobsmacked, eyes wide open. Clearly this was news to her. 'I always look my best, Karla. I work my tits off in this place, so don't be having a go at me because you're in a bad mood. Jordan loves the way I entertain the punters, so stop shit-stirring. It's you with the problem, not him. He loves my dances, he's told me.' This girl had attitude alright. She wiped the trickle of sweat from her brow with a quick flick of her wrist. 'If you think it's so easy, why don't you give it a go and dance yourself? Then you'll see what it really takes.'

Karla's jaw dropped. Her voice was knife-sharp. 'Me, dancing? I don't think so. I wouldn't lower myself to do your job, ever. I'm a classy woman, not a tart.'

Jenny placed her hands on her hips and smirked. 'You couldn't pull it off anyway, so maybe you're best standing with the rest of the men watching. You carry on being some man's bit on the side, begging for scraps. I can earn nearly five hundred pound a night. Not bad for a dancer, is it?'

Karla went quiet. Surely the girls didn't earn that kind of money? She must be lying. 'Yeah, five hundred quid to drop your knickers and let them creepy old pervs grope you would never be enough cash for me. You have to be desperate to do that.'

Jenny kicked her silver heels from her feet and picked them up. She held one up for Karla, and giggled. '*Jimmy Choo's* these are, love. No fakes here. What make are yours?'

Karla reddened and shot a look down at her footwear. They weren't designer, far from it. She watched Jenny leave the stage and, after a few seconds, followed her. She'd show this tramp who the boss was. As soon as she got the chance, this scrubber was getting her marching orders.

In the dressing rooms, the other girls were walking about semi-naked. There was no privacy here, no point being shy when you spent the rest of the night with everything on display. Jenny watched Karla stalk in and plonk herself down on a chair before she spoke.

'Right, girls, we want a top-notch performance tonight. Jordan is already stressing, so be it on your own back if he has a go at you.'

Jenny raised her eyes at Angela, one of the other girls. Who the hell did this girl think she was, calling the shots here? She was just a leg-over, Jordan's sack emptier. She knew nothing about the business and how things worked. Jenny nudged Angela and kept her voice low. 'Ignore her. She's had a pop at me out there already, telling me how I should dance.'

Angela covered her mouth with her fanned fingers and replied, 'I can't wait until she's carted. Jordan won't keep her around for long. I've been here years and seen his women come and go. He's never come near leaving his wife for any of them. God help her if Pam finds out he's at it again, she'll scratch her eyes out.'

Karla spotted them talking and stood up from her chair. 'Are you listening, you two? Jenny, I've already told you your job's not safe, so it's up to you how you want to play this.'

Jenny stepped forward and almost growled at her, eyes glassy. 'Yes, and I've told you I'll take it up with Jordan. I talk to the organ grinder not the monkey. We all work hard here, so don't come with your fucking attitude, otherwise we'll all be gone. *The Marigold* is always looking for new girls, and Marty has already told me there's a job there if I want it. So, if I was you, I'd fuck off out of here and let us do what we're good at. You go and lick Jordan's arse like *you're* good at.'

The other girls were behind Jenny now and they stood back waiting to see what Karla had to come back with.

'Jenny, keep your smart remarks to yourself. If you want beef with me then bring it on. You're forgetting who the boss is here. Jordan will do whatever I tell him, so keep that big gob shut before I shut it for you. And might I suggest you stop shoving that shit up your nose every night?' she added as she watched Jenny rub the back of her hand across her face. 'If the police raid us, you'll be nicked on a drugs charge.'

Jenny flicked her long red hair over her shoulder. Drugs were a big part of this industry and without cocaine in their bloodstreams some of these girls would never dance the way they did. They needed the powder for confidence, to keep them awake, to help blank out what these men did to them. Jenny smirked. Karla didn't scare her, not one bit. 'I'm stating the facts, that's all. If you want me to find work elsewhere, just say the word and I'm gone. But you know as well as me that Jordan will never let me go without a fight.'

Karla was losing the battle. 'Just get fucking ready, and get out of my face.'

The war was won by Jenny today. Karla dipped her head low and tried to regain some composure. She walked over to Angela and lifted her hair up in her hand.

'Put your hair up tonight. You have a lovely face. Let the guys see what they're paying for.'

Angela nodded. She just wanted an easy life with no drama. After all, she'd been a dancer here for over two years. She knew the role inside out and, when a new girl started here, she was the one who showed them the ropes. Angela was like the mother of the dancers. She kept them under her wing and protected them from the world she knew existed outside this room. She had her own story to tell and nothing surprised her any more. After all, she'd been Jordan's woman once; his bit on the side. He'd promised her the world, too, and told her that one day he would marry her. What a load of bullshit. As soon as a new girl came on the scene, he'd dropped her like a ton of bricks. She had nothing: no money to her name, no home that wasn't with him. She had nothing when she met him, and he left her with nothing. But he did offer her a job at the club, and she knew paying her rent was more important than walking out over being replaced by a fresher model. It was that or back to square one. A part of Angela still loved Jordan, still craved his touch, his warm lips pressed against hers. There wasn't much room for romance in this game, but it didn't hurt to daydream.

Jordan sat working in his office as his wife strolled in. His eyes flickered. Pam never turned up at the club unannounced. He sat up straight in his black leather chair and forced a smile on his face.

'Hello, darling, what are you doing here? To what do I owe the honour?'

Pamela stepped further into the office and sat down. Her perfume was strong, and its scent filled the small room. It was none of that cheap stuff the dressing rooms reeked of, this was a three-hundred-pounds-a-bottle job. 'I thought I would put my glad rags on and come and see you for a bit. That's alright with you, isn't it?' She watched him from the corner of her eye: he seemed anxious. 'It's ages since I've been here. I've missed the place. I miss this world.'

Jordan inhaled deeply and replied, 'I'm pretty busy, so you'll have to look after yourself for a while. You look gorgeous, by the way. Is that dress new?'

Pamela draped her long fur coat from her shoulders and kicked her long, tanned, slender legs onto the table at the side of him. She still knew how to make an impact.

'Yes, I treated myself. I went and had my hair done, too. I mean, I need to keep my husband interested, don't I?'

Jordan gulped. Did she know something? Why was she here? Usually, if she was alone in the house, she would put her feet up with a bottle of red wine and have an early night. He'd have to be careful tonight, make sure Karla was hidden away.

Pamela stroked a single finger down the side of her long silky leg. 'Lock that door, and come and give me a kiss. It's not often we get a few minutes together.'

Jordan was edgy. This was all he needed. But what could he do? He smiled and followed her orders. His wife looked mint tonight and everything about her was calling to him. Her red dress clung to her curves and her breasts strained against the fabric. She was a diamond, he had to admit: she had everything going for her. So, why the hell did he cheat on her? Before he could hold onto that thought, Pam stood up and moved closer to him. Jordan locked the door and stood with his back pressed firmly against it. Her lips met his and slowly she kissed him, teased him with the end of her tongue. His hands were all over her. He was lost in the moment as his hand slid up her dress. The passion was still there. He wanted her, just as he always had. She was his woman, and he was king in his world. Then the office door handle rattled. Someone was banging on the door. Voices from outside. They both froze and Jordan placed a single finger over his mouth. 'Sshh,' he whispered.

Pamela ignored the knocking on the door and carried on biting her husband's neck.

But the voice from outside was getting louder. 'Jordan, open the door, will you! I need a word with you about that

Jenny. I swear I'll swing for her if she carries on with her attitude.'

Pamela kissed her husband one last time and straightened herself. 'Better let them in, it sounds important.'

Fuck, fuck, fuck, what was he going to do now? He didn't want Karla and Pam in the same room – they'd size each other up instantly. Jordan quickly fastened his jeans and opened the door, hoping to stop Karla before she crossed the threshold.

Karla burst inside, raging. 'You need to get rid of her, Jordan, on my life, she's a gobby bitch.' Karla froze as she clocked the woman sat there. She looked over at Jordan.

He put her in the picture before she opened her big trap. 'Karla, this is my wife, Pamela.'

It was obvious these two had been up to something. Jordan's cheeks were bright red, and sweat glistened on him. Karla looked the other woman up and down, and stuttered, 'I didn't know you were busy. I'll come back later.'

Pamela flicked her hair over her shoulder and sniggered. 'It's fine, love. We were having a bit of a kiss and cuddle, that's all. We can't keep our hands off each other. Even after all these years, we still have the hots for each other.'

Karla looked like she'd been punched in the stomach, the colour draining from her face. No words, nothing, she just left and slammed the door behind her.

'Oops, what's her problem?' Pamela chuckled.

Jordan shot a look at his wife and tried to smooth things over. 'She's a funny one, that one is. She blows hot and cold all the time. Just ignore her.'

Pam studied her husband, sat straight in her chair with her legs crossed. Then she stood up and made her way to the door. 'I'll go and get a drink. Maybe I'll go and see the girls. I bet they wonder where your wife is all the time, don't they? I'll see who it is who's causing all the trouble, too.'

Jordan gulped and ragged his fingers through his hair. 'You go to the bar. Leave Karla to sort them out, that's what she gets paid for.'

His wife left the room and Jordan let out a laboured breath. Tonight was going to be a long night, a very long night indeed.

Chapter Three

Elsa Bradshaw sat on the edge of the bed and looked at herself in the mirror, head turning left then right. She was a pretty little thing: angelic, some would say. Her long honey-blonde hair nearly touched her waist; her crowning glory. She glanced down at her phone and threw it onto the bed. Reaching for her black mascara, she leant nearer to the mirror and fanned her long dark lashes out. Her eyes stood out now. Big blue enchanting eyes just like her mother's.

The bedroom door opened and made her jump. Mary, her grandmother, stood there. She was always barging into her bedroom without knocking.

'Where are you going tonight? You better not be late again. I don't sleep until you're back home and in bed. Honest, I toss and turn all night until you're home.'

Elsa carried on applying her make-up, her mouth open as if she was catching flies. 'Nana, stop stressing out, will you? I'm just going out with my friends. You know, like every other teenager does? My mam said, as long as I look after myself and I don't get into trouble, I'm more or less okay to come in at any time I want.'

Mary shook her head and walked about the bedroom. 'Ignore what your mother tells you. As long as she's alright, she doesn't care about anybody else. This is my house and my rules, so I want you in at a decent time. God knows who's out on the streets. You need to be safe in here with me. So, be in for eleven o'clock.'

Elsa's jaw dropped. This was a joke: she was eighteen years old, not a baby. 'Nana, are you being serious? It's Isabelle's party tonight and things will only get going at that time. It's not like when you were young, Nana. Times have changed and I can look after myself. I'm not coming home at eleven o'clock, no way. I'll be a laughing stock.'

'Bloody hell, you sound just like your mother when she was your age. She thought she knew it all, too. Do yourself a favour and don't be messing about with any boys, either. Keep them legs shut and your knickers on. The last thing I need is you getting tubbed.'

Elsa blushed and giggled. 'Nana! I am not like that. I'm not a slapper. I wish you would trust me. I'm not my mam, you know?'

'I know you're not, but I can't help but worry. I don't want you making any daft mistakes like she did. She could have had so much more. She was very clever, your mother, the top of her class she was.'

Elsa looked down at the floor, all the fight gone out of her.

'I don't mean you were a mistake, sweetheart. A happy accident, I call it. The mistake was picking a man who didn't want to stick around to raise a beautiful girl like you.'

Mary plonked down on the edge of the bed and looked around the bedroom. It was a pretty bedroom, candy-pink walls, cream curtains. 'Elsa, I don't mean to be hard on you. It might be my age, but I just know there are some bad people on the streets and it's easy for you to get tangled up in the world they live in. You read about it in the newspaper all the time, young girls going missing from home and being dragged into a life they never wanted. I'd never forgive myself if I didn't protect you from that world.'

Elsa moved closer to her nana and leant her head against hers. She took Nana's wrinkled hand in hers, lifted it to her mouth and kissed her fingertips. These were the hands that had held her when she was a baby, the same ones that picked her up when she fell, and the same ones that wiped her tears away when she was upset. Karla had never been a great mother: she would rather buy her child something than spend time with her, when she had the cash, that was. Whereas Mary had always been the one she could rely on, the one to show Elsa affection, always kissing and cuddling her. Elsa snuggled deep into her nana's chest now, inhaling the mix of soap and tobacco that often lingered about Mary.

'I love you, Nana. I know you're only looking out for me, but I'm fine, honest. I'm just going to a party at Belle's. I'm only drinking WKDs. They're not even strong. Some of the girls drink neat vodka and you should see the state of them at the end of the night. I always watch what I drink, and I know when I've had enough.'

Mary stroked her hand over her granddaughter's hair, slow gliding movements over her silky locks. 'I know you're a good girl, but be careful. People can spike your drink. I watched a drama on the TV last week about some guy who was spiking young girls' drinks and doing god knows what to them. Honest, it curled my toes. I didn't sleep all bleeding night thinking about it. On my life, there are some nutters out there, love. Tapped in the head, they are.'

Elsa sighed. 'Nana, if I listened to you, I would be too scared to even leave the house. Why don't you go to Bingo or something? I think you need to get out a bit more and start enjoying your life instead of staying in all the time, looking at four walls.'

Mary smiled and looked into Elsa's large blue eyes. 'I wish I had the money, love, to go out every night. The bills are piled high. I can't seem to get myself straight anymore. It's in one hand and out the other. And your mother gives me nothing. I'm sure she thinks I've got a bleeding money tree growing in the back garden. She needs to cough up and start giving some money towards running this house, instead of leaving it all to me.'

Elsa knew Mary was right. Her mother always declared she was skint, yet there she was, buying clothes and make-up all the time. 'You should tell her, Nana. You let her get away with it for a quiet life. She's out nearly every night. Where does she get her money from for all that?'

Mary licked her bottom lip, stood up and pulled her grey knitted cardigan tightly around her thin body. It had been a long day and she was drained. 'Her fancy man pays for that, she tells me. But, come on, I'm not green. She gets her benefits every month and where does that go? Surely she could put a bit of that by for food or the leccy?'

Elsa agreed. 'She's always getting new clothes. She very rarely buys me anything. If it wasn't for you, Nana, I wouldn't have anything. You wouldn't think she's my mother, the way she acts. But now I've finished college, I'm going to get a job soon – I'll help you out.'

Mary bent and kissed the top of Elsa's head. 'I'm not sure what job your fancy "performing arts" is going to get you round here. You need a nice little shop job – one of those fancy boutiques you're always looking in the windows of, maybe. Something classy, quality. But I'm going to bed, love. I've got an early start in the morning. I can't wait for the day to come when I'm not cleaning toilets and wiping up other people's piss.'

There was a knock at the door. Elsa smiled at Mary. 'Will you let Candice in for me, so I can finish getting ready, please?'

Mary checked her wristwatch and sighed. 'It's half past nine. In my day we'd be half-way through a night out by now. I don't know what this generation is about anymore. Crazy, you lot are. You don't even get started til past my bedtime. Have a good night, though – and remember what I said: take care.'

'Thanks, Nana, love you,' she giggled.

Mary left the bedroom, and you could hear her pottering down the stairs, huffing and puffing. Elsa reached her hand underneath the pillow and pulled out a half bottle of vodka. She unscrewed the red cap from it and lifted it to her mouth, taking a large gulp. She quickly wiped the side of her mouth with her wrist and smiled at her reflection in the mirror. She held her ear to the door as she heard her friend Candice talking to Mary in the hallway. She chuckled to herself. Her nana was a right chatterbox. She could talk a glass eye to sleep when she got going. Elsa reached for her dress and quickly slipped it over her slender body. She leant down and pulled out her silver heels from underneath the bed and placed them near her feet. She felt good. Her make-up was on point, hair glossy and bouncy, and she was ready to shine.

Candice walked into the bedroom and called over her shoulder, 'Night, Mary.'

Elsa slipped her shoes on as Candice went to the mirror and checked her make-up. She was a pretty girl too; long caramel hair and conker-brown eyes. 'This party is going to be mint. I swear to you I'm getting steaming drunk. I've told my mam I'm staying here with you tonight, so make sure you remember that, if she starts asking questions.'

'Are you planning on staying over at Nat's?' Elsa asked.

Candice pushed her breasts out in front of her and smirked. 'Of course I am. I've bought new underwear; red lacy bra and the knickers to match. Anyway, I have to keep my eye on him. There are loads of girls there tonight and that Annie Morris is the biggest slag walking on this earth, so I'll be near Nat all night long, making sure she doesn't get her claws into him. The girl is ruthless, I tell you. She has no respect for anyone. She slept with Joanne's boyfriend and thought nothing of it. I swear, if that had been Nat, I would have scratched her eyes out.'

'Do you think Nat would ever cheat on you?' She knew her friend had only been seeing Nat a few months, and trust had to be earned.

Candice chewed on her bottom lip. 'I wouldn't trust him as far as I could throw him. Once he's out with the boys, he thinks he's a player. If I so much as hear a whisper about him cheating, I'll cut his balls off. Anyway, never mind me. Clayton is there tonight. Are you excited to see him?'

Elsa blushed and quickly held a single finger to her mouth, her voice low. 'Sshh, Motor Mouth. My nana listens to everything we say. These walls are paper thin, and she can hear a mouse fart from down the road, that woman can.'

Candice covered her mouth and opened her eyes wide. 'Sorry,' she whispered. 'So, are you going to make a play for him, or what? He's fancied you for ages, everyone knows it. He can't take his eyes off you.'

Elsa flicked her hair and picked up a small silver sparkling handbag from the bed. 'Clayton can whistle if he thinks I'm an easy catch. I've heard stories about what he gets up to with the girls, and there is no way he's adding me to the notches on his headboard. When I lose my virginity, I want it to be special. I want to meet someone who deserves it.'

Candice grinned. 'You sound like someone out of those Sunday night telly programmes. You need a ballgown and a fan!' Then she looked wistful. 'That ship sailed for me a long time ago. I was only thirteen.' She paused for a moment. 'I think I've slept with seven lads up to now. But you know me: I'm a fool in love. I think each of them is going to be the one I stay with for ever. I just fall too easily.'

Elsa's eyes opened wide. She knew Candice had a few men in her past, but she'd not known her that long and hadn't realised how much more experienced than her she was. 'Seven fellas!'

Candice shrugged off the comment and smirked. 'My mam told me to enjoy my life to the full. Look at her, and how many men she's had in her life. I know she's my mother, but she's had more knob-ends than weekends.'

Elsa burst out laughing and held the bottom of her stomach. 'You can't say that about your mam, Candice. She'd whack you one if she ever heard you talking about her like that.'

Candice sniggered and playfully punched Elsa in the side of the arm. 'I'm only saying it to you. I would never dare say it to anyone else. But it is true: she's had more pricks than a second-hand dartboard.'

Elsa covered her mouth with both hands and burst out laughing. The two girls had been good friends for over a year now. They'd met at a party and Candice just clicked with her. Elsa was pretty shy, and Candice was a loud-mouth. Chalk and cheese. Elsa liked it this way and often hid away in her friend's shadow. The vodka was pulled out now and both girls gulped at the bottle until it was gone. They looked in the mirror and smiled. They were ready to leave: well, after four or five selfies were added to their Snapchat.

The party house was booming with music as the girls walked along the street towards it. Every light in the house was on and they could see people stood in the garden as they approached. The curtains were twitching in the neighbourhood. It was only a matter of time before one of the neighbours rang the police and had this party closed down.

Candice dug Elsa in the waist. 'Right, let's make a decent entrance so these slappers know the talent has arrived. Get them tits pushed out, girl, and swing those hips.'

Candice was oozing confidence and Elsa seemed to be loosening up, too. They walked through the gate and turned their heads as they heard shouting from across the garden. Candice smiled and pouted. 'Nat's here already. Come on, let's go over.'

She didn't wait for a reply, but dragged Elsa to where Nat and his friend stood. Clayton clocked Elsa straight away, edging forward. Candice smirked and nodded at Clayton before she rushed to Nat's side and draped her arms around his neck. She kissed him and turned to face the rest of the people in the garden. She was putting her mark on him, letting everyone know this guy was taken.

Elsa blushed as she felt Clayton's eyes burning into her. Her heart was beating faster, and her palms felt hot and sweaty. She always felt like this when she was near him: he made her heart flutter. His dark-brown hair skimmed his forehead with a neat parting at the side. He had all the latest designer clothes on, and a brilliant-white smile that complimented his tanned skin. She had to stop herself from staring.

'Do you want a drink, Elsa?' he asked with that big, cheesy smile spread across his face.

She stuttered, 'Erm, yes please. Vodka, if there is some.' She felt warm as she found him looking deep into her eyes.

Candice jumped into the conversation and added her request. There was no way she was budging from her place with her man. 'Can I have one, too, please? Two big shots of vodka in mine, please. In fact, make it a treble.'

Nat shook his head as Clayton wove through the people. 'Don't think you're coming back to mine when you're rat-arsed, Candice. My mam went mad last time you were there.'

Candice chuckled and started to dance as a tune hit the decks. 'I'm living my best life, Nat. I was only being happy. Tell your mam to loosen up.'

Nat shook his head as he watched her step out to show off her moves. This girl could dance. All eyes were on her. Clayton came back with the drinks and stood next to Elsa. His eyes were the only ones not on Candice as she ground her hips and moved her body from side to side. He stood next to Elsa, his warm breath tickling her neck as he moved in closer. All the hairs on the back of her neck stood on end. It was happening again: he was making her heart flutter.

'You look gorgeous tonight, Elsa. You always look nice, but tonight you look stunning.'

Her mouth was moving but no words came out until she gulped. 'Thank you. You look nice, too.'

Clayton smirked and replied, 'So, that's a start. At least I look nice. Does that mean you fancy me, then?'

Her cheeks were on fire and her mouth became dry: he'd put her on the spot. She took a mouthful from her drink. She had to act cool, play hard to get. 'I wouldn't go that far. I just said you looked nice.'

'Do you fancy coming back to mine later? My mam and dad are out and, well, I have a free house. We can chill for a bit, if you want?'

'Let me see how I feel later. Plus, you might find another girl by the end of the night. I know what you're like.'

'Oi, I'm a good lad. Ignore the rumours. I only have eyes for one girl, and that's you.' Oh, this lad had game alright. He moved in closer to her and softly moved her hair to reveal her bare shoulders. He bent forward slowly, and gently kissed the base of her neck. Her legs nearly buckled as she felt a warmth riding through her body. Every inch of her was tingling. Her breath seemed locked inside her. Clayton raised his head and their eyes met. Before she had chance to stop him, his lips pressed against hers.

Candice clocked them straight away and stood looking at them both, grinning.

But Elsa was lost in the moment. She was in a world of her own, eyes closed, enjoying every second of the kiss. She'd wanted this to happen for months. She'd imagined it so many times and here it was, really happening. As the kiss finished, Clayton dragged her closer to him, draping his arm around her neck. This was his woman now. Mission completed.

By midnight, it was clear the party had been a hit. Elsa was steaming drunk, she'd danced the night away and now was complaining her feet were covered in blisters. Sensing his opportunity, Clayton had finally got her to agree to come back to his house, after hours of persuasion.

When they reached his place, Elsa stood back and her jaw dropped. 'Oh my god,' she slurred. 'Do you really live here? It's like a mansion, like one of them houses you see on the TV. I don't live in a place like this,' she said.

Clayton nodded his head, proud. Everyone who knew him knew his family was wadded. He wanted for nothing. He stood tall and began to speak. 'Glad you like it. I'm used to it, I suppose. It's just where I live.'

They made their way up the garden path, Elsa looking at the small bright lights that lit up its edge. Clayton fumbled about in his tracksuit bottoms for the front door key and, once he found it, he tried to focus on the lock to insert the key. He wasn't a big drinker, and he could normally only manage a few beers before he felt sick. He was a lightweight, really, not the big party animal he made out to be. He preferred the party drugs; magic, ketamine – that was his idea of a good night out. Being twisted and off his napper was much more fun than filling his body with alcohol.

The large wooden front door finally opened, and Elsa stood back, looking inside. Marble floors, large silver vases, and a beautiful floral scent greeted her.

Clayton took her hand in his. 'Come on then, I don't bite.'

Elsa was inside the house now, but she seemed glued to the spot. 'Should I take my shoes off?' she asked in a timid voice.

'Yes, and everything else,' he joked.

She playfully punched him in the arm. 'Stop it. I feel so nervous and I don't know why. I never go back to anyone's house. I must have drunk too much vodka.' Her eyes shot to a silver photo frame. She walked slowly to the silver table and picked up the photo frame with a gentle hand. 'Are these your parents?'

He came to her side and smirked. 'Yep, that's my old man and my mother.'

She studied the photograph. 'Your mother is gorgeous. Your dad is a dish, too. They are so well suited. They look like they belong on the cover of *Hello!* magazine.'

Clayton walked into a room to the left. 'They think they're red-carpet merchants. Honest, my dad is the worst. He never queues for anything. He owns a nightclub. We hardly see him, to be honest. He doesn't even come home, some nights. My mam hates it, but there's nothing she can do about it. I hear them arguing about it all the time.' Sadness filled his eyes as he continued. 'You see, it's a lap-dancing club, and my mam reckons my dad's shagging the dancers there.'

Elsa's eyes opened wide. 'What, sleeping with the girls who work there?'

'Well, to hear my mam talk, yes. She always thinks he's up to no good, but up to now he's never been caught. Not that I know about, anyway. He's either very good at hiding it or he's being wrongly accused. You know what you women are like when you get something in your heads.'

Elsa wasn't sure how to reply, so she looked around the living room and, once again, she was gobsmacked. So, this was how the other half lived. Everything was matching, nothing out of place. The sofa was massive. She couldn't wait to sit on it, it looked so comfortable. She massaged the bottom of her blistered feet.

Clayton was still standing. 'I'm starving. Do you want me to bang a pizza in the oven?'

Elsa was hungry too, and she hoped having something to eat might sober her up a bit. 'I'll have some if you are. I must be drunk: I don't usually eat in front of people when I don't really know them. I'm funny like that. Ask Candice: I rarely eat in front of anyone.'

'I'm honoured, then. Things are looking good for me tonight, aren't they? First a compliment, then being made to feel special. Go on, lad, you're doing great,' he joked as he punched his clenched fist into the air.

Elsa took the time while she was alone to digest everything around her. This house stank of money. Nothing was old or outdated. Everything was top-notch. One day she hoped to have a home like this, a place she could be proud of. She could feel her eyes closing: the drink was taking effect. The room began to spin. Around and around it went, spinning at incredible speed. She opened her eyes quickly and sucked in a large mouthful of air. She needed fresh air before she spewed, she could feel it in her stomach. She stood up and wobbled through the room. She called, 'Clayton, I need some air. Where is your garden?'

His head popped out of the next room and he sniggered. 'Come through here.'

Elsa stumbled through the kitchen. She looked ill, sweat forming on her forehead. She rushed past him as he opened the back door. A warm gush of clear liquid sprayed from her mouth as the fresh air hit her face. She didn't know which way to turn and settled on the side of the garden near some bushes.

Clayton walked over to her and held her hair back. His hand was flat on her lower back, rubbing up and down. Elsa lifted her head up. 'I'm so sorry. My nana told me not to drink on an empty stomach. Oh my God, I'm so embarrassed.'

'Well, you should have listened to her. It looks like she was right.'

Elsa stood up fully and sucked in large mouthfuls of air. She was shivering now, teeth chattering together. 'I feel so rough. Can we go back inside, please? I do feel a bit better now I've been sick.'

Clayton led her back inside the house and showed her where the bathroom was while he went back into the kitchen to check on the pizza.

Elsa looked at her pale face in the mirror, swilled some water and tried to straighten her hair. She dashed back to the sofa and pulled her legs up to her chest. How embarrassing was this? Here she was on her first date with this lad, and she was steaming drunk. Surely, he wouldn't be attracted to her anymore? He was probably looking for a posh bird, someone who was well educated and never got into an intoxicated state like she had.

Clayton came back into the front room, holding a plate. He was munching on a piece of pizza. 'Here, get some of this down your neck.'

Elsa reached over for a piece and he could see her hand shaking.

'You're in a proper state, aren't you? If it's any consolation, I spew up after a few beers, too. You're lucky I wasn't stood next to you doing the same.'

They sat filling their faces. Elsa looked a lot better than she had minutes before. The colour was returning to her cheeks. She smiled over at him. 'I'm so sorry. It's a good job your parents weren't in. Imagine if they were and I was acting like that?'

Clayton stretched out fully on the sofa and patted the space next to him. 'Come and get next to me here and have a cuddle.'

Elsa didn't move straight away. 'What time is it? I'm not staying for long. If my nana wakes up and I'm not back, she will have kittens.'

He smirked and rolled his eyes. 'Just lie here for a bit. Come on, you can keep me warm. Stop worrying, I don't bite.'

Elsa crawled next to him and looked straight into his eyes. It was happening again and that feeling she got when he was near took over her body. She melted into his arms and she felt safe as he pulled her close to his firm chest. Clayton kissed the top of her head and moved down to her lips. It was as if there was a magnet drawing her closer, she couldn't help herself. This was a passionate kiss, a spine-tingling, heat-building kiss. Elsa opened her eyes quickly; this was all happening too fast. There was no way she was going to sleep with this guy after one night. She'd be like all those girls she spoke about with Candice. No, her legs were staying shut. The first time she had sex was going to be a wonderful experience, special, something she would remember for the rest of her days. Maybe some candles, and soft music playing. She pulled away from him.

Clayton ran his fingers through his hair and sighed. 'Bloody hell, you pick your moments, don't you? I was getting carried away then.' He gripped his crotch.

She panicked and sat up, straightening her clothes. There was no way he was shoving that thing anywhere near her: it looked massive. 'I need the loo. Which door is it, again?'

'Up the stairs and the first door on the left. Do you want a drink of something?'

Elsa stood up and smiled at him. 'Please can I have a cold drink? No alcohol, though. I couldn't stomach another drop.'

She made her way out of the door as Clayton got up and went into the kitchen to make a drink. When Elsa reached the top stair, she stood looking one way then another. Did he say left or right? She wasn't sure. Her sore feet slowly moved over the thick grey shag-pile. It felt so comfortable and she couldn't help but stand for a few seconds and stroke her foot over the fluffy carpet. Realising she'd better try her luck, she stepped forward and slowly turned a shiny silver door handle. She dipped her head inside the room, but it was dark as she fumbled about on the wall, trying to find the light switch. At last, she located it. And stood still in surprise.

This wasn't the toilet. The walls had long mirrors on them, and in the middle of the room was a silver pole. Elsa looked behind her and edged further into the room. She'd always loved dance – it had been her favourite part of her college course, even if she couldn't match the technical skills of the girls who'd had the money to do ballet and tap since they were tiny. The teachers always said what she lacked in training she made up for in talent. But she'd never even thought about pole-dancing. She walked to where the pole was. Her hands slowly gripped the cold metal bar and she just couldn't help herself. Her body swung around it slowly, her hair streaming out behind her. Around and around, she went. She felt in a world of her own, lost in a fantasy. She finally looked at her reflection in the mirror, and she liked what she saw. A woman, not a shy girl. She flicked her hair over her shoulder and bent her body around the pole. Then she heard noises behind her. Somebody was coming. She panicked. What on earth had got into her? She rushed out of the room and quickly found the toilet. She could hear Clayton's voice coming up the stairs.

'Elsa, are you alright? You've been ages …'

She replied in a shaky voice. 'Sorry, I needed to wash my face to sober myself up. I will be out in a minute.'

She hurried and when she came out of the toilet, she almost bumped into Clayton.

'Do you want to come to my bedroom and chill for a bit?'

Elsa knew his game straight away and she wasn't falling for it. 'No, I have to go home. My nana will be waiting for me. She's a right worrier and doesn't rest until I'm in bed. Honest, she'll be walking the streets if I'm not home soon.'

Clayton knew this was the end of any passion he was getting tonight.

She smiled at him and started making her way down the stairs. 'I'm not like that, Clayton. If you want me, then it's not going to happen overnight. I'm a good girl and I don't spread my legs for anyone.'

He started to follow her and replied, 'Nah, I know you're not a dirt-bag. That's why I'm attracted to you. I just thought you could have a lie down on my bed for a bit and kick back. You know, listen to a few tunes and that.'

She was at the bottom of the stairs now and waited for him to come down to join her. 'Can you ring me a taxi, please?'

Clayton pulled his mobile phone out of his pocket and smiled at her with cheeky grin. 'Give me a kiss first and I will.'

Elsa shook her head: she couldn't help but like this guy. 'I'll kiss you, not because you're ringing me a taxi, but because I have had a great night.' And she meant it. But not only because of him. She could still feel the power and the freedom of spinning around the pole. A fire had been lit inside her.

Chapter Four

It was past midnight, the sky pitch black, as a Range Rover with tinted windows roared down the country lane. Johnny nodded his head to the beat of the music and kept his eyes glued to the road. The last time he'd driven this way he'd knocked a sheep down. At least, he hoped it was a sheep. He was lucky he had a mate who sorted out the dent in the car, no questions asked.

Johnny was singing, but he stopped for a few seconds and listened carefully. Moaning and groaning, a soft sobbing came from behind him. He looked at his reflection in the rear-view mirror and licked his pearly-white teeth. New they were, two months ago he'd been over to Turkey and bagged himself a full set of veneers. These teeth gave him confidence, made him stand out from the crowd, made sure the girls were all over him. Fanny magnets his best mate called them. Johnny nudged Dave who was half asleep in the passenger seat next to him.

'Have you heard her? Fuck me, she's not stopped crying for over an hour.'

Dave yawned and stretched his arms above his head. 'I'd do more than scream if I'd been through what she had. The man is sick in the fucking head, Johnny. He's a beast, the things he does to them girls are unheard of. Don't get me wrong I'm into a bit of kinky sex now and again, maybe slapping their arse and all that but, fuck me, the guy is beyond the limit. He needs locking up. Don't bloody tell him I said that, though.'

Johnny slowed down as the lighting on the lane disappeared. He put his headlights on full beam. 'Tell me about it, Dave. He's always telling me to drop them off down here when he's finished with them. But he pays me a decent bit of cash to keep my mouth shut so who am I to take the high ground? These girls know what they're getting into when they take the cash, just like we do.'

Dave shook his head and folded his arms tightly in front of him. 'Sure they expect a bit of fetish stuff, but not that what he does to them, tying them up and all that, taking photographs, that's on another level. I'm just waiting until I get some better graft and I'm gone from this job. My Mrs would divorce me if she knew what I was involved in. She thinks I do a bit of security work, not heavy shit like this. I have a daughter myself and it doesn't sit right with me what goes on at the farm. I want to sleep at night without this shit on my conscience.'

Johnny opened his window slightly, he was burning up, his conscience getting the better of him, too. 'We're just the foot soldiers, Dave. We pick girls up and drop them off, that's all. All that sex shit is fuck all to do with us and if it ever comes out I'll tell the police straight that we had no clue what went on behind closed doors.'

Dave rubbed at his arms as the night air crept inside the window and bit at his arms like tiny insects. 'Just put your foot down and let's get her out of here. It gives me the creeps listening to her crying. Turn the music up again, so I can't hear her.'

Twenty minutes later, the car came to a halt. Dave reached inside the glove compartment and pulled out a long silver torch. He looked over at Johnny and shook his head. 'Right, let's make this quick. If we get clocked on this road by anyone we're fucked. Just get her out and gone as soon as.'

Johnny zipped his coat up and opened the driver's door. He met Dave at the boot and they both gave each other another look before they opened it. A young girl who must have only been sixteen was lying there, shaking, shivering. Her bony arm reached out towards them. 'Please, I want to go home, my family care about me, please take me home.'

Dave swallowed hard as he clocked the bruises all over her legs and arms. A small trickle of red blood, rolling down the side of her lips, her dress ripped. Dave bent down to grip her by the arm, her eyes dancing one way then the other, white powder stuck to the side of her nose. She was in a bad way, twisted out of her head.

'Come on, you can go. Fuck off back to where you came from. You knew the script when you come here. What did you expect?'

Johnny wasn't as patient as Dave. He gripped her by her long hair and dragged her out from the boot of the car and flung her to the roadside into the thick brown mud. He launched a bag at her, a passport fell out of it and a small roll of notes. He sighed as he watched her scramble into the big bushy hedges clutching her bag. She was petrified, still crying.

'Where am I? This is nowhere … where do I go?'

Johnny looked over at her 'Start walking, sweetheart. Just be glad you're in one piece. You're loaded now, anyway. Get a fucking cab – just don't say a word about where you've been. Not if you know what's good for you.'

He looked over at Dave. 'All for a few quid and a bag of sniff.'

Dave was already on his way back to the car, he shouted behind him. 'Come on, let's get back to the farm before he does the same to another one. Honest, I need out of this job, sooner rather than later.'

Johnny bent down and dragged the young girl up by the scruff of her neck, her head falling one way then the other. 'You go back home, do you hear me, don't ever come back here again, because next time you won't be as lucky.'

Johnny got back into the car and flicked the engine over. The car screeched off. He looked into his rear-view mirror and he could see the young girl wobbling about in the middle of the road. He put his foot down and decided to not look back again.

Pam lay on the bed and watched Jordan getting ready to go out. She watched him spray his Hugo Boss aftershave across his chest. Who was he out to impress? Not her, she knew that much. Probably his floozy, the one she knew he'd been boning when he didn't come home until the small hours. From the corner of her eye, she watched his every movement; the boxer shorts he'd chosen, the shirt he'd placed on the end of the bed. Yes, he was definitely getting spruced up for some other woman, probably one of the dancers from the club, he never went anywhere else, so it had to be one of those girls.

'It should be a good night tonight in the club, I've got a few lads coming in on a stag party.'

Pam rolled her eyes at him. 'So it's another late night, then?' she moaned.

'You know the deal, love. More punters drinking, means more money in the bank for us.'

'It's always about the money with you, Jordan. Don't you ever think, I'll take the wife out tonight for a romantic meal and surprise her?'

He scoffed. 'Nah, sod that, why spend money eating out when we can get a takeaway and save buckets of cash? No need for all that palaver anymore.'

She let out a laboured breath. 'It is my money too, you know. And I want to go out sometimes instead of being locked away behind these four walls every bastard day.'

'Quit your moaning. We have holidays, don't we? And you have more than enough money to make yourself happy. Book a bleeding facial or something. Get a wax.'

'Maybe I need your time, Jordan, not money, or clothes, or facials.'

'Time is money and if you want to go on these snazzy holidays then I have to work my nuts off to get it, don't I?'

'I'm a good businesswoman, Jordan, I can help make Passion bigger and better, just cut me a bit of slack and let me change a few things. I've done it before and I can do it again.'

'We don't need to change anything at the club. If it's not broken then there is no need to change anything. I want more of the same, not a makeover. Simple.'

Pam pulled her laptop from under the bed and placed it on her legs as she watched Jordan finish getting ready. 'I suppose it's another boring night lay in bed for me then isn't it, watching TV and drinking wine. I remember the time when I was out each night, eating in the best restaurants and never got home until after three in the morning. The good old days, ay?'

Jordan shot a look over at her, a look that told her she needed to button her lip. He picked up his car keys from the dressing table and marched back to the side of the bed. 'Right, I'm off, put a film on and stop moaning. Clayton will be in soon. He'll talk to you if you're bored.' He bent down, kissed the side of her cheek and strutted out, ready to be king of his club.

Pam rammed two fingers up at the back of her husband as he left the room, mumbling under her breath. 'One day, mate, someone will come for you.'

Pam listened as she heard Jordan pull out of the driveway. He was gone now, she was alone. She jumped out of the bed, rushed over to the wardrobe and pulled out a small black wallet. She returned to her bed and used the passcode she'd stashed away in the wallet to log on. The light from the computer screen lit up Pam's eyes; she was immediately engrossed. Pam pulled out a bank card and smiled at it as she ran her index finger across the top of it.

'We all have secrets, don't we, Jordan? I told you I was a businesswoman. You just watch this space.'

Pam logged on to her online banking and checked her statement. Years of saving, years of cunningly saving money from the guilt-money he threw at her had final come into blossom. Pam looked at her bank balance and nodded. This was her time now, time to get the things she wanted. With speed in her fingertips, she logged out of the account, deleted her search history. She hurried back to the wardrobe and placed the wallet back in its secret location.

Lay on the bed browsing shopping sites on her phone, Pam switched to YouTube and started to watch some pole dancers. She sat up straight, alert, remembering how it felt to be on the stage, how the men lusted after her. She'd not felt that way for a long time now. Her friends from back in the day had often commented on her leaving the stage.

'Why have a Porsche and have it banged up in the garage every day?' they told her. And, they were right, she had it all still going on. Sure, she was older and a mother now, but did that mean she should curl up in a tight ball and just hide away from the world? No, did it hell, she told herself. She should be out there in the mix before it was too late. She had plans that would get her right back on top. She flicked back to the homepage and froze as she spotted a headline. 'SEX TRAFFICKERS JAILED.' The colour drained from her cheeks as she continued reading about a young girl who had been brought into England by men and sold to the sex trade for a few hundred pounds. The girl was only sixteen years of age, the men had told her she would be working in a factory for good money, they had lied to her, plain and simple. But this wasn't just another girl, another story – this girl looked just like the kind of girl that kept turning up at Jordan's club. She slammed the laptop shut and reached over for her glass of wine. She complained when Jordan cut her out of his business dealings, but did she really want to enter that world again?

Chapter Five

Pamela sipped her coffee and waited for her husband to come into the kitchen. The steam from the cup was like a trail of smoke rising. She stood gazing out of the window. It was a lovely view, she could see the full length of the garden. She'd never really had a passion for gardening, and that's why she employed someone to come once a month to keep this area looking nice. Appearances mattered, Pam knew that. She stared, lost in thought. Jordan had been quiet last night and not his usual self. He'd been edgy. He never really spent any time with her when she was at the club, and she had spent most of the night stood at the bar, watching the dancers, on her Jack Jones. It had been her up there once and she missed the stage. She felt free when she danced: calm, in control. All of her stresses disappeared, electric energy surging through her body.

By anyone else's standards, last night had been a success. The club had been busy all night, and there had been no trouble. The punters enjoyed the night and, judging by the takings, Jordan would consider it an evening well spent. But it wasn't the cash in the till that she'd been focussing on. Pamela longed to be back on the stage dancing, but knew Jordan would never allow it. He'd told her straight a thousand times before. She was his wife and there was no way in this world he was having any dirty perverts looking at, let alone touching, her body.

Jordan strolled into the kitchen now and opened the fridge door. He looked moody. 'Have we not got any fresh orange, love? I'm not into coffee this morning. I want something fresh and clean.'

She lifted her head and answered him. 'Yeah, we should have. I bought two cartons the other day.' She watched him from the corner of her eye. He seemed stressed this morning, mumbling under his breath. Pam reached for her cigarettes and popped one from the packet. She flicked her silver lighter underneath it and sucked on it hard. 'Did you enjoy me being at the club last night?'

Jordan swallowed hard and moved to where she sat. He bent his body slightly and kissed her cheek. 'It's always lovely to see you there, darling, but I don't rest when you're there, in case it kicks off. You know better than me how nasty it can get if we get some idiots come in. It was only last week I had to twist some fucker up who got above his station. Honest, I give it him. He was in a bad way when I was done. But he won't fuck with me or my girls again. Lesson learned.'

She stroked her long talons around the rim of her coffee cup as he sat down next to her. 'That Jenny girl can dance. She reminds me of myself when I was dancing.'

Jordan opened the newspaper and rustled it about nervously. 'Yeah, she's got a good following, too. I knew when I discovered her she was going to be a good earner.'

Pamela studied him, trying to detect anything in his voice or body language. 'You know I'd love to come back dancing, babe. Seeing the girls on stage last night reminded me of who I used to be.'

Jordan flung his newspaper down on the kitchen table. His voice was loud and firm. 'Are you for fucking real, or what? How many times have I told you? You are the mother of my child, and you think you can go showing all you've got on that stage? Get a grip, woman – you're twice the age of some of those girls.' He gasped. 'Sometimes I think you've got a fucking screw loose. Imagine our Clayton's face if he thought his mother was a pole-dancer. Get a fucking grip. It will never happen as long as I've got breath in my body. I can't believe you even mentioned it. I'm sure you look at me and think, oh he's in a good mood, I'll just fucking ruin it.'

Pamela screwed her face up and challenged him. 'Listen, I may be forty, but I am still in great shape and I'm better than any of them girls you have dancing for you. What?' She paused and stubbed her cigarette out in the ashtray at the side of her. 'It's alright for you to lust after the dancers, laugh and joke with them, but when it's me it's a different story? I'm sick of it, Jordan. I'm not your prisoner and I'm sick of you ruling my life, telling me what I can and can't do.'

He slammed his large hand on the side of his chair, his eyes meeting hers, ears pinned back. 'Fuck off, Pam. I'm not going over this again. How many times have I told you, the club is our bread and butter? What, do you want to live in a crummy flat like we used to? Stop now before I lose my rag.'

She gripped her mug of coffee and squeezed her cupped hands around it. Maybe she was imagining it was her husband's neck. But he had a point and she knew it. Jordan had worked hard to get them out of the rut they were in back in the day. They'd had fuck all, always living from hand to mouth. But that didn't mean everything about those days was bad. Dancing had given her freedom. Of a kind.

'Do you know, it would be nice if for once you didn't swear when you were talking to me. I'm not a dollop of shit on the bottom of your shoes. I'm sick of it. I hear how you talk to everyone else, and you're all nicey-nicey with that lot in the club, but when you get home here, it's all attitude and talking to me like shite.'

He ragged his fingers through his thick locks and sighed. He was losing it and, if she carried on like this, he'd waste her, like he always did when he lost his temper. 'Shut up!' he screamed. 'Just be happy with what you have, and do what a wife is supposed to do. Stop wanting to change us.'

'I look after everyone in this family, Jordan. Everyone except myself. I need something other than cooking and cleaning every day. Every time I mention anything that involves me going out of this house you come up with some excuse to make me stay in. When are you ever going to support me and push me to do something I will be proud of? Go on, tell me why you don't want anything more for me?'

Jordan huffed. Was she on this planet, or what? He was old school, and his wife would be tied behind the sink, if she liked it or not. Women in business was not something that sat well with him. This was a man's world, and that's the way it was going to stay. 'Join a fucking baking club or something. I'm sure there are groups you can join if you're bored. Needlework, there you go, make some cushions or something.'

He was lucky the cup in her hand wasn't smashed right over his sexist head. There was no way she was letting him get the better of her. She wanted a life too and, now the kids were grown up, she was going to get one, if he liked it or not. 'Piss off, Jordan. You know I'm right. Do you think it's fair that you're out every night and I'm sat in here staring at four bastard walls?'

He bolted up from his seat and started rummaging on the side for his car keys. This was not what he wanted to hear before he'd even had his breakfast. 'And you wonder why I'm never around much. You're always moaning about something. Give it a rest, will you. You're turning into your mother.'

Ouch, another low blow. Pamela's mother had had a hard life and there was no need for him to slate her.

'No, I won't. You don't listen to me, you just run away from it all the time. I've spelt it out to you that I'm not happy and all you do is brush it under the carpet. Don't be surprised if you come home one day and I'm not here.'

Jordan froze, the purple vein at the side of his neck bulging from the skin. He slowly walked to where she sat. She was on thin ice and she knew it. She swallowed hard, knowing he could strike at any minute. That was all she needed, another black eye.

His voice was animated. 'Be happy with what you have. And, for the record, if you ever think you can leave me, remember that I have contacts. I will search high and low until I find you. And God help you when I do.' He went nose to nose with her, his hot breath spraying her face. 'Do you hear me? Am I coming in loud and clear?'

She knew not to say another word.

Pamela stood at the window and watched her other half leaving. She leant against the silver crushed velvet curtains. Her fingers gripped the cold fabric and squeezed it. Her eyes prickled and, slowly, a fat salty tear rolled down her cheek. Life wasn't fair sometimes and she knew she'd paid a high price for the creature comforts that surrounded her. Money did not buy happiness; she'd told Jordan this a million times, but her words fell on deaf ears. As long as he was happy, he didn't give a flying fuck about anyone else. She'd show him, she'd show him big time. She was more than only a mother and a wife, she was a woman on a mission. She walked away from the large window and sat down on the sofa. Her eyes read the words engraved on the silver picture frame: 'If you do what you have always done, you will get what you have always got.'

Clayton came barging into the room. 'Mam, I've got a girl coming over later, so can you try and make yourself busy somewhere? I don't want you sat there being a third wheel. Can you go to bed early or something?'

Pamela shook her head. Like father, like son. Did they both think they could walk all over her? 'No. This is my house. If you want to see some girl, then take her out. There is no way I'm staying cooped up in the bedroom all night long. Are you embarrassed about me or something?'

Clayton looked closely at his mother. Was she upset? He wasn't sure. His voice was soft. 'Mam, you know what I mean. This girl is mint, and I don't want to mess it up. I've been grafting her for ages.' He sat down next to her and knew he'd have to do some persuading. 'I need a bit of alone time with this one. She's not like the others, she's a good girl. Wife material, even.'

Pamela sucked hard on her gums. 'Do you mean she doesn't drop her knickers?'

Clayton chuckled. 'Correct. So please can I have a bit of privacy tonight? Then I can try and work my magic on her.'

'I'll tell you what, Son: you're just like your dad, you are. He can charm the knickers off any woman when he puts his mind to it. The apple never falls far from the tree, does it?'

Clayton could sense something in her voice and knew he should sit and chat with her for a bit. 'Mam, what's up? You seem sad. Have you had an argument with Dad? Because if you have, you know he'll be back here later with a big bunch of flowers and chocolates for you.'

'It will take more than flowers this time, Son. I'm going to make myself happy and stop waiting hand and foot on him. I need a life, too, don't I?'

Clayton secretly pushed his cuff up and checked his wristwatch. He needed to get off. 'Mam, do what makes you happy. End of. Anyway, are we sorted for tonight, or what?'

Pamela started to smile. She looked deep into her son's eyes and smirked. 'Yes, but you owe me a bottle of wine and a takeaway. If I'm staying upstairs all night, at least I can get pissed.'

'Done.' Clayton got to his feet and quickly checked his reflection in the silver mirror. 'I'll tell you what, Mam, you've got a handsome son, you have. Come on, tell me I'm not good-looking?'

Pamela burst out laughing. 'Oh my God, you are such a poser. Just don't spoil yourself by being up your own arse like your dad is. Girls love romance, kind caring guys, not big-heads all about themselves.'

Clayton rushed back to his mother's side and kissed her cheek. 'Love you, see you later.'

'I love you too,' she replied.

The house seemed so quiet these days. No children laughing or running about. An emptiness filled her body and tears flooded her eyes again. Pam let out a laboured breath. 'Things are going to change. I'm not being a prisoner anymore,' she muttered.

She went upstairs and opened the door to her sanctuary. She stared at the silver pole. Jordan had it built for her, saying now she could dance whenever she wanted with no one leering at her. But it felt more like a silver cage – the mirrors reflecting back how trapped she was. But at least it meant she hadn't lost her touch. Every day she danced in here, she made sure her body remained flexible and supple. Pam looked at her reflection. She was dressed in black hot-pants and a small red belly-top – she looked as good as the younger girls she'd seen at the club. With a burst of energy, she ran at the pole and gripped it with all her might. It made her feel powerful to know she could move like this.

Her body melted into the pole and she was like an acrobat. She used her long slender legs to position herself on the pole. Losing herself in the rhythm, the sweat soon poured from her body as she moved up and down. This was *her* time in this room, *her* rules. Nobody could tell her what to do when she was dancing. She was strong, fearless. She finished the dance and collapsed onto the floor; she'd worked hard this morning. She sat up with her legs pulled close to her chest, recovering from the workout. The corners of her mouth began to rise, a sparkle returning to her eyes. She jumped to her feet and left the room.

Jordan opened the club doors and the smell of stale tobacco and beer hit his nostrils. This place needed a good deep clean. He looked at his wristwatch and checked the car park behind him. The cleaner should have been here by now. He walked inside the club and went behind the bar. He stood staring at his empire for a few seconds and nodded. He'd worked his nuts off to get this place up and running. Yes, he'd upset a few people doing it, and he'd lost a few decent pals too, but business was business, and friendship was friendship.

His mobile phone started ringing and he rummaged deep in his jacket pocket to get it.

'Hello, what's happening, Robbie? I've been waiting for your call. What have you got for me?' Jordan listened to the voice at the other end and smirked. He nodded as he spoke. 'Give me about twenty minutes and I'll fly over. Make sure you keep the decent ones for me.' The call ended and he shoved his mobile back in his pocket. The door opened and Angela stood there looking windswept.

Jordan stepped onto the stage and turned to face her. 'Bloody cleaner hasn't turned up. You wouldn't give those side-rooms a good clean, would you? A guy was sick in there last night.'

She huffed. 'You don't pay me enough, Jordan, to do that. I'm here to look after the girls, not clean up after punters.'

Jordan sighed and walked about the stage, checking the lights. 'For fuck's sake, Ange, I'll pay you extra to do some cleaning today.'

'OK, I'll do it this once.' Angela added, 'Not for you, but because I don't want the girls working in squalor. They deserve better. We all do. We're not pieces of meat, Jordan. Treat us like shit one too many times, and one day you'll regret it.'

Chapter Six

Karla lay sprawled on the sofa as Mary entered the room. Last night's make-up was splattered under her eyes; thick, clumpy, black mascara. Mary, meanwhile, was soaking wet and looked bedraggled. She gasped as she shook the rain from her hair. 'It's pissing it down out there. Twenty minutes I've had to wait for that bus.'

Karla reached for another chocolate and stretched her arms out. 'I've told you, I'll ask Jordan for a cleaning job at his club, if you want, then you can ditch the other one. You don't like it, anyway, do you? Long hours and shit pay. Tell them to shove the job up their arse and get some other mug to do it.'

Mary dragged her coat off and plonked it on the back of the chair. 'Don't waste your breath. I wouldn't work for that womaniser if my life depended on it.' She changed the subject quickly. 'Oi, what happened to you staying out last night? Did Mr Full-of-Shit have to go home to his wife?' Mary folded her arms tightly with a told-you-so face on.

Karla folded the cushion under her head. 'I came home because I wanted to. People can change their minds, you know.'

Mary wasn't wet behind the ears and let out a sarcastic laugh. 'Pull the other one, it's got bells on, love. Don't try and kid me, because I can see right through you. Go on, tell me he didn't go home to his wife last night. What excuse did he give you?' Mary knew she was right; she could tell by her daughter's body language.

Karla had to bite her tongue, keep her cool, not respond to Mary's comments. Luckily, just then, Elsa appeared in the room wearing a white short t-shirt and some bed shorts. She could clearly sense the atmosphere as soon as she walked in. Her eyes flicked one way then the other. 'Mam, can you leave me some money today before you go out? I'm going for pizza with Candice and a few of the other girls.'

Karla fanned her fingers out in front of her and examined her long almond-shaped nails. 'I've not got a carrot, love. My money hasn't been paid yet.'

Mary nearly choked. 'What, no money again? You never got paid your benefit last week, or so you told me, so it's due this week, isn't it?'

Karla started fidgeting and sat up straight, no eye contact with her mother. 'They always mess my money up. They said I should have gone for a job interview they'd set up a few days ago and, just because I wasn't feeling too good and didn't go, they suspended my benefit. If you don't believe me, you can ring them up. Bleeding hell, you're like Miss Marple, you are. You should ring the police station and ask if they're recruiting any detectives.'

Elsa screwed her face up and shot a look over at her nana. 'So, what am I supposed to do, then? Mam, it's every time I ask you for something. It's always go and ask your nana, or you have some excuse about having no money. You bought new clothes last week, so where did that money come from?' Elsa stood waiting on an answer. She knew her mother was lying,

Karla bolted up from the sofa and quickly tied her hair back. 'I'm skint, it's not my fault. I do my best for you, and over the years I've gone without so you could have nice stuff. Why don't you get a job and start buying your own clothes? That's what I had to do when I was your age.'

Mary huffed and sparked a cigarette up. She smirked at Elsa and rolled her eyes. 'Ignore her, Elsa. When she quit school, after having you, she worked a few weeks then jacked it in. Every morning I was trying to wake her up and she wouldn't get out of that bed. Yep, two weeks tops she worked, so don't let her make out she worked her socks off to support you, because she bloody well didn't, it was me.' She pointed a finger at her daughter. 'I worked three jobs to buy your daughter everything she needed, Karla, and what thanks did I get for it, eh?'

Karla was flustered. 'Bloody hell, do you want a gold medal or something? That's what families do.' She paused before she continued, 'They help each other out. I'll tell you what, I'm going back to bed. I might get a bit of peace there. On my life, I can't do right for doing wrong in this house.'

Karla stormed out of the room and Mary shook her head at Elsa. She folded her arms tightly across her chest and let out a long hard breath. 'It's like pissing in the wind trying to talk to that one.'

Elsa dropped her head low. She could hear rustling behind her and, from the corner of her eye, she could see Mary digging into her tattered red leather purse. 'Here, take this tenner. It was to pay the gas bill for this week, but I'm sure it can wait. Well, it will have to wait if I've spent it, won't it?'

Elsa edged over to her nana and kissed her. 'I don't know what I'd do if you wasn't about, Nana. I'm going to look for a job, anyway. My mam's right, I need to be bringing some money into this house, too.'

'You ignore her, love – I know you'll be paying your way soon enough. You just have to find the right job. Not like your mum. She's bone idle and, if she carries on with her attitude towards me, I'll end up giving her her marching orders. The gob on that one is terrible. It's a wonder I'm not six foot under with all the stress she gives me.'

Elsa folded the ten-pound note neatly in her hand and stood looking at Mary with sadness. 'If I had my dad around then maybe he could help out. I don't know why she doesn't go and see him and ask if he can put his hand in his pocket. He is my father, after all.'

Mary swallowed hard. 'Over my dead body will anybody ask that bastard for money. We've managed this long without him, we're not going to start begging now.'

'But I can go and see him. My mam said he knows about me, so why shouldn't I go and see him and ask for help? Tell me who he is – I'm old enough to know now, surely.'

Mary's eyes widened and her cheeks flared. 'Elsa, promise me now you will never go in search of that scumbag.

There's a reason why we've kept you well clear of him. Even if you did track him down, I wouldn't want you within six feet of that man. He's a wrong-un. Someone who can't be trusted. You don't know anything about him and, believe me, you don't want to. He's the lowest of the low. Keep well away.'

Elsa shot her eyes towards the telly and didn't reply. Flustered, Mary stood up and started to clean the front room, mumbling under her breath as she picked things up from the floor. Elsa carried on watching *The Real Housewives of Cheshire*. She loved the world they lived in: designer clothes, big houses, women doing things their way and bossing it. This was where she wanted to live if she ever got the chance. She was sick of scrimping and scraping every day to try and keep up with all the other girls her age. One day, her life would change, and then she wouldn't want for anything. She just had to find a way.

Chapter Seven

Jordan parked his black Land Rover and quickly scanned the area. He locked the car up, looking over his shoulder. A man stood at a door not far from him and waved his hand to get his attention. Jordan took one last look to see if he was being watched, and headed towards him.

'How's it going, Wesley?' Jordan asked.

The man nodded slowly and smiled. 'It's going good, pal. You're first here so you can have first refusal. I've got some beauties here for you today. I'll tell you straight though, the price is set, so don't be umming and ahhing like you normally do.'

Jordan slapped Wesley's back in acknowledgement. The man was built like a shit-house door: solid, thick-set neck and a head like a donkey. They walked into the house. The corridor was dimly lit and held an eerie silence. Wesley froze and held one finger up at his mouth. 'Wait here a minute while I make sure these girls are ready for you. A few of them have been playing up a bit, so I'm going to warn them before you go in.'

Jordan examined the few pictures hung on the wall near him. Yellow sunflowers, purple lavender growing widely in a field. He held his ear to the door; he could hear raised voices and Wesley shouting. He grinned and stood cracking his knuckles. Wesley ran a tight ship here, but the way he treated some of these girls was shocking, even to a man like Jordan. He'd backhand any of them without giving it a second thought. Oh yes, this man was a bully, a woman-beater. It made Jordan feel better, though – he was saving these girls from worse treatment.

The door opened and a bright-yellow light hit the corridor. Wesley's head appeared from behind the door. 'Ready when you are, mate. Are you having a beer while you have a look at this bunch?'

'Nah, mate, I'm alright. I'm in and out today, not sticking around.'

Jordan entered with caution. The room was painted in a deep red. Table-lamps positioned in each corner gave a gentle glow at odds with what he knew often happened here. There was a thick cream sheepskin rug by the fire. Soft music played in the background as Jordan sat down on a black leather chair.

Wesley cracked open a can of Budweiser and gulped a large mouthful. It was showtime. He opened the door behind him and shouted, 'Right, one at a time. Remember what I told you, keep your mouths shut. This man can earn you some decent money, so I want you at your best. No fucking about or making mistakes.'

Jordan sat back in his chair with his legs opened slightly. A pale girl walked into the room dressed in a red bikini. Bleeding hell, she looked young. Her body was thin: you would have seen more fat on a chip. She was shaking, and she nearly fell over on her red high-heeled shoes, too large for her feet. She walked past Jordan and he was sure she was crying.

'This is Polly. She can dance a bit, but you'd have to train her. She knows English and she doesn't have a problem understanding you.' Wesley twisted his body and made sure Polly could see him. 'You know how to move, don't you, girl?'

There was no reply. Wesley used the remote control and changed the music. A loud baseline tune began pumping through the speakers. 'Dance, Polly. Show him what you can do,' Wesley hissed.

Polly closed her eyes slowly and walked back to where Jordan sat. She bent over fully, and Jordan inspected her like he was at a cattle market. Her long legs were perfect, no blemishes or telltale scars. The young girl came to face Jordan and opened her legs over him. Her cold, scrawny fingers stroked the side of his face, and slowly her body rolled down his. This was business, but he found he was still enjoying the dance; his dick stood up like a soldier ready for war. He tried to cover his excitement before anybody else could see it. Polly looked deep into his eyes as the tune reached its climax. Big treacle-coloured eyes, clouded over as if she was all cried out, met his. He dipped his head slightly and turned his glance away from her. This was no time to be having a conscience. This was all about the money.

'Right, get me the next one, Wes. I'll have Polly, so put my name on her.'

The girl walked away, and her legs seemed to buckle underneath her as she left the room. Jordan nodded his head in approval. 'A bit of feeding up and she'll be mint, her. She's got great moves, too; the punters will love her.'

'I told you I had some top girls, didn't I?'

Jordan chuckled and prepared for the next dancers to strut their stuff. All in all, he picked two girls. The rest of them were not up to standard. They looked like druggies, he told Wesley: spotty skin, greasy hair, dodgy teeth, and he was sure he clocked track marks on the last girl's arms. Drugs were a big part of the world he lived in, but party drugs, not the hard stuff, the smack, or the spice.

Jordan stood up after the last girl had awkwardly tried her moves. She was crap, nothing sexy about her at all. He didn't even let her finish her dance, he carted her and told Wes to take her away. Two other men entered the room. They spoke in their own language and looked over at Jordan. He jerked his head at them, paranoid they were talking about him – it sounded like Romanian.

'What's up, lads? Is there a fucking problem?'

They looked at each other and carried on talking. Jordan's nostrils flared. He slowly guided his tongue across his top lip. His knuckles turned white. If these two wanted any beef with him, he was ready to knock ten tons of shit out of them. He stood up, rolling his shoulders back.

Wesley rushed over and tried to calm him down. 'It's sorted, mate. They don't speak much English; they mean no harm.'

'You'd better word them up about me, then. I can't stand it when these cunts start muttering. They could be saying anything.'

Wesley patted Jordan's shoulder. 'Come on, we'll go to my office and you can weigh me in.'

Jordan straightened his clothes, but never took his eyes from the men as he left the room. He never trusted anyone as far as he could throw them. He'd been had over in the past, and nearly lost his empire through taking his eyes off the ball. That would never happen again. He was always alert and questioned anything that didn't seem right, anyone he didn't know. He was on the juice and, even if his behaviour was probably partly due to the steroids he pumped into his body every morning before he got ready, it didn't hurt to be on your guard. He'd rather that than the competition think he was a soft touch.

Jordan plonked himself down in Wesley's office. He was happy with his purchases today. He reached into his black leather jacket and pulled out a wad of cash. Dirty money it might have been, money obtained from people who could ill afford it, but that was the circle of life round here. 'I hope there'll be no comeback from these girls. They better be legal to be in the country and all that. The last thing I need is the dibble on my case for immigration.'

Wesley sat back and smiled. Today was a money earner and he was happy. 'It's sweet, mate. These girls got shipped in last weekend. All official, above board. They know the crack when they agree to come over to England. What do they have back home? At the end of the day, we're doing them a favour, aren't we? We're saving them from poverty. Fucking guardian angels, we are, mate.'

Jordan agreed and started to count the money out. He wet the end of his finger in his mouth and flicked it through the cash. Wesley's eyes never moved away from the stack of money until the last note had been counted. Jordan was his friend, yes, but in this game even your closest friend would have your eyes out, given the chance.

'I'll send Karla over tonight to pick the girls up. They can stay at the house I have for the girls. But make sure you tell them it's not a free ride. They have to pay rent out of their take. I'm not a fucking charity.'

'Yes, I'll let them know. A few little extras for your punters here and there and they will be wadded. They'll have more money than they know what to do with.'

Jordan reached over and shook Wesley's hand; hot, sticky palms clenched together. 'I'll see you in a few weeks, Wes. Remember, always let me have first look at the new arrivals. I've got plans to open a new club in the near future, so I need some top-notch girls to get the punters inside the doors.'

Wesley opened his eyes wide and shoved the money into the desk drawer. His voice lowered and he spoke, knowing the reaction he would get. 'Does Lenny know you're set to launch another club?'

Jordan snarled. His words were slow and full of meaning: he hated the man they were talking about. 'I'm not arsed if he knows or not. It's got fuck all to do with him what I'm doing. If he wants beef, then he knows the dance. It's game on, isn't it? But I'm not a kid anymore, like I was back in the day. This time I'll take him to the fucking cleaners. I'll put him in a body bag.'

'As long as you know what you're doing, mate. Lenny is a force not to be messed with. The guy's off his napper. The stories I've heard about him and his boys would make your toes curl. He's ruthless, a law unto himself.'

Jordan walked to the office door. His cage had been rattled and his eyes were dancing with madness. 'You let me worry about that prick, mate. I've got my own team ready to go, if he wants war. We all know fucking nutters who are willing to take the cunt down for a few quid.'

'Just tread carefully, that's all I'm saying. I'd sleep with one eye open if I was you. The guy gives me the creeps, honest, mate. Even the way he looks makes me shit my pants.'

'He doesn't scare me, mate. Catch you later, Wes, speak soon.' Jordan marched out of the house and headed for his car. Once he was sat inside, he gripped the steering wheel and squeezed it with all his might. If Lenny Jackson thought he was stopping him building his empire, he had another think coming. *He* was the main man now, not Lenny Jackson.

Chapter Eight

Elsa pressed the brass bell and stood back from the door. Her heart was beating ten to the dozen. She could hear footsteps inside. A female voice, talking to herself, coming nearer. Elsa straightened her hair and tugged her leather jacket down. The door opened and a woman stood looking at her. Never said a word, she just kept looking her up and down, examining every inch of her.

Elsa stuttered, 'Is Clayton in?'

Pamela smiled, but still didn't open the door fully to let her inside. 'So, you're the girl who's got my son running about like a headless chicken. I've never seen him like this before.'

Elsa tried to clear her throat. How should she answer her? She had to think on her feet. 'Why, what's he said? All good, I hope?'

Pamela chuckled and opened the door wide, inviting her inside. 'He's not shut up about you. I've been banished to my bedroom tonight so he can have a romantic date with you. You must be special, because he's never acted this way before over any girl. He was in the bathroom for hours. Usually he spends every hour God sends on his phone or at the gym.'

Elsa blushed. She flicked her hair over her shoulder and followed the woman into the front room. She'd been here before, but acted like this was her first time in the house. There was no way she was having Clayton's mam thinking she was some slapper who went back to every lad's house.

'I'm Pamela, but call me Pam. As you may have worked out, I'm Clayton's mother. He's a lovely lad, you know. Kind, caring, and knows how to treat a woman.'

'He's spoken about you. I can tell he thinks a lot of you.'

Pamela stood proud: her boy, her first born. She'd rip every hair out of their head if any girl ever crossed her boy. She was like a lioness, she never kept still; her eyes on Elsa all the time. 'Clayton's still out, but he told me you were coming. He had an emergency, he said. He's always out helping his mates, or doing odd jobs for his dad. I'm going to have a glass of wine; do you want one?'

Elsa wasn't a big drinker, especially on a weekday, but she didn't want to be rude. 'Yes please, if you don't mind.'

Pamela went into the kitchen and Elsa could hear cupboard doors opening, glasses clanging together. She sucked in large mouthfuls of air: breathe, girl, breathe. She stood for a few seconds debating what to do next. Should she sit down? Should she go and help with the drinks? Too late – Pamela was back, holding two glasses. She looked even prettier than her photograph. Her skin seemed flawless, hair like silk and a figure to die for.

'Come and sit down. I don't bite,' Pam purred.

Elsa tried to walk straight, but she was nervous and she couldn't hide it.

'So how long have you been seeing Clayton?' She caught Elsa off guard.

Using her telephone voice, Elsa replied, 'I've known Clayton for ages. We've been speaking for a few months, but we've only just started dating, really.'

'So, is he your boyfriend, or what?' This woman was like the Gestapo, she'd have her finger on her pulse next to check if she was lying.

'It's early days, so we don't have a label on us yet.'

Pam sipped her red wine and pulled her feet up under her on the sofa. 'Are you on the pill, love? I'm only making sure, because I don't want our Clayton's life ruined by getting someone up the duff when he's got to think about choosing a career and that.'

Elsa bit down on her tongue. The bluntness of the question had taken her by surprise. 'I don't need to be on the pill, Pamela, because I'm not having sex. And I'm planning a career for myself. I don't want any children either, yet. Not that it's any of your business.'

They locked eyes and neither of them blinked. Pam ran a finger around the rim of her glass. This girl was a dark horse. She looked as innocent as anything, at first glance, but there was a core of something much tougher inside, she could tell. Pamela eased up on her. 'You are stunning, you know. No wonder my boy is trying to bag you. So, what are you studying, what career do you want?'

Elsa took a large mouthful of the red wine. 'I'm into the

arts. I love dancing and singing. I've just finished at college doing Performing Arts. But I don't know if I'll be able to find a job like that around here.'

'What kind of dancing are you into?'

'I love street dance, but I like salsa, too. Any kind of dancing, really. I get lost in the music and it sort of takes me away in my head to a place that's sort of peaceful and safe.'

Pamela reached over and touched Elsa's shoulder. 'That's exactly how I feel when I dance. It's funny because I've never told anyone that, but yes, it makes me feel safe, too.'

'What kind of dancing do you do?' Elsa tried to make her question sound innocent and felt guilty that she'd stumbled on the mirrored room upstairs.

Pamela held her lips tightly together. She was debating what to say next. She tapped her fingers rapidly on the corner of the sofa. 'I've done lots of dancing. I like express-ing myself.' There you go, she didn't need to tell her son's girlfriend that she'd been a lap-dancer.

'Do you still dance?'

Pamela dropped her head and twisted her fingers. 'Come on, drink up. I've got another two bottles waiting for us in there.'

Elsa necked the rest of her wine and already she could feel the cool liquid travelling down her body, making her feel calm, more confident. A mobile phone started ringing and Pam rolled her eyes as she looked at the screen. 'It's Clayton's dad. I won't be a minute.' She stood up and headed out of the door.

Elsa could hear the conversation, and she could tell by her tone that Pam wasn't happy.

'But, you said it wouldn't be a late one tonight. Bleeding hell, do what you're doing. It's not like you listen to me, anyway.'

Elsa tried not to look directly at Clayton's mother when she came back into the room. She pretended she hadn't heard anything. 'Did Clayton say what time he was coming home? Maybe I should come back later.'

Pamela sat back down with the bottle of wine held close to her. 'No, he said for me to entertain you. It's nice to have another woman around to talk to. Have another glass.'

Over an hour passed, and Clayton still wasn't there. He'd texted Elsa, telling her he was running late and how sorry he was, but Elsa found – as the wine flowed – she was having a fun time with his mother.

Pamela wiggled her finger at Elsa. 'So, come on then, show me your dance moves.'

'No way, I'm too shy. I don't really dance in front of anyone outside college.'

Pamela was slurring her words now. 'You're not shy, you just think you are. It's all in your head. Listen, when I'm dancing, I have a few glasses of wine and I can dance in front of anyone, and I mean anyone.'

'You go first then, and show me what you're all about.'

Pamela loved a challenge. She loved that someone wanted to see her dancing again. She didn't need asking twice. She jumped to her feet and quickly made her way to the door. 'Come on then, but let me warn you, our Clayton would go mad if he knew I've been dancing in front of his new girlfriend.' Pamela was alive, her eyes shining, and every inch of her skin seemed to be glowing. She stood at the bottom of the stairs and urged Elsa to follow her. 'Don't stand there gawping at me. You want to see me dance, prepare to be surprised.' She paused. 'But this is our secret, girl stuff. Pinky promise?' She curled her little finger and interlocked it with Elsa's. The deal was done, their secret was safe.

Pamela rushed up the stairs like a young girl. She opened the door to her refuge and stood with her back against the cold wall. Switching the coloured lights on above them, she yanked her top off over her head. This woman was sculpted and toned, no bingo wings or love handles. Pamela stood in her grey vest top and black jogging bottoms. 'I'll find a song and then I'll show you the kind of dancing I do.'

Elsa watched her with eager eyes. Lady Saw's 'Heels On' started to play through the speaker. Pamela rubbed something onto her hands and sprinted to the silver pole in the middle of the room. The speed of this woman: she gripped the pole at the top, her fingers clenched tightly and her body spun around it. Wow, she was so flexible, Elsa was amazed. Pamela's legs came over her head with such elegance, and then she was upside down on the pole, sliding down it slowly, seductively. Oh my God, her legs were wide open as her body melted down the pole. Elsa was mesmerised, she never took her eyes from Clayton's mother. She was amazing, every movement precise. The strength on this woman was unbelievable. She was using all her body to caress the pole. This was more than a dance; she was like an Olympic gymnast. Elsa knew, from her own time in rehearsal studios, there was no room for error. If you took your eye off the game, a dance could be ruined in a moment. Focus, focus, focus.

The song came to an end and Pamela sank to the floor. Her breathing was rapid and strands of hair stuck to the side of her face as she dropped her head down on the top of her knees. Elsa slowly brought her hands together and started clapping. This was no ordinary dancing, this was sexual, more than a strip tease, more than any twerking she'd ever seen. There was energy in the moves, confidence, power.

'That was amazing, Pam. Oh my God, I've never seen anything like that in my life. You're so fit. I could never do that. You must be so strong. Honest, you were mint.'

Pamela held her head up. She looked at Elsa and patted the floor with a flat palm, beckoning her to come and sit down next to her. The alcohol had loosened her lips and she wasn't bothered what she was saying anymore. 'I used to be a pole dancer. The best in town, I was. Men used to travel from miles out to see me.' Her eyes opened wide. 'Just to see me. I'm a bit rusty, but I've been practising at home. Why don't you have a go? I could teach you some moves.'

No way in this world was Elsa getting up on that pole in front of anyone else. She declined the offer point blank. This woman had put her to shame and there was no way she could match her performance. Sure, she knew she could move, and she knew how much she'd enjoyed that first illicit time on the pole – but that was alone, no audience, and certainly no professional, watching her. But she wanted to know more.

'So, tell me about being a dancer. Where did you work? Was the money good?' So many questions burst out in one breath. Elsa was more than interested in this woman's story.

'Pass me my wine and I'll tell you about me, the real me. Not the one everyone thinks I am; the old me my husband wants to lock away for ever and never talk about.'

Her eyes flooded with tears and Elsa panicked. Bloody hell, what should she do? She couldn't sit there looking like a spare part, she had to comfort her.

Elsa reached over and touched her hand softly. 'Don't get upset. Everyone has a past. It's who you were, then. Look at you now: you're gorgeous, you have a family, and look at where you live. I would give my left arm to live your life.'

Pamela wiped the tears away with the side of her wrist. She cringed as she remembered her past. She looked in pain. 'I've done things I'm not proud of, love. Things everyone tries to brush under the carpet and pretend don't exist. But they do, they will always be there.' She poked her index finger deep into the side of her head. 'They exist in here, they'll always be here, and nothing will ever blank them out; no amount of money or wine or drugs. Nothing will ever make them go away.'

Pamela folded her arms and squeezed her body. She lifted her head slowly, closed her eyes and her expression changed. In her mind, she was back there, back in the world where she was trying to escape. The smell, the noise, the hands on her young flesh were all there for her to see. 'I was only a kid, back then. My home life was shite. You know the story, Mam and Dad had split up and my mam hit the bottle hard. When I look back now, I would say she had big problems, but I was too young to understand it all, then. She'd just given up on us, left us to fend for ourselves. There was never no food in the cupboards, and she was always propping some bar up in the local boozer. It was child neglect; we should have been taken into care. And,' she sighed, 'you don't even want to know about the number of men she brought home night after night. Dirty old men, the dregs of society, they were. The men nicknamed her VD Vera. They used to shout it across the road at her whenever she walked past them. VD Vera, don't go near her, they'd scream.'

Elsa rubbed her arms as the soft blonde hairs there stood on end. This was a real story, not made-up crap that she was used to watching on the TV. This was someone's life. Pamela slowly opened her eyes. She picked up her glass and took a large mouthful of wine. Elsa wanted to know more but there was no way she was going to rush her, that would have been rude. No, she just sat there patiently waiting to hear more.

'I started getting into trouble with the law to start with, bits of shoplifting, fighting. The usual stuff you'd expect a teenager to be involved with. Then one night I met a man when I was waiting for my mother outside the boozer. He seemed to take an interest in me. You should have seen the car he got out of, it was like nothing I'd ever seen before. We all thought the geezer was royalty or a famous person when we saw him get out of the motor. He smelt so good, too. I'll never forget that smell, ever. It was fresh and clean, like peeled oranges. He smelt of money. It was the way he stared over at me, the way he touched my face. He was a good-looking guy, too.' Pamela smiled. 'He promised me the world from the moment I met him. He told me he could change my life and keep me safe. I was a kid, how was I supposed to know what I was getting into? He told me to meet him the next day. It was a secret, my first ever secret.' Pamela sat twiddling her hair as she continued. 'Anyway, I met him the next day and he took me shopping. He bought me new underwear, clothes, shoes, make-up. I'd never had as many presents in my whole life. It was like Christmas and my birthday all rolled into one. I loved it, I felt special. Once we'd been shopping, he took me to a house; a big, posh house in the countryside. It was like nothing I'd ever seen before. There were other girls there, too, and I couldn't see the harm in staying there with him for a bit longer. After all, he'd treated me to new clothes and that. One of the older girls took me under her wing, and she couldn't wait to get me into my new clothes and tidy me up. I had my hair washed, make-up applied. I looked amazing. That day I felt clean, a feeling I'd not experienced in a long time. I loved the new fabric next to my skin, no stale smells, or big holes in my clothes, I felt like a princess.'

Elsa was fascinated, hanging on her every word. She tried not to think how close it came to her own story – the life she'd have led if she'd not had her grandmother looking out for her.

Pamela continued, her fingers never still, tapping on the top of her knee. 'Then one night there were three of them. Dirty old bastards they were, hands touching my body, touching places that they shouldn't have been touching me, pressing their dry old lips against mine. I can still taste them in my mouth, and it turns my stomach.' Pamela froze and sucked in a large mouthful of air before she continued. 'That night changed me for ever. I was never the same after that. They took my youth, my innocence. I was forced to have sex with each of them. Nobody listened when I screamed for help. No one helped me when I was fighting to get them off me. I was alone and scared.'

Elsa covered her mouth with both hands. Pamela had been gang-raped. She thought of how she'd been planning to lose her virginity – and how Pamela had hers snatched away.

'They gave me money before they left and told me they would be back for me. One of the other girls came into me after they'd left, and it was her who told me the real reason I was there. Gina was lovely. She was a wise head, and she taught me how to shut the pain away and think what I could turn it into: money. Real money, more money than I could have ever made shoplifting, or even by going straight. Gina was a pole dancer, and she worked the clubs. I owe Gina a lot. She trained me every night for months. She promised me that when I was ready, she would take me with her to perform. She kept to her word, too, and before long, I was on the stage, and I was earning tons of money. The guy who brought me to the house always kept his eyes on me, though. I was his, he told me, he'd made me. And I agreed because he'd taken me away from my shitty life and made me rich. I always planned to go back to school and get educated, but it never happened. I'd had to grow up quickly and couldn't face looking back. Then Gina vanished. I still hope she found a way out – a better life. But I'll never know.

Still, it made me sort my life out. Without her watching out for me, I needed someone else who would – someone who'd make sure I never ended up being taken advantage of again. The first night I met Jordan I knew he was my knight in shining armour. He never took his eyes from me when I was dancing and wherever I went he wasn't far from my side. He freed me, you know. He fought for me with the man who said he owned me. It was terrible, blood everywhere, windows smashed, glasses smashed. It was like World War Three when it kicked off. But I never looked back after that night. Jordan was my protector. He made me feel safe, loved. And together we built the *Passion*. I found him the girls to dance and I was the one who managed everything in the beginning. But,' she paused, 'he changed after a while. I wasn't the most important thing in his life, anymore. His eyes were always on some other girl. I have no proof, but I know he's cheated on me. He keeps me locked away in here all the time and never wants me to have a life. So, in reality, I went from one jailer to another. Sad really, and I know I should stand up to him but, once again, I owe him.'

Elsa's eyes prickled with tears and she swallowed hard trying to hold them back. What a sad story. Here she was, thinking this woman had everything she could ever want for in life. But, in reality, she couldn't have been further from the truth.

They heard noises from downstairs, and looked at each other. Pamela's colour drained from her face. She was as white as a ghost. 'Quick, get downstairs. It will be Clayton. Please, please, don't ever breathe a word of what I have told you. Promise me.'

'I promise,' Elsa whispered. She ran down the stairs to the living room, sat down and tried her best to calm down. She could hear Pam opening the front door and she sat forward in her seat as she met the smiling face of Clayton. He bounced towards her.

'I'm so sorry I'm late. I got mixed up with some shit that was going on in the gym and ended up losing track of time.'

Pamela walked into the room and she smiled as she watched the two love-birds. The way her son looked at Elsa, the way his eyes filled up with bright lights; he was smitten for sure. Her husband used to look at her the same way. He didn't do that anymore.

'So, Mam, what do you think of her?' Clayton chuckled.

Pamela swept her hair back and went to sit down next to Elsa. 'She's lovely, Son. Make sure you look after her, she's special, this one is. I've interviewed her, and she passed all the tests. So, in the words of Simon Cowell, it's a yes from me.'

They all laughed, and Clayton sprawled his body down on the sofa. He shot a look over at his mother and raised his eyes.

She got the message and smiled at him. 'Right, I'm going to watch a film upstairs. You don't want me sat here with you two, do you?'

Elsa was blushing. 'I don't mind, honest. You can stay here if you want?'

Clayton coughed loudly and that was enough for his mother to leave them alone. He didn't need a third wheel. As Pamela neared the living room door, she turned back and spoke in a gentle voice. 'It's been nice meeting you, Elsa. Perhaps we can go out for lunch sometime and get to know each other better?'

Elsa did not need asking twice. 'I'd love that. I will get Clayton to give you my number.'

Clayton looked at Elsa and then his mother. It seemed like they'd known each other for years. Once Pam had left the room, Elsa smiled at Clayton. She examined every inch of his face, and she couldn't wait to kiss him, he was so attractive.

'You two got on, didn't you? She never really talks to people you know, so you're lucky. She must have warmed to you.'

'She is lovely, honestly, she made me feel so welcome.'

'What was she saying about me? Singing my praises?' This lad was full of himself, so confident.

'I'm not telling you. It was girl talk,' she giggled.

Clayton rolled towards her and gripped her tightly in his arms. 'I've been dying to kiss you all day. I swear, you're like a drug, and I can't get enough of you. What's the chances of you staying over?'

Elsa wriggled about in his grip. 'I can't tonight, but maybe … soon …' she replied.

'Playing hard to get, are you?' he joked as his lips pressed against hers. The kiss was even better this time. She tingled from head to toe, sensations deep inside her that she'd never experienced before. But she wasn't ready to take it further – not tonight. Sensing she wasn't going to be persuaded, Clayton relaxed his grip. The two of them cuddled up on the sofa to watch a film. But if anyone had asked Elsa what it was about, she'd have been lost for words. Between the desire she felt for the man sitting next to him and the story Pam had told her, the film seemed a pale comparison to real life. And beyond all of that, she thought about the music, the pole, the moves. She wanted to dance – she was sure of it.

Chapter Nine

At *Passion*, Angela was waiting for the new girls to arrive. Jordan always trusted her with the latest recruits and knew she would whip them into shape before they hit the stage. Jordan walked in. Angela sat up straight, pushed her breasts out in front of her and crossed her legs. This was her time with Jordan, a time when she could have him all to herself without that daft cow Karla swinging around his neck.

'What time are the girls landing, Jordan?'

He plonked down on a chair next to her. 'Wes is on route with them as we speak. You know the drill, get them checked out and make sure they're clean before anyone touches them. I don't want any girls working for me who are riddled with the clap. It's not good for business.'

'I'll sort it out, just like I always do,' Angela said. 'And while you're here you need to sort Karla out. She's going to end up getting her lights punched out if she carries on with her mouth. Jenny was going to rag her out last night, if I hadn't stopped her. Honest, she's getting above her station. You need to get her in line or get rid.'

Jordan raised his eyes to meet her gaze. 'Tell me about it. Why do I always get myself caught up with women like her? You'd think I would have learned by now.'

Angela sensed her chance. 'Oi, I wasn't like that. I looked after you and never pressurised you to do anything you didn't want to do. I know Karla thinks you're going to leave your wife; she's got a big shock coming when she finds out you're going nowhere. Even I know that. You promised me the same thing, didn't you? But I knew it was all talk.'

Jordan jerked his head up and stared at Angela. 'We had a fling, Angela. We both knew it wasn't long term. So I might have got carried away and said a few things in the heat of the moment, but it was a shag, nothing more, nothing less.' He yawned and stretched his arms over his head. 'I'm not in no mood for this ball-ache today. Wherever I go lately, I seem to be getting headache from you women. Fuck me, I just want a quiet life.'

Angela was fuming. 'You get ball-ache because you're a player. You're full of bullshit. All these women think you're going to leave your wife and live happily ever after. You should be straight with them from the start and tell them they're just a leg-over, then your love life wouldn't be hectic, would it?' Angela stared at Jordan, waiting on a reply. She was beginning to see that she would never get this man back in her bed. Maybe it was time to move on and get him out of her head for good.

Jordan casually stood up, aware that there was an atmosphere. 'Get the girls ready for tonight. Mickey wants a few girls around at his gaff. He's throwing a party and wants some eye-candy there for his guests. Don't put the newbies on their own, either. Make sure a couple of the other girls go, too. Now I've got to be somewhere, so I'm trusting you to sort tonight. I don't want any fuck-ups. There's too much at stake.'

Jordan pulled up at a long, low building and pulled the keys from the ignition. He was eager to get inside and have a look around. This was his next project, his next club. Jordan could see a man in the distance waiting for him. He was late so he jogged over to him. He stretched his hand out to greet the man.

'Sorry I'm running late, Gary. It's been one thing after another today, mate.'

Gary smiled, and shook his hand. 'Before we start, Jordan, I need to tell you there are a few people after this place, so don't drag your heels making a decision.'

Jordan raised his eyebrows. This guy must have thought he was green or something. He knew the score and how things worked. This plonker was just trying to get a deal done today. 'Show me around and then we can sit down and talk about money. Who are the other people interested, then?'

Gary shook his head and straightened his jacket; he held a poker face. 'You know the code of conduct, pal. I can't break confidentiality. It's more than my job's worth.'

Jordan sniggered: he knew this man was after a back-hander. 'I'm sure a few quid will loosen them lips, Gary. I'll sort you out. You look after me, and I'll look after you. You know the Bobby Moore.'

He followed Gary into the building. This place was the dog's bollocks. It was everything he thought it would be. He stood in the middle of the room and pictured how it could look. 'Yep, a stage could go there, dance floor here, and the bar over here.'

Gary agreed. 'It's got lots of potential. I can see your vision, and I like it. This is a gold mine and, with some work on it, I can see it being one of the best clubs in Manchester.'

Of course, Gary was pitching the place. He wanted a sale here today and Jordan could see him trying to work out if he was going to make an offer.

Jordan's eyes lit up. 'I can see it all. I'm going to call this club *Peaches*. The name will be in lights over the bar and over the stage. Now let me see the rest of the place, so I can get a full picture.'

Gary was talking non-stop, chatting shit, nothing of real importance, but trying to sound like a player. Jordan let his chatter wash over him and opened the fire exit to look at the parking spaces. There was enough ground here to park at least a couple of hundred cars and a few coaches. His nostrils flared as the cold, crisp air hit his body and his chest expanded as he took a deep breath. His empire was growing and, once he had this club under his belt, the sky would be the limit. Gary was lingering, never far from his side. Jordan reached over and patted his shoulder.

'Let's talk about money. How much are you looking at? And don't be insulting me with daft figures. This isn't the only place I'm interested in, so don't think you can have my eyes out on this.'

'Mate, since when have I had you over? I have the guide-line price, and that's all I can tell you. Put an offer in. I'll ring the seller and see what they're saying, that's all I can do.'

Jordan chewed on his bottom lip. He knew that, to get the best price here, he had to play it cool and not be so eager. 'I'll ring you later with an offer. I'm going to look at some other buildings first before I make my mind up.'

Gary was deflated. He'd thought this was a done deal. He stuttered. 'That's fine, but sooner rather than later, pal. Like I said, there are other interested parties.'

'Blah fucking blah.' Jordan chuckled. 'Like I said, I'll ring you later, so keep your phone handy.' Jordan walked back to his car and got straight on the blower.

———

Over at *Passion*, Angela greeted the new girls: Polly and Anneka. They were like two scared animals stood in car headlights. They could barely talk through shaking. Angela came to their side and spoke in a quiet, calm voice.

'Hello, girls. Don't be scared, I won't bite. You're going to like it here, and I'm going to look after you both.'

Polly edged away from her and tried to raise a smile. Her voice was low. She seemed so timid. 'Do we get to use the phone now? We were told we could phone home and tell our family that we are safe when we arrived here?'

Angela brushed the comment off. She knew these girls would never phone home again after they started work. Who would want to tell their parents they were selling their bodies and dancing for dirty old men?

Leaning against the wall, Jenny watched the newcomers with her hands on her hips. She was the main attraction here and that's how it would stay. She looked the new arrivals up and down, and spoke in a cocky tone. 'So, can either of you girls dance, and I mean really dance, not just fuck about on the stage doing pussy shots?'

Polly's eyes were wide. 'I can dance. I love dancing.'

Jenny shot a cunning look at Angela. 'You girls have only just landed here; you need to do your induction first. Good luck with that. I hope you know what to expect because, whatever you think, it's probably a hundred times worse.'

Polly looked confused. 'So, we're not dancing tonight, then?'

Jenny howled laughing and sat down on a silver-padded stool. 'Not yet, darling. You have a lot to learn before you step on that stage.' Her position as the top dancer was safe for now, and Jenny knew she had nothing to worry about.

Angela snarled over at her and gave her a look that meant, shut your gob. The girls followed Angela backstage to meet the others. The room was loud and noisy and there were semi-naked women walking about everywhere you looked.

'Right, Polly and Anneka are down to do Mickey's party tonight, so I want them looking top-notch. Grace, can you sort them out and make sure they're ready to go in a couple of hours? Jade is going with you, too, so that's four of you at Mickey's tonight.'

Grace had long red hair and sea-green eyes. She shouted over to Angela. 'Fucking hell, Ange, why am I going there again? The guy is a pervert. I told you what he did last time

I was there, the dirty git. I said I would never go there again. Come on, send someone else. I can't stomach the man. I'd rather move clubs than face that perv.'

Angela walked over and eyeballed her. 'You're going, end of. Jordan picked you to go, so, if you don't like it, pick your bottom lip up from the floor and go and take it up with him.' Angela was used to the moaning from the girls, and if she had a pound for every time one of them said they were leaving she would have been a rich woman. She looked at the two new girls. 'Right, get in the shower first and make sure all your bits are shaved. Even your arse crack. I don't want any hair down there whatsoever, do you hear me? A clean landing strip, no Hitler moustaches, no nothing, bald as a badger. Grab a robe each from the back of the door and go and get sorted. When you've done that, I'll get one of the girls to do your make-up and style your hair.'

The girls all looked amazing when they were ready. The outfits they wore were revealing, tantalising. Jenny had chosen a red sparkling bikini tonight for her main dance and she was hoping to pull some decent cash in from wearing it. Of course, Jordan took money from each girl's wages to pay for these outfits. He wasn't a charity and told them straight that the more they invested in new outfits to wear, the more they would earn.

There was a silence as Karla opened the door and stood looking at them all. She held her head high and took a few seconds to speak. 'Have any of you seen Jordan tonight?' Not one of them answered her. She walked further into the room and started to check the girls over. 'Angela, have you seen Jordan?'

'Nope, last I seen of him was this afternoon. He said he had business to take care of. You know Jordan, he's probably stuck up some new girl.'

The dancers giggled and whispered under their breaths. This was a low blow from Angela. There was no love lost between these two, none whatsoever.

'Keep your smart remarks to yourself, Angela. And why would he even look at someone else when he has me?'

The dancing girls whispered amongst themselves and Karla clocked them.

Angela smirked. 'Are you dropping Grace and Jade off with the new girls at Mickey's?'

Karla let out a sarcastic laugh and shook her head in disbelief. 'Do I look like a fucking taxi driver, or what? I'm a manager here, not a driver. Phone Malc, or one of the other lads, and ask them to.'

Karla walked out, still searching for Jordan. The moment she walked through the double doors she clocked him on the other side of the room on the blower. She approached slowly, trying to look casual, in the hope she could hear his conversation.

'Gary, stop fucking about with me. I told you before I was ringing you. You can't piss about with me when you know money is involved.' Jordan walked in a small circle as he continued. 'So, tell me who bought the building. Surely you owe me that?' His ear was pressed firmly to the mobile phone as he listened. Clearly he didn't like the answer. He lashed out, sending a silver stool flying. Then he booted another chair. 'I want that club. Don't fucking tell me you can't help when I've helped you out in the past. Get on the fucking phone to whoever it is that's bought it and tell them you've made a mistake. Honest Gary, you mess with me and I'll put you in a fucking body bag. Get it sorted, pronto.' He slammed the phone down on the bar and dropped his head into his hands. Karla stepped out from the shadows. Jordan lifted his head and spit sprayed from the corner of his mouth as he raised his voice at her. 'Some twat has bought the building I wanted to open another club in. Gary won't tell me who it is, just that they paid a good few quid for it. He's a shady twat, him, and when I see him face to face, he's getting told. I swear to you, I'm ready for going to find him and snapping his fucking jaw.'

Karla knew not to add fuel to the fire. She tried to calm him down. 'You can look for another location. If it's not meant to be, then it's not meant to be, is it?'

He shook his head at her and cringed, her voice going through him. 'Fuck off, what do you know about business? It was perfect.'

'Don't speak to me like that, Jordan. I was only trying to help.'

'The only way you can help me is by fucking off out of my face. I've had a bad day and, the way I'm feeling at the moment, I'll end up smashing some sod's face in. So do yourself a favour and do one before it gets ugly.'

Karla was fuming. She stared at him and never flinched. Oh, the words were there, alright, but she didn't have the balls to say them. She knew from everything she'd seen that Jordan Maylett could be a very dangerous man to get on the wrong side of.

Chapter Ten

Elsa sat in the coffee shop, waiting for Pamela to arrive. When she was younger, her mother used to bring her in here for a hot chocolate with big, fat pink and white fluffy marshmallows sprinkled on the top of it. That was a long time ago, though. There was no mother and daughter bonding time anymore. Elsa longed for those cosy chats with her mam, to tell her about boys she liked, to speak about fashion and perfumes, or curl up on the sofa and watch a chick flick together, but that never happened. It was all about Karla and her dramas. Elsa had tried lots of times to arrange a girlie night in with her mother, but something always cropped up that was more important. Karla always made an excuse why she couldn't spend time with her daughter, and always said she would make it up to her. She never did. Mary liked a cosy night in, though. She was always there when her granddaughter needed her. And, if she'd had a few lagers at the weekend, she would sit and talk for hours about days gone by. But she'd end up crying, sobbing her heart out about the choices she'd made in the past, regrets. Mary always held one secret close to her heart, though, and Elsa had long stopped trying to get her to tell her father's name.

Elsa looked around the coffee shop and smiled. When she was working and earning a few quid, she would come here with her friends and sit and drink coffee with them and talk about their problems. Everybody looked so happy and engrossed in conversation. Elsa looked at the group of girls near her and tried to listen in on their conversation. Pamela was over twenty minutes late. Elsa hated being late for anything. The cold wind rushed inside the coffee shop as the doors swung open. At last, Pamela was here, although she had her phone pressed to her ear. Elsa waved to get her attention. Pamela spotted her, smiled, and joined the queue to order her drink. She shouted over to her.

'Elsa, do you want a coffee or something else?'

'Can I have a hot chocolate with marshmallows on the top, please?'

Pamela nodded and carried on speaking on the phone. Whoever she was on the phone to, they were making her smile. She was laughing out loud.

Elsa moved a couple of empty glasses from the table and waited for Pamela to join her.

'I'm so sorry I'm late. I got caught up in something and couldn't get away. To tell you the truth, I'm so excited today. Don't ask me why, but I feel full of life again.'

Elsa was confused. The woman had just told her not to ask, so how on earth could she join in the celebrations if she didn't know what they were celebrating? Pamela looked dressed to the nines today. Her make-up was on point and her curly blow was bouncy and silky. She took her coat off and settled in her chair.

'Elsa, I've found somewhere for you to learn to pole-dance. The place is going to be done up. I've had a word with the owner, and he has agreed for us to use some space until it's ready.'

Elsa gulped: this woman didn't mess around. 'That's amazing. Do you really think I will be able to do it? I'm used to much more – erm – traditional stuff. And I'm not very flexible.'

Pamela smirked. 'That's why you can start doing some yoga to get supple. You can download an app on your phone and start doing it every day.'

Elsa agreed. She was swept up in the older woman's excitement. Pamela was alive today and, whatever had happened in her life, it had done her the world of good.

'We can go shopping after we've had a drink, if you want?' Pamela said.

'I don't have any money and my nana doesn't get paid until Friday, but I will come with you and window shop.'

Pamela looked at the young girl in more detail. 'Tell me about your parents, Elsa. You know lots of things about me and I barely know anything about you.'

Elsa was on the spot. What should she tell her? That her mother was a slapper and that she didn't really bother with her? Should she tell her that her father had never been in her life? She wasn't sure. She started off with the basics. 'I live with my mam and my nana. To tell you the truth, without my nana I would probably have ended up in care. My mam is a party girl. I've heard my nana shouting at her, telling her to keep away from married men, but she never listens, it's just one mistake after another. Apparently, my father was some rich older guy who nobody ever wants to talk about. They think I'm daft and don't hear what they say about him, but I do. My nana said he was a barely better than a paedo: he liked young girls.'

Pam sipped her drink before she spoke. 'So, you don't know who your old man is, then?'

'I know he's a bit of a name around the area, but that's it. They just feed me lies to keep me quiet, I think. Whenever I tackle anyone about his full identity, they go ballistic and tell me that the past should be left in the past. I think he was married, too. My nana always says we're better off without him and his money, but I still think about him – wonder what he's like.'

'That's terrible. It's kind of the same story I have with my mother. Sometimes they're just so selfish and don't see what they're doing.' Pamela swallowed hard. She'd been this girl, and she knew more than anyone how it felt to have nothing. She put on a big smile. 'Well, today I will treat you to some new clothes. I've had a bit of good luck and I'd like to share it with you. Let's shop until we drop.' Elsa was smiling from cheek to cheek. There was no way she was refusing any shopping spree. Pamela bit her bottom lip. 'Sometimes us women have to make our own luck. Love messes you up when it doesn't work out. You can't *make* someone love you, no matter what you do. And, when it fades, it's very rare you get it back. I'd love to feel again that way you do when you first fall in love. It's priceless. Promises get broken, though. Women sense things, you know, we feel it deep in our guts. And, when you suspect your man is playing away from home, you're probably right. They let their dicks rule their heads.'

Elsa was going bright red, people were looking at Pam and her voice was getting louder. 'Jordan has cheated on me. He thinks I don't know but, come on, I'm not green. I know the score more than he thinks.'

Elsa kept her voice low and didn't know if what she was going to say next would be out of order. 'Why don't you leave him and start again? You don't deserve to be treated like that. You could get any man you wanted. Look at you, you're stunning.'

Pamela ran her index finger around her cup. 'He's told me that if I leave him he will find me. I've tried before to leave him, but he beat me within an inch of my life and locked me away in the house for months. He's a head-the-ball when his cage is rattled.'

Elsa was shocked. 'What? He's hit you?' She wondered if Clayton knew.

Pamela swallowed hard. 'I know what you're thinking, but it's not as easy as you think to walk away from a man you have loved. Clayton needs his father in his life. I've always said that when he was old enough I'd piss off and start again. That time is nearly here, so I have to plan my life out. There is no room for any mistakes. I have to make sure I've got everything covered, make sure he can't touch me when I'm gone. And the only way I can do that is to have money. I've been saving for years from my housekeeping; he doesn't miss it. Money does not buy happiness, love. It's not all it's made out to be. Trust me, I know.'

Elsa sipped the creamy hot chocolate. Pamela sat in silence for a few seconds. 'Anyway, I'll land on my feet, I'll make sure of it. But for now, let's put our problems to the back of our minds and do some serious shopping.'

Chapter Eleven

The man poured himself a large glass of brandy and took a big mouthful before he topped the glass up again. Dave and Johnny were sat in the room with him and they looked like they'd just had a bollocking. The boss loosened his collar and sat in his black leather chair, crossing his legs before he spoke. 'I want to run all the clubs in Manchester. I've not grafted my balls off for years for some prick to come along and think he can take it all from me.'

The two men just sat listening. They knew he was a greedy bastard who had too much already – but nothing would ever satisfy him. His house was like a show home, the curtains were probably worth more than anything they owned. The boss dressed in all the top clothes, his watch was insured for over fifty grand. There had been times when he'd left it lying about to see if any of his men would dare to touch it, to take it home, or pocket it to sell on. They never did. He was always testing his lads, always wanting to catch them out. He trusted nobody. The large windows behind him showed off a breath-taking view of the country-side, the sheep peacefully grazing the nearby hills, but in the distance, the city lights glittered. Some people were never grateful for what they had in life and this man was one of them. He would never have enough, always wanting more. After another large swig of brandy he pulled out a little gold box full of white powder. A small key dug into it, and its contents went straight up his nose like a vacuum. The boss held his head back as the drug filtered through his body. He rammed the box back into his pocket, not offering his workers a sniff.

'I want you two both out there looking for the best girls, the best dancers, the ones that make the end of my cock wet, the ones who can seduce men without even touching them. Nobody should have better girls than me. Do you hear me, fucking nobody.'

Johnny raised his eyebrows and rolled his eyes at Dave when the boss wasn't looking. The man was talking to himself now, mumbling crap. The drugs were taking effect. 'Go and bring me a young one down,' he barked. 'Something pretty and with a bit of meat on her, I'm sick to death of these thin, scrawny ones.'

Dave and Johnny stood up, playing for time.

The man dropped his head down, looking at the empty glass. Maybe he thought the answer to his problems was there. 'Make sure all the security is switched on tonight. Keep the men on the gate and keep me updated if anything happens.'

'Will do, boss,' Johnny replied.

'Hurry up and get me some pussy down here as soon as.'

They both left the room and Dave made sure his voice was low as he walked slowly down the corridor. 'He knocks me sick, he wants for fuck all and he's still moaning for more.'

Johnny sighed. 'Life deals us a hand of cards, pal, and it's up to us how we play them. Sometimes we get bum-deals, sometimes jokers, or the lucky ones get a royal.'

Dave sniggered and playfully punched Johnny in the arm. 'Shut up with your wise words, you wanker, and go and get old dirty bollocks a girl before he kicks off. I wonder if he needs anything to keep his old fella hard tonight because, let's face it, he's no spring chicken, is he?

'Too much information, mate. I do my best to block it out.'

Johnny knocked before he entered the bedroom and met the eyes of the girls in there. There were at least five in that night. They looked happy enough and were all getting ready for the night ahead. The boss had invited a few friends over and it was up to this lot to keep them happy. Johnny stood at the door with his hands on his hips and looked about the room. All eyes seem to dip to the floor, knowing the reason why he had come. The boss wasn't the nicest man they'd met and some of the stories the girls told each other stuck in their mind. Some girls went up to see the big man and they returned. Nobody asked any questions. Johnny clicked his fingers up in the air over at Elena. She was a new girl, only in the country for a few months. She was pretty. Long, natural curly brown hair and flawless skin, no make-up needed. A natural beauty. She pretended she'd not seen him at first, but one of the other girls nudged her to get her attention.

'You, get ready and I'll be back for you in five minutes. Make sure you are clean and shaven. You know the man goes mad if you're not.' Johnny closed the door behind him.

All the girls huddled together whispering. They spoke in their own language, but the tone said it all.

Elena was led down the corridor by Dave. She was timid and only spoke a few words. Dave shot a look over at her and sighed. He stood at the door at the end of the corridor and paused before he knocked on. One last look at the girl at the side of him and he led her inside. The lights were down low now, soft music being played. Dave could see the back of his boss's head in his large leather chair and walked up behind him.

'A lovely new girl tonight for you.'

There was no reply. Dave waited a few more seconds and the left the room.

Elena stood in the same spot, eyes wide open, not sure of what was expected of her tonight. 'Hello, I'm Elena,' she said in a quiet voice. His hand reached over and stroked her leg, up and down, up and down. Tears welled in her eyes as she stood there not knowing what to do. His voice was firm as he pulled her onto his lap.

'You do as I tell you to do, do you hear me? I own you now, you obey only me.'

Chapter Twelve

Angela sat in Jordan's office and looked around. She could hear a voice outside and knew he would be joining her soon. His voice was getting louder and louder, and whoever he was talking to, he was giving it to them with both barrels. The office door crashed open and he stormed inside. Angela waited until he settled and cringed as she added fuel to the fire. He was going to go ballistic when he heard the latest news. 'There was a few problems in the club last night, Jordan. I'm not sure if the boys have filled you in, but Lenny's boys were in causing a scene. Cheeky bastards, they were blatantly groping the girls and being loud.' Jordan was alert, ears pinned back. She had his full attention. 'Lenny's boys were talking to our girls, especially Jenny, trying to poach them for their club.'

Jordan smashed his clenched fist on the table, papers flying to the floor.

'He can fuck right off if he thinks he's taking any of my girls. I've invested time and money into each of them.'

Angela spoke quietly. 'I've heard whispers. A few of the girls are thinking about it. To tell you the truth, they're sick to death of Karla and how she speaks to them. I can't blame them really. She's a bleeding nightmare.'

'Angela, I thought you were my wingman with these girls. Sort them out, will you? Offer them a few quid extra. I can't lose girls, not when the club is doing so well.'

Angela sat cracking her knuckles. 'Cart Karla, and the girls will fall into line. Honest on my life, I've had to hold Jenny back a few times. She wants to leather Karla, like I've told you before.'

Jordan inhaled deeply. 'Leave Karla to me. I'll have a word with her. But for now, I need to show Lenny that my girls are off limits. What the fuck is he playing at, sending his boys in here? The guy is a slimy rat. He's up to something.'

'It's a dog-eat-dog world, Jordan, you know that without me telling you. The girls will go where they get treated the best and, from what I've seen, you'll be lucky if they stay until the end of the month.'

Jordan held his head in his hands and sat thinking for a few seconds. 'I might pay Lenny a visit. If he thinks he's being a smart-arse sending his boys in here, I'll walk straight through his front doors and see what he has to say. Yes, I'll go team-handed and show the wanker I'm ready for whatever he's got to give.'

Angela stood up, walked to Jordan's side and placed her hand on his arm. She inhaled his aftershave. It was the same one he used to wear when he was seeing her. 'Jordan, Lenny Jackson is a lunatic. Take my advice and stay well away.

You've worked hard to get where you are today, don't go and lose it because of pride. Just forget about it.'

Jordan lifted his head and looked deep into her eyes. There was fear there, for sure, and he swallowed hard. 'I have to defend what I have. He knows that more than anyone. He's an old devil who's ready for the knackers' yard. I'd rip him in two, given the chance. But maybe you're right. I'll send the boys in first.'

Angela backed off and headed towards the door. 'Like I said, be careful what you're starting. Lenny won't take anything lying down.'

'Shut the door behind you, Angela, and go and have a word with the girls for me. I'll be in soon to see them.'

Jordan and his boys parked up outside *Lush Laps* night-club. It was busy tonight and they could hear the music from their cars. Jordan turned to face the hulking guy in the passenger seat. The guy was like a giant.

'Right, go in and order a drink. I'm sure within a few minutes Lenny will get word that you're in there. I only want to keep them on their toes, nothing major, just a little warning.

'Consider it done, mate. If any of them pricks think they can do anything, I'll snap them in two, pal.'

It was music to Jordan's ears. This was dangerous ground and there was no room for hesitation.

Jordan stayed put and left his men to do his dirty work. There was no point in him showing his face, not yet anyway. Let the foot soldiers do their work before the generals met. He watched. His men hadn't even walked into the club and already their presence was felt. A few of the bouncers were whispering to each other and he could tell his boys had unsettled them. Satisfied he'd defended his honour, he drove off.

Jordan arrived back at *Passion* and immediately clocked his wife sat at the bar. He shook his head and marched over to her with a face like thunder. He dragged her by the arm to the end of the bar away from the punters. 'What the fuck do you think you're doing here again? I didn't mind the other night, but I'm not having you here every fucking night. Get home.'

'Take your hands off me, you idiot.' Pamela growled at him, and wriggled free. She straightened her short black dress and flicked her hair back. 'I can come here whenever I want. This club is half mine, or are you forgetting that?'

Jordan gritted his teeth tightly together. He didn't like the backchat. He looked around him before he dragged his wife out of the club. Her voice was loud and she was making a scene. 'Shut the fuck up,' he sneered. Once he was outside, he gripped her by the scruff of the neck and flung her over his car with force. Her body crashed against the cold metal and she screamed out in pain.

'There's no need for this! Stop thinking you can tell me what to do, when you can't. I've told you, time and time again, you don't own me. Carry on and I'll be in here every night. What's wrong, eh? Are you scared I will uncover the trollop you're banging? Don't think I don't know, Jordan. I know you of old, and I know when you're screwing somebody else.'

He ran at her and squeezed his right hand around her jaw, spit spraying from his mouth. 'Don't do it, Pam. Keep your mouth shut. Get in the car and go home. You know what will happen if you don't be quiet, don't you?' He pushed her away and watched her with eager eyes.

'Do what you're doing, Jordan. If beating me is the way you get your kicks, then fucking do it. I'll always get back up, and then what? I've told you before, you can't hurt me anymore.' She went nose to nose with him and spat in his eye. This was bad, very bad indeed.

Jordan moved quickly, gripped his wife by her hair and swung her around like a ragdoll. Screaming, howling in pain, Pamela tumbled. Once she'd fallen to the floor, he brought his foot back and booted her again and again, each kick landing deep into her lower body. Why did nobody hear her screams? Surely somebody must have seen or heard something? Or worse, was it all being witnessed and people were too scared to get involved?

Jordan bent his knee and looked down at his wife. The corner of her eye was bleeding. He wiped his finger across the gash and stuck his tongue out to taste the blood. What kind of person did something like that? Jordan let out a menacing laugh and ran his finger down his wife's face, smearing the bright-red claret all over her cheeks. His voice changed, chilling tones now. 'I can carry on, or take you home. Speak to me, woman. What do you want to do?'

The poor woman could barely answer. She croaked, her words almost inaudible, 'Take me home.'

Jordan gripped her by the hair and dragged her head back. 'Do you know how much shit I've got going on at the moment? And here's you thinking you can come into the club flirting with all the punters. Do you think you can still pull the men, eh? Is that what it is, you want somebody new?'

Pamela was struggling to breathe, her eye closing as a pocket full of fluid filled over it, the swelling distorting her face. She was dragged to her feet and flung into the back of his car.

Once Jordan started the engine, he dipped the rear-view mirror so he could see her in it. His nostrils flared and the vein at the side of his neck was bulging through the thick skin. 'Look at what you made me do again. Didn't I tell you to keep your mouth shut? But you didn't listen, you never fucking listen, woman. You always push me over the edge.' His voice was getting louder: he was winding himself up. 'You've probably been shagging someone behind my back, haven't you? You dirty little slag. Is that what it is? It all makes sense now. That's why you're all fucking dressed up. Have you been with him? Go on, tell me now, have you been getting fucked by someone else?' He slammed the brakes on and twisted his body around in his seat so he could grab her. But his large hand struggled to reach. He looked at her and his eyes had changed. He'd lost the plot, for sure. 'Tell me his name. Tell me who it is.'

Pamela just lay there, summoning the energy to speak. 'You'll get what's coming to you one day, Jordan Maylett. For every tear I've cried, you'll cry a bucket. Trust me, this won't go on for ever. Stop turning it on me like you always do. It's you who's fucking about, not me.'

Jordan froze and looked deep into her eyes. Whatever he could see in them he didn't like. There was no fear anymore, he could sense that. She wasn't apologising, wasn't backing down this time. He skidded out onto the road like a maniac, nearly smashing straight into another car. He never spoke another word all the way home.

Clayton and Elsa lay on the sofa, watching a film. It was nearly time for her to go before she got tempted to cross a line. Clayton held his head up and listened carefully. 'That's a car pulling up outside.' He stretched his neck and tried to get a look out of the window. 'It looks like my old man's car. I wonder why he's home early? We never usually see him until the morning.' He looped his arms behind his head and carried on watching the film.

Elsa straightened her clothes and sat up. She had to look respectable, make a good impression. The front door opened, then quickly slammed shut. The walls shook, and Elsa looked over to Clayton. Loud voices in the hallway. Clayton bolted up from his seat.

'Wait here a minute.' He ran into the hallway.

Elsa could hear raised voices, but not what was being said. There was a man's voice and, whatever he was saying, he was furious. A woman crying, then screaming at the top of her voice. Oh my God, it was Pamela. Had there been an accident? Elsa sat tapping her fingers. What the hell should she do? Should she go and help, see if she was alright?

Clayton rushed back into the room. 'You need to go. I'll walk you home. I need to get out of this fucking house before I stab that cunt.'

Elsa didn't ask any questions, she slipped her shoes back on and stood up. Clayton was fuming. He punched the wall a few times, and let out a scream from the pit of his stomach. What on earth was going on? Elsa walked to his side and placed a hand on his shoulder, but he pushed her away. 'Nah, I don't need any comfort, Elsa. I'm a big boy now and I can deal with my own shit.'

There were no words left for her to say. She waited at his side.

'You don't know my dad. He's a bully, always has been. I ...' Clayton stopped, as if there was something it hurt him to say.

He led her through the hallway. Elsa could hear Pamela whimpering and crying from upstairs. The hairs on the back of her neck stood on end. She wanted to go to her, but Clayton opened the front door and waited for her to step outside.

'You mark my words, there'll be truckloads of presents here tomorrow. Flowers, chocolates, jewellery. He always licks arse when he's panned her,' Clayton fumed. 'He's fucking wrong in the head. I swear I'll never, ever, hit a woman in my life. It's the lowest of the low.'

Elsa knew now what had gone on. After all, it wasn't rocket science, was it? 'Will your mam be alright? We should have taken a look at her before we left. What if she's seriously hurt?'

Clayton sighed. 'My dad has a medical kit. He'll be putting ice on her eyes as we speak. It's usually for the boys – if his lads get in a bit of bother, or the bouncers handle some dodgy punters. But it's not the first time he's used it on her. It's always the same old story. I don't know why she puts up with him.' Clayton stopped walking and zipped his coat up. The wind was picking up, and he could feel small drops of rain starting to fall on his cheeks. He stopped in a bus shelter.

'Come over here and sit for a minute, Elsa. I've never discussed my family life with anyone before. But I feel you will be around me and my family for a long time, so you need to know what you're letting yourself in for. About what he does. And about what I ...' Before he could say any more, Clayton's phone lit up with a text message and he turned away from her before he read it. It was obvious he didn't want her to see it. Elsa sat down on the small red plastic seat. The traffic seemed to have gone quiet and she could hear him loud and clear when he turned back.

'He's always battered her. He's got anger problems; I think the drugs make him worse, though.'

'What, he takes drugs?' Elsa was gobsmacked Clayton was so open about it. And here she was thinking her family was fucked up.

'They all sniff, Elsa. It goes with the territory. Don't get me wrong, he's calmed down a lot these days. In his day, he was snorting cocaine from the moment he opened his eyes to the minute he went to bed. His jaw was always swinging low. He's been in rehab, cleaned himself up, but he always goes back on it. Mum didn't tell me that, I heard her saying it to him when they were arguing. They forget I can hear everything. I've heard a lot more, too.'

'I'm shocked, Clayton. Honest, on my life, I thought you had the perfect family when I first met you. Can't we get your mam some help? Phone the police or something, get Women's Aid involved? I know a woman who got help from them when her husband was abusing her. She was a right mess when she finally left him, honest, she was ready for a nervous breakdown.'

'No way! The dibble are the last thing we need in this family. We're not grasses. My dad would string me up if he thought I was a Judas. Our family does have values, you know, and snitching is not something I even want to talk about. And this isn't just about family, it's about business. I've got to see both sides.'

She touched his cheek with her long cold fingers. 'So, where does it stop? He can't keep battering your mam every time he's having a bad day. Your mother is beautiful, she doesn't deserve it.'

His sprang to his feet and shouted, 'Don't you think I know that? I've lay in bed listening to her sobbing her heart out. Do you know how that feels not to able to do fuck all?' He booted the side of the bus-shelter, causing it to shake. 'It feels like I'm a coward. No balls to tackle my old man. I should be whacking a baseball bat over the fucker's head. It's coming though, Elsa, oh yes, it's coming. He knows it, too, he could see it in my eyes tonight. I've put up with too much for too long – first because my mam told me to, then because I had to, if I wanted to show him I should have a seat at the table one day when it came to the business. But he's gone too far this time ...'

'Can I come around tomorrow and see her? Please, I just need to let her know that she is not alone.'

Clayton smiled softly and his voice was calming down. 'You're special, you are, Elsa. Look, I'll ask her, but she'll be black and blue. She might not even let me in her room for a few days. But whatever happens, please, keep this to yourself. Like I said, it's private family stuff that I want to stay between us.'

'My lips are sealed. I'll never breathe a word, but please tell your mam I'll be around tomorrow. I feel sick, Clayton, the thought of her being hurt has made my stomach turn.'

He stood and pulled her to her feet. 'Come here and give me a squeeze.'

Elsa could feel his solid arms wrap around her body, and, despite everything she'd heard tonight, she felt safe.

Mary lay in bed, and tossed and turned. Sleep seemed a million miles away tonight. First Karla had been out on the tiles even more than usual, and now Elsa was out late. She reached over and flicked her small bedside light on. For a few seconds, she lay there staring into space. Then she opened the small drawer at the side of the bed and pulled out a letter from a white envelope. She checked her door was closed and slowly began to read the letter, over and over. Finally, it fell to her chest and she closed her eyes for a second. Her fist curled up slowly as she spoke to herself. 'It's about time I paid you a visit, isn't it?' She rolled onto her side and flicked the lamp off. The silver shimmer of the moon shone into the bedroom, lighting the whites of Mary's eyes. She was up to something.

Chapter Thirteen

Elsa had barely slept. She'd sneaked into the house late, and sneaked back out again early this morning before her nana could catch up with her. She'd not slept properly all night. She walked up the path to Clayton's house now and her hand trembled as she knocked softly on the door. Clayton had told her to let herself in, but there was no way she was doing that: what if Jordan was there? She stood back from the door, playing with the cuff of her sleeve. The front door opened and Clayton stood there looking at her, paler than she'd ever seen him, dark circles under his eyes.

'Come in, I'm just talking to my mam. She knows you know, so she'll be fine with you being here.'

Elsa swallowed hard. What would she say to her? Should she hug her and call her husband a prick? Because that's what he was. A bully. Elsa followed Clayton into the front room, bracing herself as she walked in through the doors. Pamela dropped her head low, ashamed she had let this happen to her again. Clayton sat down and waited until

Elsa sat down next to him. This was awkward. Elsa smiled softly over at Pam. Her eyes prickled with tears as she clocked the deep-purple bruises around Pam's eyes, visible even though she was staring at the floor. Elsa had to say something. Why should she pretend this wasn't happening? She inhaled deeply and looked directly at Clayton's mother, who still hadn't looked up.

'I think you should leave him, Pam. There are places you can go where he won't find you. I've researched it on the internet and people will help you. It's against the law what he is doing to you. It's domestic violence.' These were wise words from such a young girl.

'I'm fine, Elsa. Shit happens, but I can tell you now that it won't happen again. Things are changing and, with a bit more planning, he'll be out of my life for good. Every dog has its day, and mine's been a long time coming.'

Clayton shuffled about in his seat: this was obviously news to him. 'Mam, don't be on the phone to the dibble. You know we don't work like that.'

'I would never involve the police, Son. I've got ways and means to get my revenge on someone like your dad, and, trust me, this is something I've been planning for a long time. It's not just for me, Son. It's for both of us. You're ready to take a step up in the business.'

Clayton looked at his mother. Was she going to do him in, or what? But he knew more than anyone what his father was capable of: she had to be wise, out-think him. 'Be careful, Mam. You've got to hit him in the wallet. We want the house. This is our gaff and, if he's the one who's fucked up, then he should be the one who leaves.'

Pamela moved and her expression changed. Pain, deep piercing pain in her body.

Her son cringed as he watched her trying to move. 'Has a doctor checked you out?'

'No, love. I probably look a lot worse than what I am. I bruise easily. I'm fine. A few days' rest is all I need, and I'll be fighting fit. I'm a tough cookie, I am.'

Clayton rolled his eyes. She wasn't fine at all and he was used to her pretending everything was rosy in the garden. He could remember when he was younger, when he used to watch her barely able to get out of bed to make his breakfast before he went to school. He knew the code of conduct from an early age and he knew to say nothing to nobody about what happened at home. Because, if he'd spilled the beans, social services would have been all over him and he'd have been flung into care, without a shadow of doubt. Or that's what his old man had told him, anyway. This kid feared his old man. He would never admit it, but he was nowhere near ready to challenge his father for his title. He checked his watch. 'Mam, Elsa is going to stay with you while I nip out. She said she's more than happy, if that's alright with you?'

Pamela nodded and sighed. 'I am able to look after myself, Son. Stop fussing about after me.'

He stood up and walked about the front room, peering through the windows, edgy. Another message pinged on his phone. 'I know that, Mother, but as from today I'm making sure you're safe. That prick needs to remember I'm not a kid anymore and the day will come when I stand up to him. I'm training hard, Mam, lifting more weights than I have ever lifted. I'm strong.'

Pamela was alert, her voice distressed. 'You keep well away from him. This is my battle, not yours. Like I said, I'm dealing with it.' She let out a laboured breath. She had always tried to protect him from the full truth about the kind of man his father was. *She* knew Jordan was an animal when his cage was rattled – but what son wanted to hear that about his own father?

Clayton grabbed his black designer jacket from the chair. 'Elsa, if you need me, ring me. Any trouble here, and I'll be back before you know it. Trust me, my mate drives like a mad-man.'

Elsa swallowed hard. She wasn't used to this life. Yes, she knew this world was out there, but her nana had done a good job of protecting her from the reality of what that meant. Clayton came to Elsa's side and pecked her on the cheek. He did the same to his mother before he left.

There was an eerie silence, and Elsa didn't know what to do or say. How could she sit here with this woman, and see her suffering, and not say anything?

Pamela smiled over at her. 'Don't you be worrying about me. I've been hurt a lot worse than this and I've bounced back, so don't be worrying. Anyway, we need to get you dancing. We have the house to ourselves and I know Jordan is out of town all day. He won't dare to show his face until things have cooled down. And I'm going to take this chance. I've got plans. Big plans for me and you, girl. If you listen to me, you'll never want for anything again in your life. I want you dancing as soon as possible. Help me upstairs and let's see what you can do. Oh, and on Friday, don't book anything in. I want you to come with me to meet someone. This guy is one of the best in the business and he can open doors for you. Just pencil it in for now. I'll let you know the details.'

Elsa tried to stop her. 'Pam, you need to rest. Look at you, you're black and blue. Honest, I don't know how you put on a brave face and can even think about dancing when you should be thinking about getting help, getting away from all this. I don't think you're safe here. It will get worst, and then what?'

Pamela knew if this was her giving advice to a friend, she would have told her one hundred percent to leave his sorry arse and move on. But she never once took her own advice. 'Babes, you are a young girl and you have a lot to learn. Shit happens in relationships and, when you love somebody, you're blinded to the reality of things. Love is a horrible emotion sometimes. It messes with your head. One minute you hate their fucking guts, and the next you couldn't be happier.'

'But I don't ever think I could take my boyfriend or husband hitting me.' Elsa shuddered.

Pamela closed her eyes. 'You have to walk the walk first, love, and then you can judge me. Now come on – help me upstairs.'

Pamela made herself comfortable in the large chair facing the pole. She winced as she tried to protect her ribs and gave a half-hearted smile. It was obvious her body was aching. She was doing her best to put on a brave face. 'Let's get started, and, for the record, I do appreciate your advice and that you care for me. It's been a long time since anyone has put their neck on the line for me and I won't forget that, ever. But I'm not teaching you to dance as a distraction –

this is what's going to set me free. So take that big coat off and let's see what you're wearing. You need to be able to move about.'

Elsa pulled her red coat off. Underneath she was wearing a pair of black leggings and a short lime-green top.

'Perfect. I need you to warm up first. You can't just get on the pole and expect to move about. Your body needs to be ready. So, let's start with some stretches. Put your arms above your head and reach for the stars, keep your feet flat.'

Elsa looked awkward. She made a half-hearted attempt at stretching – something that didn't impress her mentor. Pam screwed her face up and clapped her hands together loudly.

'Right, let's get some ground rules sorted. I can't work with you if you're going to be like this. You need to overcome your shyness. You are stunning. Please, look in the mirror and see how gorgeous you are. You have to believe in you, tell yourself every day how beautiful you are. It might be hard at first but, trust me, when you love yourself, all them punters will love you, too.'

Elsa blushed: she was crumbling with embarrassment. She always struggled with her confidence, and nobody had ever spoken to her like this. Blown away by Pam's words, she barely registered what she meant by 'the punters' …

'Tie your hair up and tuck your T-shirt up under your bra. Get used to showing some flesh. After all, when them geezers are leering at you, you are going to be half-naked.'

Elsa sucked in a large mouthful of air. She had to concentrate, she could do this. She had to overcome her lack of body confidence and face her fears. She pulled her shoulders back like a gymnast getting ready to make her entrance into the arena. Wow, this was better: she looked like a dancer now. Her breasts looked firm, her chin was up and she held a look that told Pamela she meant business. Pushing to the back of her mind the thought of ever doing this in front of an audience, Elsa just wanted to be able to move like Pamela had. She wanted that strength, that freedom.

Elsa was exhausted by the end of the training session. This was the hardest she'd ever trained in her life. She fell to the floor and dropped her head onto the top of her knees, deep breaths.

Pam clapped her hands. 'You smashed it, just like I knew you would. You need to start doing some weight training to get your upper body strong. I've got some weights in the garage that I can set up for you. This is not going to happen overnight. It's going to take dedication and discipline to get you ready. Your diet needs to be looked at, too. You need to sack off the takeaways for a while, and sugary drinks.'

Elsa lifted her head. She loved a fizzy drink and fast food. She looked down at her body and stroked her hand slowly down her legs. 'I don't think I'm overweight?'

Pam tutted. 'I never said that, but I need you to look the best you can. We can work on lowering your body fat. Once that starts to come down, that's when we will start to see some decent muscles, perky bum and toned arms.'

Elsa was in no mood to argue; she was breathing out of her arse. This was what she wanted and, if these were the rules, then so be it.

Pam got to her feet and walked over to the small fridge in the corner of the room. She dipped down, opened the door and gripped a cold bottle of water. She held the bottle up and made her way over to Elsa. 'You need to start drinking a lot of this, as well. You'll piss like a donkey at first, but when your body gets used to it you'll be fine. Plus, water is great for your skin. It flushes all the toxins out from your body.'

Elsa took the cold water and, the minute she got a grip of it, she quickly screwed the lid off and gulped a large mouthful, just like she did when she had a hangover. Bloody hell, it was nearly all gone.

Pam rubbed her flat palm over Elsa's head. 'You were amazing, sweetheart. It's a long road ahead but, trust me, it will be worth it. I know you might not think so now, but you will smash it. They will travel far and wide to see you, and you'll be the talk of the town.'

Elsa looked up at Pam. She was hesitant and she stuttered, 'I don't want people touching me. I'm not into stuff like that. And I'll never dance nude, no way in this world. My nana would shit a brick if she thought I was showing my private parts off to every Tom, Dick and Harry.'

Pamela chuckled. 'No one will ever touch you. It's all about the tease, looking in their eyes and making them think they are the only person you want. Your job is to arouse them, make them drool and, the most important thing, make them part with their money. If you get some followers, you watch the money they throw at you.'

Elsa tried to raise a smile, but she was apprehensive.

Pamela walked to the door. She giggled and rubbed her hands together in excitement. 'I can't wait to show you off. You're like my own flesh and blood, and I feel so proud of you already.'

Elsa rushed up behind her, flung her arms around her and kissed her cheek. 'No one has ever really believed in me like you have, not even my mother. If I could have picked my own mother, I would have picked someone like you. Maybe my life would have been different then and I wouldn't have struggled all the time.'

Pam held the young girl, her heart still thudding from the session, but there was a look in her eyes she was glad Elsa couldn't see. Pamela might have been the one with broken bones and bruises, but Elsa was like a helpless bird in her grasp – ready either to fly or else be trampled underfoot.

Chapter Fourteen

Mary sat at the kitchen table with her head held in her hands. Bills, bills, and more bleeding bills. Final demands, letters telling her the bailiffs were coming. When was it ever going to end? No sooner had she paid one bill and another one landed on her doorstep. She couldn't answer her front door without fear anymore. If she heard the loan-sharks were on the estate she always closed the curtains, turning the lights off so the men didn't know if she was in or not. But it was only a matter of time before they caught her coming home, or even turning up at her work. Mary sat staring into space, wondering how on earth she could get some money together fast to help her out of the big dark hole she'd fallen into again. She knew what was coming.

Mary hurried up the stairs and dragged the double bed away from the wall. It was heavy and she struggled. Pulling the carpet back, she lifted up the loose floorboard with the end of her thin fingers. Her hand disappeared into the dark hole and she moved it about, searching. Finally she pulled out a ten-pound note, clearly disappointed that was all that was left under there. Mary quickly placed the floorboard back and pushed the carpet back over it. She was exhausted, sweat blooming on her forehead as she dragged the frame back. Sitting on the edge of the bed she held the ten-pound note out in front of her and let out a laboured breath. Maybe she could chance her luck and buy a scratch card, double her money, even treble it? No, her luck had run out months ago. She'd won nothing for ages down the bingo hall, not a carrot. She rushed back down the stairs and went into the living room. She grabbed her handbag and pulled out her mobile phone and sat thinking. With shaking hands, she sent a text message.

> I need to see you. Elsa needs things.
> Can we meet @ the side of Queens Park
> tonight at 9?

Mary pressed the send button and held her mobile phone to her chest. She'd promised herself that she wasn't going to ask that bastard for another penny now Elsa was eighteen, but she couldn't manage without his help; she needed a lifeline and the kid deserved a proper start at adult life. Money had always been tight in this household and why shouldn't her granddaughter's father put his hand in his pocket when she couldn't make ends meet? She took no pride in it – every time she met him, she told him she was only asking because she was desperate. Up to now, he had always put his hand in his pocket, even if it came with a lot of grumbling. Elsa had needed a lot of things growing up, things she couldn't have afforded; new clothes, new shoes, he didn't get how much money it cost to bring a child up. And Karla never helped. She was as much use as a chocolate fire-guard, absolute bobbins. No, all the responsibility was left to Mary. Well, today she was going to see Elsa's father and tell him straight that he needed to give her a decent amount of money to help look after his daughter until she found work and could fend for herself. Alright, she might have treated herself to a few nights at bingo from the money in the past, but who would have denied her that?

Mary sat down and clocked the photo album on the edge of the sofa. Elsa had been looking at it last night and she must have forgotten to put it back where it belonged. Her fingers stroked the cover and she smiled as she opened the first page. There they were, photographs of when they were all younger; happier times – simpler, certainly. Mary sat down and placed the album on her lap, she loved looking back. She spotted one of herself with an old friend. She chuckled to herself and shook her head. 'Bleeding hell, look at the state of you there, Mary, what on earth were you wearing?'

It was good to have memories of days gone by, times when people were happy, seeing friends she had lost contact with and remembering the nights out they had all had together. Mary turned the page over and her expression changed. There was Karla, her baby, her girl, stood outside a shop with her friends smiling from cheek to cheek. She spoke to the photograph in a low voice. 'You were pregnant then, weren't you? That dirty bastard had his hands all over you. I wish I had known, I would have stopped it, cut his balls off or had him done in.'

She had to close the book, bad memories flooding her mind. Mary blamed herself for the way Karla had turned out. By her own admittance she hadn't exactly been mother of the year, far from it. Maybe she should have cuddled her daughter more, told her how special she was and how beautiful she was? But she was in a bad place herself back then and the drink had got a grip of her. She shook her head – she was never going down that road again.

Mary had been sat ready for over half an hour. She'd had a wash and combed her hair in an effort to look half decent. There was no way she was having him calling her names again. The last time she'd been to see him, he'd told her that she stank of fags and to open the window in the car because she was knocking him sick. Cheeky bleeder. Nobody was at home yet and if anyone was to ask her where she'd been she could always say she was at the bingo hall. Nobody would question her on that, they never did.

It was dark outside as she left the house. Mary zipped her coat up as she rushed down Rochdale Road. Her head was dipped low, she didn't want anyone to see her. Queens Park was a place Mary used to take her granddaughter when she was younger. For hours she would push her on the swings. But now Mary could see a silver Mercedes at the end of the road in the layby. He always hid away in the shadows of the night, never wanting anyone to see him. She lifted her shoulders back and inhaled deeply. It was showtime.

You could have cut the atmosphere with a knife when Mary sat in the car. She didn't look at him, eyes facing forward looking out of the window. She inhaled and twisted the edge of her coat.

'I'm struggling to look after Elsa. I know you said that last time was the end of you giving me anything, but she needs something to help her leave the nest. She's your blood and it doesn't matter how old she is, she still needs supporting.'

His voice was firm, chilling. 'It's always been about bleeding money with you, Mary; take, take, take. I told you I would support her until she was eighteen and that was it. You're lucky I've even put my hand in my pocket at all.'

Mary finally turned to face him, the smell of his after-shave was strong, catching in her throat. 'And you're lucky I've not been banging on your front door telling your Mrs about her.'

His hand seized her neck, squeezing at her windpipe. His teeth clenched tightly together as his words fired out like bullets. 'Don't pull this shit with me, Mary, because you'll end up in a fucking body bag. I'll just take you one dark night and nobody will have a clue where you have disappeared to. Trust me, you old tart, I'll make sure nobody ever finds you. You'll be six foot under.'

He let his grip loosen and moved his hand away from her throat. She was coughing and spluttering, her eyes budging from the sockets.

'Don't you ever lay your hands on me again. This is your child that you created – by having your dirty way with my daughter. She was barely more than a child – I could have you lynched for that. But, like I have always said, as long as you do right by your daughter then my trap will be shut. Are you forgetting about everything that I've done for your child, all the things I've gone without? I could have had her banged in care and walked away from her but I didn't, I chose to stay and support her unlike her bleeding mother.'

'Don't ever try and blackmail me, Mary. Have I made myself clear?'

Mary tried not to show the panic rising in her and sat back in her seat with her arms folded tightly in front of her chest. She had to change her tune, speak nicely to him. 'I just want her to be happy. To have what every other girl has. My hand is always in my pocket for her, and I do my best to make sure she never goes without. I lie awake at night worrying about how I'm going to pay bills, put food on the table. I'm not rolling in cash, you know.'

'Don't give me all that, Mary. Everyone knows you're always down at the bingo.'

Mary listened to the sound of rustling. She side-eyed him. He placed a stack of twenty-pound notes on her lap and growled over at her. 'This is the last time you ever come and see me for money. If I see you here again, you'll be in the boot of my car and taken where nobody will ever find you. Don't ever ring me again.'

Mary was silent, her hands slowly picking up the cash from her lap. She knew well enough what this man could do. She was doing this for Elsa – but if she ended up dead, who would care for her then?

Chapter Fifteen

Jordan stood at the bar, snarling at anyone who looked at him. He was like a bulldog chewing a wasp. God help anyone who crossed his path tonight, he was in a foul mood. White powder clung to the edges of his nostrils. Angela walked up to him and knew instantly she should give him a wide berth when he was in this frame of mind, but she needed to talk to him; she had no option. His head turned slowly.

She swallowed hard before she began. 'Polly and Anneka were at Mickey's house last night and you should have seen them both when they left the gaff. They're in a right state. Mickey's boys had a field day with them and, to hear them speak, they are lucky to be alive.'

Jordan gulped the final mouthful of brandy from his glass and got to his feet.

'Why is this the first I'm hearing about this? Does every-one around here think I'm a fucking mind reader, or what? If nobody tells me, how the fuck can I sort shit out?' He marched off, kicking bar-stools over and slamming doors behind him.

Angela struggled to keep up with him as he stamped towards the dressing room. She was still talking behind him, trying her best to fill him in. 'It was the early hours of this morning that they got out of there. I went to pick them up and they told me what had gone on. Some of Lenny's boys were there, too, and they were as bad as Mickey.'

Jordan booted the bottom of the dressing room door, nearly taking it from its hinges. He stood growling at the girls, his chest expanded as if someone was pumping it up. 'Polly, Anneka, get your arses over here. I want a word with you both. Make it fucking snappy. I don't have all day.' He went into the side room and sat cracking his knuckles. His eyes were dancing with madness and he looked like he was going to blow any second. Polly walked in first, shortly followed by Anneka. Jordan clocked the bruises on their arms and legs straight away. 'Polly, park your arse down there and start talking. I want to know everything that happened from start to finish, and don't leave fuck all out. I'll tell you now that heads will roll for this. Nobody fucks with my girls, fucking nobody.'

Angela stood next to the young girl and placed a hand on her shoulder to comfort her. The poor thing was shaking like a leaf.

Polly stuttered, 'I told them we were going home, but they wouldn't let us out of the room. Mickey made me stay. He dragged me about by my hair, and he let the others do things to me. I told them no, but they did it anyway. The four of them wouldn't stop. Anneka tried to help me, but they done the same to her, too. They had sex with us, one after the other. I want to go back home, I want to see my family. You told us we would be looked after here, you lied, you lied,' she sobbed.

Angela took it into her own hands to make sure justice was served here today. She blurted it out, 'Jordan, these girls need to be safe when they go to these parties. The police should have been called, and the bastards should have had the book threw at them. This should be a rape charge, not a tit-for-tat fight between your boys and Mickey's. Nobody used to touch your girls, they knew better, but lately it's like nobody gives a flying fuck who you are any more. Lenny's boys are saying you're a has-been. Are you going to let them treat your girls like that? Because if you are,' she paused and swallowed a large mouthful of air before she continued. 'We'll all be off out of here. Trust me, none of us will be staying with you if we're not safe. That's your job. You should be making sure none of us girls are ever left at a party alone. They should have been picked up and taken home. End of.' She was going for gold. She knew he was raking the money in from these dancers and the least he could do was protect them.

Jordan sprang to his feet and roared, 'Shut the fuck up! I'll sort it. Do you hear me, I'll fucking sort it? This shouldn't have happened, and I'll make sure it doesn't happen again. But for now, get out of my face and let me fucking think. Do one.'

Angela stood with her back to the wall and her heart pumping inside her rib-cage. She needed to be careful. She'd lasted this long at *Passion* because she knew when to speak up and when to shut up around Jordan. But had she pushed it too far this time? Jordan edged closer to Polly and touched her cheek. She cringed and shrank away from him. The thought of another man touching her again sent waves of terror down her spine. You could see the fear in her eyes.

His voice changed. He looked directly into her eyes. 'Polly, trust me, this will never happen again. Take tonight off and rest. Angela, give them a few ton each and let them treat themselves. In future, I want to know not only who is hosting the parties, but who the guests will be, before they go anywhere. I'll make sure that each girl is picked up, too. Nobody messes with me or my girls, fucking nobody.'

He left the room and slammed the door behind him. Angela stood for a few seconds regaining her breath. She sighed and looked over at Polly and Anneka. 'The shit's going to hit the fan now. I told you he would sort it out. Come on, let's get you two home. Go and have a nice warm bath and relax tonight. When he's calmed down, I'll speak to him about maybe letting you go back home for a few days.' Polly was shaking from head to toe. This young girl looked like she was ready to have a mental breakdown. None of them spoke as they left the room. But as for going home for a few days, come on, that was never going to happen. They were damaged goods now; they'd never be the same again.

Jordan was on the phone, but no one was picking up. Whoever he was ringing, they were blanking him. He walked to the window and looked out into the car park. It was dark and the wind had picked up. A few leaves were blowing about, and he felt himself calming down as he watched them dance on the ground. The office door opened slowly, but he never turned around to see who it was. A hand touched the side of his waist.

'Hi, babes, you look like you've got the worries of the world on your shoulders tonight. Is everything alright?'

Jordan turned around slowly and met Karla's eyes. 'It's nothing I can't sort out. Just a bit of bother with Lenny Jackson's boys.'

Karla turned away from him and changed the subject quickly. 'We need a night out away from this place. You just work, work, and work. Let's go away for a few days and chill. We can book a nice log cabin in the Lake District. You loved the last one we went to, didn't you?'

He tutted and shook his head. 'I can't leave this place and go anywhere, not now these wankers are testing me. How many times do I have to tell you, Karla? Are you thick, or what?'

She screwed her face up. 'Why do you think you can talk to me like I'm nothing? I'm sick of it all, Jordan, sick to death of it. One minute you're all over me like a rash and the next you won't give me the time of the day. It's make-your-mind-up time. You either want me or you don't, because I can't go on like this, it's doing my head in big time.'

Jordan pushed her out of his way with a flat palm. He had no time for her drama; he had problems, big problems. 'Fucking move out of my way and let me get back to work. You've turned into a right moaning cow.'

She rushed to the door and stood in front of it, eager to get her words out. With her hands on her hips, she gave a cocky stare. 'I don't think so. You can wait until I've finished saying what I have to say.' His expression changed and his nostrils flared. He was on the verge of ragging her about when she dropped the bombshell on him. 'Don't you dare try and hurt me again. I'm carrying your child. I'm pregnant.'

Jordan froze, his eyes wide open, his jaw dropped. He went nose to nose with her, his hot breath spraying into her face. 'Shut up lying. I'm warning you, I'm in no fucking mood for mind games tonight.' He watched her closely: she never flinched.

'I have been feeling sick for a few days now and my period is late. I bought a test before, and I haven't done it yet, but I remember how I felt with Elsa, so I reckon you're going to be a daddy, whether you like it or not.'

Jordan paced around the room ragging his fingers through his hair. 'Nah, you're joking with me. You're on the pill.'

'Well, I forgot to take it a few times, didn't I?'

'What do you mean you forgot to fucking take it? Are you for real, or what?'

Karla sat down on the chair and crossed her legs, twiddling her hair. This was her shout now. She was the one calling the shots. 'So, go and tell the Mrs about us, and we can live happily ever after, like you promised me. You were divorcing the daft bitch anyway, so what does it matter?'

'Fuck off talking shit. How many times do you need telling that things take time?'

Karla sat forward in her seat and licked her teeth slowly. 'So, let me get this right: you're not leaving Pam?'

He swallowed hard. He had to keep this woman sweet before she blabbed to the world and his wife that she was carrying his baby. He had to think on his feet. His tone softened. 'Karla, do you know how much pressure I'm under? I could lose it all if I take my eye off the ball for a single second. Lenny has been after this club for as long as I can remember and, if I let things slip, he'll be all over me before I know it.'

'Lenny Jackson is an old man, babe. What on earth could he ever do to you?'

'How the hell do you know? You don't even know the guy. He's a force not to be messed with. He knows a lot of heads around this area and, if he really wanted to, he could have taken me down years ago.'

'So, why didn't he, then?'

Jordan was thinking out loud. 'My wife used to work for him and he kind of had a thing for her.'

Karla was listening, her expression changed. 'Your wife knows Lenny?' She let out a sarcastic laugh. 'And, since when did Pam work? She's been sat on her arse for as long as I can remember.'

Jordan was getting hot and bothered, and he wasn't going to sit down and tell her the full story. His wife was a grafter back in the day, she worked hard. Not like this free-loading bitch. 'Karla, I'm not ready for another pan lid. Do the test, and if it's positive, get it sorted out. In a few years, when we're settled, maybe then we'll have one.'

Her eyes opened wide. 'Are you actually asking me to consider an abortion?'

He sat down next to her and moved the hair from her face. 'Babes, me and you have a good thing going on here, and I don't want us to ruin it. I was planning to take you on holiday in a few months. The full works – five star, all inclusive, proper tropical paradise. Wherever you fancy – Barbados? The Maldives? And anyway, you'd hate being pregnant again, admit it.'

Karla sucked hard on her bottom lip; she gave him a cunning look as she replied, 'Jordan, why are you only telling me now that you're taking me on holiday?'

He smirked at her. 'Because I wanted to surprise you.'

She put her head back and closed her eyes as he rested his head on her lap. She was thinking. 'Jordan, do you honestly love me? I mean, am I really what you want?'

He kept his head on her lap and squeezed his arms around her tiny waist. He had to pull this out of the bag if she was ever going to believe him. He spoke slowly, 'Babes, I've always loved you. The moment I set my eyes on you I knew you were the one. I want to stay with you for ever.'

She gulped, and tears prickled her eyes; she was getting emotional. 'Do you really mean that? I know things have been hard for us lately, and I wasn't sure if you felt the same about me as you did about you.'

He squeezed her tighter. The bullshit rolled from his tongue without any effort. 'Of course I do, you nutter. How could I not love this face?' He lifted his head and looked directly into her eyes as he spoke again, 'Just sort it out, babes. You can have some money to go shopping, too, if you want? Go and get some new holiday clothes.' He watched her from the corner of his eye, and he could see she was thinking about it. He needed to persuade her, and money talked. 'Karla, give me time. Things are really bad at home at the minute and I'm only waiting for the right time to tell Pam that we're over. If you love me like you say you do, please let me sort my shit out and then you'll have my full attention.'

'But what if I am pregnant, Jordan? We could be a real family.'

Jordan stood up and inhaled deeply. He walked to the desk and used a small silver key to open its drawer. She watched him like a hawk. Rustling, his head was dipped low as he counted out the cash. He fanned the money out in front of her and smiled.

'Go shopping, baby, and buy something to cheer you up. It's your choice what you want to do if you are pregnant. But, if you are tubbed, I'm not booking a holiday. I want to keep you safe.'

Oh, this was a cunning move by Jordan. He knew this girl well and he could see her scanning the money held in his hand. She smirked and walked towards him. She picked the notes out of his hand and licked her lips in a sexual manner. 'Book the holiday, babes. I'll do what I need to do.' This girl was such a money grabber, he thought, as he watched her stalk out of the room holding the notes in her hand.

Jenny was in the corridor and she looked cocky as Karla approached her. 'See you've sold your soul again?'

'What do you mean by that?' She quickly stashed the money in her handbag.

Jenny kept her voice low and whispered into her ear. 'I heard what you said to Jordan. Just be careful I don't run around to his wife and tell her the good news, too.'

Karla gulped and swallowed hard. 'I don't know what you think you heard, but keep as far away from me as you can, because given the chance I'll land on you like a ton of bricks and scratch your eyes out.'

Jenny burst out laughing and started to walk away. 'I'll believe it when I see it, darling. You're just a daft bitch who's shagging the boss. Girls like you will come and go, trust me, I've seen it happen time and time again.' She sucked on her heart-shaped lips. 'Eh, I might even have a pop at him myself. I've seen the way he looks at me when I'm dancing, He's dying for a piece of me, I can see it in his eyes.'

Karla nodded slowly. 'Give your head a shake, woman. Jordan wouldn't touch you or your baggy fanny. You keep on dancing for the old men, babes. You'll always be a brass, a dirty slapper. Do you think Jordan would ever look at a slut like you?'

Jenny let out a sarcastic laugh and you could hear her heels clipping along the corridor. 'Whatever, you'll get what's coming to you, lady. I just hope I'm here to see you fall flat on your face.'

Karla hooked her bag over her shoulder and stalked into the club. She was in a mood, for sure.

Jordan pulled up at his house and stormed inside. 'Pam! Where are you, Pam?' he shouted at the top of his voice. He sprinted into the living room and quickly scanned the room, the same in the kitchen. He motored up the stairs and barged into the bedroom.

Pam was startled and sat up in the bed.

'Why are you not answering your phone? Six times I've rang you!'

Pam lay back in the bed and rolled on her side. 'You're not my master. I don't have to answer my phone to you. Go back to the club and do whatever you're doing.'

He sat on the edge of the bed and stared at his wife, eyes not moving. He could see the bruises on her arms, the side of her face. Slowly, he shook his head and sighed. 'I'm sorry, Pam, alright. Why are you making me feel worse than I do already? What, do you want me to beg for forgiveness? Because if you do, then I will.'

Pam looked at her husband, and she could no longer see the man she once loved. He looked older; he was an animal. A dirty no-good bastard who treated her like a doormat. She prepared herself for Round Two, because she had to tell him how she felt. 'Save your words for someone who cares, Jordan. I'm immune to your bullshit. Shove your apology where the sun doesn't shine. Your words mean nothing to me anymore. Any man who raises his hand to a woman is a coward. You used to call your dad that for hitting your mother when you were growing up, and look at you now, a chip off the old block. Like father, like son, eh?'

His eyes were glassy. 'Don't compare me to my old man, Pam. I'm not like him. Don't ever say I'm like him, because I'm not. You're trying to hurt me now. What kind of woman are you?'

She sat up straight in the bed. 'You *are* like him, deal with it. And, for the record, remind me what really happened in that marriage?' She smirked as she continued, 'Am I right in saying that your mother left him and he fell to pieces? A washed-up drunken wreck. He was nothing without her.'

His eyes flooded with tears as he dropped his head into his hands. He snivelled as he spoke to his wife. 'Pam, don't do this to me. I love you more than anything in the whole wide world. I know I have problems, but you are the only stable thing in my life that keeps me going. I do everything I do for us. Nobody else, just us. We're the dream team, remember?'

'Fuck off, Jordan. Go and tell someone who gives a fuck, because I don't anymore.'

The man was desperate. He fell to his knees at the side of the bed and reached to hold her hands. She quickly moved away. 'Don't touch me. You make me cringe inside. Honest, my stomach turns every time you are near me.'

He was quieter now, begging her. 'Please, Pam. I'll change. I'll get help. I'll do whatever it takes, but please don't treat me like this. I can't think straight without you.'

Pam stared at her husband. She'd always forgiven him in the past, but tonight she was sticking to her guns.

Jordan rolled on to bed next to her, and he was sobbing. He stared at the ceiling and poured his heart out. 'It's the drugs, babes. It gets a grip of me and I turn into a person that I have no control over. I don't ever want you to say I'm like my dad, Pam, never. I watched that man beat my mother black and blue, and there was nothing I could do to protect her.'

She rolled her eyes. 'You mean like our son has watched you leather me? It's history repeating itself, isn't it?'

'No, Pam, no more. I promise you now that, if you give me one last chance, I'll never lay a finger on you again. I'll be your Jordan, the old Jordan who you loved. Remember him, Pam? Me and you, together for ever?'

Pam listened, but she never replied. She was used to her husband's self-pity, and it looked like she wasn't buying his story tonight. Slowly, she closed her eyes. Jordan watched her sleep, then sat staring into the darkness of the night. She was his woman and, if he couldn't have her, nobody could.

Chapter Sixteen

M ary sat chugging on her cigarette as Elsa walked into the room. She turned to her and rolled her eyes. 'Is your mother still in bed? It's nearly midday and both of you are just getting up. What's happening to the world? In my day, I was up, dressed and ready, and couldn't wait to get out.'

Elsa tightened her house-coat belt around her waist and snuggled her neck deep into the pink fluffy fabric before she sat down on the sofa. 'Please don't start going on, Nana. If you have a problem with my mam, then go and tell her, not me. I'm sick of getting dragged into this.'

Mary hunched her shoulders and chewed on her cheek. 'Three days now she's been in that bed. Period pains, she says she has. I've never heard anything like it in my life. If every woman took to their bed when they were on the rag, nothing would ever get done in this world. She's a drama queen, that one is. I bet if lover-boy rings her she'll be up out of that bed as if someone has poured boiling water all over her. She thinks I'm bleeding daft.'

Elsa sighed. 'Nana, I'll be starting work pretty soon. It's good money, too.'

Mary looked confused. 'And where are you working? This is news to me.'

'I know a few girls who work in a nightclub and they have a couple of shifts that I'll be working as a trial. Collecting glasses, cloakroom, that sort of thing. So don't be stopping up late if you're worried about me – I'll be earning enough to get a taxi home.'

Mary stubbed her fag out in the ashtray, just as Karla came in. Her hair was tied back loosely in a pony-tail and she looked pale. Mary never took her eyes from her as she wobbled into the room to sit on the sofa.

Karla nudged Elsa. 'Move up, will you? I feel like I'm going to pass out.'

Elsa moved up on the sofa and looked at her mother. She did look ropey. 'What's up, Mam?'

Karla plonked down on the sofa and scooped her hair back from her face. 'I'm dying with period pains. I've been like this for a few days. I'll be alright after a couple of pain-killers and something to eat.'

Mary disappeared into the kitchen and came back holding a glass of water and two paracetamols. She opened her hand out and offered them to Karla. 'Here, get them down your neck. They're strong ones that I get from the doctors for my back pain.'

Karla squeezed her fingertips together to grip the small white pills. 'Cheers, Mam.'

Mary backed away and sat down on the chair facing the sofa. 'So, tell her about your job.' But before Elsa could get a word in edgeways, Mary took centre stage. 'She's going to be working in a nightclub. She'll be bringing some bread and butter into this house, too. There's only you now who needs to get a job, and we'll be laughing all the way to the bank.'

Karla growled over at her daughter. 'Which club? Since when has this happened?'

Elsa was bright red. She spoke through clenched teeth. 'Nana, you've got such a big mouth on you. I might have wanted to tell her myself, and you've gone and blabbed already. Thanks a bunch.'

Mary looked flustered. 'Bleeding hell, I was only singing your praises. Shoot me for being proud of you.'

Elsa turned on her heel and left, still blushing furiously.

———————

The next day, Elsa held the two cold gold keys in her hand. Pam had told her that the house would be free all day for her to come around and practise her dancing. And she needed to put the time in if she was ever going to become the dancer she wanted to be. With shaking hands, Elsa slid the first key into the lock and twisted it. Her heartbeat doubled when she opened the other lock. What if Pam had got it wrong and her husband had come home early, or even worse, what if Clayton was inside? Elsa had always been a quick thinker and if anyone was behind the other side of the door, she would tell them that she was borrowing some clothes from Pam for a big night out. Yes, they'd buy that.

The front door closed behind her and she stood frozen for a few seconds looking around the house. Even just being stood inside this house, she felt different. It smelt of money, smelt of success, all the things she craved. Elsa popped her head into the front room and then the kitchen, nobody was at home. She kicked her shoes off, imagining this was her home. Why couldn't she have all this? If she worked hard and earned decent money then one day she would have a gaff like this, nice pretty things, instead of outdated stuff that her nana had picked up at the flea market.

After a moment, Elsa stood up and waltzed into the kitchen. She opened the fridge door and grabbed a bottle of cold water. Her eyes were alive as she looked at all the fresh food in there. There were vegetables that she didn't even know the name of: big, fat purple ones. Who on earth would eat such a funny-looking vegetable? Her nana was a great cook, but it was always stews and dumplings and bloody chips and egg. This family ate pasta, steak, fresh fish. Oh, how the other half lived.

Elsa climbed the stairs, loving playing the lady of the house. After all, she'd studied Performing Arts and she was never happier than when she was being someone else. At college, she had loved how she could become anyone she wanted to be once she put her mind to it. At the top of the stairs Elsa looked one way then the other, she just couldn't help being nosy. She must have got that trait from her nana. She tiptoed into Pam's bedroom. Her palm pressed the thick memory foam mattress. This was the good life; how the other half lived. She couldn't resist opening the mirrored wardrobes not far from her. The first one must have been

Pam's husband's wardrobe: dark shirts, grey, black, navy clothes. The next door she opened, her jaw dropped low. Inside was an array of bright colours, sparkling dresses, leather pants. This was any girl's heaven. Even though she knew she shouldn't, she couldn't help herself. She needed to feel these expensive fabrics next to her skin, just once. Elsa's hand stroked a long white faux-fur coat. The feel of it sent a warm sensation down her body; she felt calm, loved, secure and, more than anything, powerful. Elsa stripped off and started trying the dresses on. She twirled her body around in the mirror and flicked her hair over her shoulder, pouting her lips at her reflection. This girl was in a frenzy as she tried on dress after dress. Then, from the corner of eye, she clocked a large silver box. With caution she lifted the lid and stood back. These were Pam's dancing outfits. No wonder men had travelled to come and see her when she was wearing outfits like these, they left nothing to the imagination. Elsa started to hang the dresses back up in the wardrobe neatly. But she kept looking over at the box as if it had some magical power over her. It wanted her to come back. She twisted her fingers, thinking. Who would ever know? Without any further hesitation, she pulled out a red and silver bikini. Sequins, sparkling jewels, thin lacy briefs – she put the lot on. Elsa stood looking at herself in the full-length mirror. Was this really the same girl looking back at her? She backed off from the mirror and smiled one last time at her reflection. It was time to dance, time to show this outfit how good she was, who she could be.

Elsa turned the music on, got in the zone, remembering everything Pam had told her, even the walk, the way she licked her lips, touched her own body. Never rushing, always teasing. Her body coiled around the silver pole like a boa constrictor as she slithered down it with ease. Her legs were stronger than they had been previously, toned. Elsa head was at the bottom of the pole, and she was trying to remember what she had been taught. Slowly, slowly, she kicked her legs over her head. At last, she'd done it. For weeks she'd been covered in bruises from this move. Pam was right: practice, practice, practice. This girl could move, sweat glistening from her skin, her eyes alive as the beat kicked in. She was in a trance now, spinning, kicking, flipping from the pole. She could see herself in the mirror and she moved her body even more to show off the parts that Pam had told her the punters loved more than anything, the pussy shots. The more of these she performed the more money she would earn. She remembered what Pam had told her. She left nothing to the imagination; this was her time to shine now, her chance to make some real money.

Elsa looked at the clock on the wall, she'd been here for over three hours. Where had the time gone? Given the chance she would have been here morning until night practicing her dancing. She walked over to the mirrors, flicked her hair over her shoulder and licked her lips. Her confidence was growing every day that passed and this feeling she held inside her was growing too. She had a dream now, something to aim for, her quest in life. She wanted to be the best dancer out there. And, she would do whatever it took to get it. She was a woman on a mission and day by day her confidence was growing.

Elsa stripped off and sneaked the outfit back into the box, doubled-checked that everything was the same as she found it and left the bedroom. She was back in her own clothes now, back to being Elsa bloody Bradshaw. She cringed as she looked down at her own outfit. She wanted more, so much more.

Chapter Seventeen

Pam walked into the club and headed straight to the bar. The past couple of weeks had seen her cuts heal and her bruises fade and, in the low light, she looked like her old self again – although, if anyone had looked closely enough, they'd have seen a coldness in her gaze. This was a woman who'd been pushed too far one too many times. Still, she seemed spooked. After a few minutes, a man tapped her on the shoulder and she nearly jumped out of her skin.

'Bleeding hell, Lenny! Don't be sneaking up on me like that. I nearly jumped out of my skin. You know how anxious I get when I'm on enemy ground.'

He sniggered, 'Welcome to *Lush Laps*.' He clicked his finger over at the busty barmaid, gave her a cheeky smile and ordered his drinks. 'Two brandies, Sandra, please.'

The woman fluttered her eyelashes and wasted no time in getting the main man his drinks. Pam smirked. 'So, you still remember what I drink, then?'

'Of course I do, Pam. How could I ever forget anything about you?' Lenny stared deep into her eyes and she had to look away from him, she didn't feel comfortable. He carried on examining her for a few seconds more.

She turned back to him. 'Lenny, I'm here on business. Don't start all that crap with me again. It was years ago, get over it.' Lenny reached over and took the drinks from the bar.

Pam looked back at him. Older than she'd remembered him – in her mind, he would always be the young gun she'd met as little more than a child all those years back. But Lenny's silver hair suited his tanned skin. He held a look of George Clooney, a bit bigger frame but he definitely had similar features. He had the charm, too – when he wanted.

'Let's go and sit somewhere quiet, Pam. Too many eyes around here. The last thing we need is that big fucking idiot husband of yours coming here shouting his mouth off.'

She agreed and followed him to a quieter part of the club. Once they sat down, she was eager to start talking. 'So, how long before the new club is ready to open?'

'Another couple of weeks yet, princess, so stop flapping. I told you when you come to me the other day that I would look after you. I'm a man of my word.'

'Lenny, I've put a lot of money into this and I want to make sure we are ready to open on time. I don't need you to look after me, I can look after myself. I just need you to be my cover until it's showtime.'

Lenny nodded. 'We need to sort some girls out quickly. Can you get away any time to come with me to sort some out?'

Pam chewed on the inside of her cheek. She lowered her voice, 'I've got you the main attraction. I'll bring her to meet you soon. She'll bring the crowds in, trust me. She reminds me of myself when I was younger. But, as you know, everything comes at a price. I've trained this one myself and put time and effort into her.'

Lenny rubbed his hand across his crotch. 'How old is she?'

'Eighteen, but only just,' Pam replied. Lenny's eyes lit up. He was well known for liking the younger girl. Even at the age of sixty, he still craved young flesh next to his. The hairs on the back of her neck stood on end and a cold chill raced down her spine. She knew that look, she'd seen it time and time again over the years and, even now, it unsettled her.

'Who'd have thought me and you would end up being business partners, Pam? When Jordan finds out, he'll shit a brick. I can't wait to see his face. I owe him anyway for stealing you away. Revenge is sweet, Pam, very sweet indeed.'

'Lenny, I have my own plans so please don't rock my boat. I'm going to earn enough money to have a good life without him, so don't go messing it up for me.'

Lenny had a mouthful of his drink. 'So, tell me more about this girl. Can we get her working the private parties?'

Pam started fidgeting, but she knew the game more than anyone and she had to put herself first. 'It's your call, Lenny. Like I said, I've brought her to you, so make sure you sort her out for me. I'm going to go to *Passion* tonight to put the feelers out on a few of the girls there who might want to move. I've heard some of them aren't happy, so we need to strike whilst the iron is hot.'

Lenny looked about the club and turned slowly to look deep into Pam's eyes. 'Is this new girl a virgin? You know I like to break them in myself before I send them out working?'

Pam cringed; her eyes closed slightly. 'Yep, as far as I know she's whiter than white.'

Lenny rubbed his hands together. 'I need to meet her. The sooner the better for me.'

Pam was anxious as she picked her drink up. 'You'll have to wait, Lenny. Let's get the other girls sorted first.'

'You know I'd do anything for you, Pam. Why don't we make this more than just business partners? Come with me and I'll give you a good life. You'll want for nothing, ever.'

Pam swallowed hard. 'Lenny, I'd rather be a million miles from this life, if I can. I know you're never going to change your spots. You're too deep into this world. You love the clubs, you love the girls, you even the love the rivalry. But look what it done to me; I'm messed up in the head. The things I've done and seen will never leave my mind. Even now I can still close my eyes and see things no one should ever have to see. I want this club to be an earner for me – not a way of life.'

Lenny sighed. 'Stop your moaning, Pam. As I remember, you loved the money you were earning when you were dancing. You couldn't get enough of it. You had it all, and you know it.'

Pam licked her dry cracked lips. 'It's not all about the money, though, is it Lenny, in the end?'

He let out a loud laugh and touched her hand. 'Can you hear yourself, woman? Of course it's about the money. It will always be about money, for all of us. You're bringing me a young virgin and ask yourself why.' He leant forward and whispered in her ear, his hot breath creeping inside her, 'The money. You're no different from me, sweetheart. No matter how much you want to sugar-coat it. The money is always the answer, so get off your high horse and deal with it.'

Pam's eyes clouded over, and she had to hold back the tears. She tried justifying herself. 'I'm doing what I'm doing for a better life for me and my son. No other reason.'

'Yeah, whatever. A young girl is getting brought into this life and she'll never be the same again, so don't tell me you have a conscience all of a sudden.'

Pam's head dropped low, ashamed. 'Oh, Lenny, just let's crack on. You have your reasons and I have mine, leave it at that. I'll meet you tomorrow night at eight, and we'll go and see some new girls. I want the best, no munters, so I'm going to be picky. I want the men to travel for miles to see our girls, like they travelled to see me.'

Lenny smirked. 'You were the best I've ever seen, Pam. I was in a trance when I watched you dance. Even now, if I think about you dancing, it makes me hard.'

She sniggered. 'I thought you needed tablets for that these days?'

Lenny chuckled. 'I need nothing but a fresh wet pussy to make me hard, darling. Trust me, it's like an iron bar when I get one in my bed.'

Pam tried to hide the shudder that ran through her. This would never change, and she knew she was dancing with the devil.

Pam glided through the doors of *Passion* and Jordan, who clocked everyone who entered his club, looked relieved. She'd forgiven him. His days in the dog-house were over.

'Babes,' he shouted to get her attention.

Pam had to stop her hand darting to the scar left by the cut above her eye. The swelling had gone down and she didn't want him to see how much he'd hurt her. Turning on all the charm she used to use under the lights, she plastered on a smile and headed towards him.

He draped his arm around her shoulder and kissed the side of her neck. 'Babes, you smell amazing. I'm so glad you decided to come in. I really thought that we were over, this time. I swear, babes, my head has been all over the place.'

Pam smiled at her husband. 'So, do I have to wait all day for a drink in this place, or what?'

Jordan was brown-nosing for sure.

Once he'd got her a drink, he sat down next to her. 'I'm going to make things right, baby. Honest, I'll never lay a finger on you again. I've been to hell and back during these last few weeks, and the thought of losing you makes me sick in the pit of my stomach.'

Pam looked deep into his eyes and gave a performance any leading lady would be proud of. 'Jordan, I want us to be happy. I know you have problems, and I'm not going to leave you to deal with them on your own. Remember when I married you, I took the vows. For better or for worse?'

Jordan looked relieved. Then he spotted Karla making her way towards him. He quickly passed his wife a drink. 'One minute, babes, just let me make sure all the girls are ready. We should have a few in tonight and I want to make sure the dancers give it their best.' He left her side and she watched him rush away.

'Fucking idiot,' she whispered under her breath. Pam could see him speaking to Karla. It wasn't rocket science to work out that she was the one he was banging; she could see it in her eyes, her body language. She gripped her glass tighter and sneered over at her husband. 'Bastard,' she mumbled under her breath.

Jordan kept looking over his shoulder at his wife. This needed to be a quick conversation. 'Karla, before you start going on. I need you to work with me on this and don't start kicking off. I've told you how I feel about you and what I want, so bear with me on this. I didn't know Pam was coming in tonight, she just turned up. What can I do, eh?'

Karla was fuming and she couldn't hide it. 'For fuck's sake, Jordan. When is this ever going to end? It seems like it's never going to happen. I mean, you promised me a holiday once I got rid of the baby, you know, *our* baby?'

'I know I did, and I will book the holiday once you've had time to heal and that. You've been through a lot and I want to make sure you're well before I book us anything.'

'It does my head in watching you with her, Jordan. Honest, I can't hold the rage in when I see you two together. You're *my* man now, not hers.'

His voice was low, calming. He was blagging her, for sure. 'So go home then, go on. Go and have the night off. I can manage here without you for one night and, if I'm being honest, you look like you could do with a rest.'

Karla frowned. 'I thought I looked alright. What's wrong with me?'

He smiled at her and made sure nobody could hear him. 'Nothing, but I know when you're not firing on both cylinders. Just listen to me and go and relax while you have the chance.' The matter was settled, and she didn't argue with him.

He hurried away from her. A pain in the arse, she was, a real bunny-boiler. He was off the hook for tonight at least, though. He could relax now and put some decent time into his wife. He was going to treat her like a princess. But when he walked back to the bar, his wife was gone. The barmaid shouted over to him.

'Pam's gone to watch the girls. She said she'll be back soon.'

The club was packed out tonight and he smiled as he watched the men ordering their drinks at the bar. The mark-up on each drink was what paid for the Rolex on his wrist – and as the girls got going, the drinks got flowing. The music started and Jenny was on stage first. 'Candy Shop', by 50 cent and Olivia played at full pelt. A rainbow of lights shot across the stage. The bass kicked in and Jenny made sure that all eyes were on her. The men gathered around the stage. They were trying their best to get a glimpse of her body. Jenny folded at the waist and made sure the punters got a prime view. She wrapped her leg around the silver pole and seduced it with every inch of her body. She rubbed against the silver metal and she could see the men drooling as they watched her.

Pam smiled from the side of the stage. It was all about tantalising the audience and this girl had hit the nail bang on the head. She worked the punters and let every man there think they were the only man she wanted. By the end of her dance, she had more than two hundred pounds stuffed down the side of her tiny knickers. The notes were scattered around her too and she smiled as she stalked off stage through them. She flicked her hair over her shoulder and nodded at one of the other girls, whose job was to clear the money up before the next dancer came onto the stage. Jenny started to leave, and Pam pulled her to the side.

'You are amazing, chick. Can we talk later? I have an idea I want to put to you.'

Jenny was still regaining her breath and it took a few seconds before she replied. 'If it's going to make me money, then I'm up for anything.'

'We're talking lots of money, honey, more than you can earn in this place, anyway. But keep your mouth shut. This is between us two, nobody else.'

Jenny winked. 'My lips are sealed; I'll go and get changed for my next dance and then I'll come and find you.'

Pam rubbed her hands together. 'Sure, go and get ready and give these punters something to think about.' Pam walked back towards the bar and sat next to her husband.

He never missed a trick. 'I saw you talking to Jenny. Is everything alright?'

She patted his arm as she sat down. 'Of course, I was giving her a few tips.'

He dragged her closer and kissed the top of her head. 'You always have my back, don't you? The one person I can always rely on.'

The last dancer was on stage, and Pam knew she needed to get away from Jordan so she could have another word with Jenny. Luckily, by now he was pissed, and she knew all those visits to the toilet were an excuse to shove more drugs up his nose. He was off his napper, and getting out from under his watchful eye would be easier now.

Pam checked one last time behind her and entered the dressing room. She caught Jenny's eye and signalled her to follow her. She knew she didn't have long to seal the deal. The minute Jenny was by her side, she kept her voice low and blurted it out. 'I've got to be quick but, if you can meet me tomorrow, I can go over the details more. This is a great opportunity for you, Jenny, and I want to help you make it in this game. I know talent when I see it.'

'I'm listening. Is Jordan not part of this?'

Pam's heart was racing. She was on edge, constantly looking behind her. 'No, he doesn't give a shit about you girls, so I'm looking after you instead. All you need to know is that, whatever you are earning here, you can double it in this new club. Plus, no mucky hands will be all over you every night.'

'That will do for me, love.'

'Meet me at the coffee shop in the Shopping Fort in Cheetham Hill at one o'clock tomorrow. Don't be late, either. I hate waiting about.' Pam's heels clipped along the corridor back into the club.

Jenny shouted after her. 'I'll be there, don't worry.' But as the words faded on her lips, she heard the side door bang shut. She ran to it and pulled it open. She looked one way then the other: nobody there. But she knew if she'd been overheard, she was in trouble, deep trouble.

Chapter Eighteen

Elsa lay snuggled next to Clayton on the sofa, arms wrapped around his waist. Her eyes kept wandering to the clock and she felt edgy. She moved her body slowly and yawned. 'What time will your mam be in?'

Clayton stretched his arms above his head, then gripped her closer. 'Wow, you seem more interested in my mam than you do in me,' he chuckled.

Elsa blushed slightly. 'No, I'm not. I just get worried about her. After everything that happened …'

'Don't you worry about my old queen; she always bounces back. Trust me, if she wasn't right, we would all know about it. I don't know what she's told you about her life, but she's been through some bad shit when she was growing up. Her mam was a pisshead, you know? And she was more or less left to fend for herself. Honest, the stories she's told me have left me in tears. She had it bad, I mean really bad. You don't know the half of it.'

Elsa sat up and pretended she didn't know anything about his mother's past. 'I mean sometimes, when I look into her eyes, I can see pain. I can't explain it, but I can see she has had hard life.'

He nodded. 'Yeah, I get what you mean. Sometimes she cries when she's laid in bed at night. I hear her, she doesn't know I can hear her, and I've never said a word to her about it. I can't seem to find the words to comfort her. Her dad was the biggest bastard that walked this earth. He led her a dog's life and, for that, I'll never forgive him.'

Elsa rubbed her arms as a cold breeze slithered over her skin. Maybe having a father in her life was not all it was made out to be, if this was how they treated their daughters. Clayton moved in closer to her. He kept his voice low.

'Elsa, do you have to go home tonight? I'm dying to have you stay over. And I think you want to, as well. Plus, I swear I'm going to burst if I don't get a bit soon.'

She moved away from him and made sure he knew there was nothing in store for him tonight. But she had to keep him interested, otherwise he would be going elsewhere for his sexual needs. 'All good things come to those who wait. I just need to feel …' she paused and thought about how she wanted to word this. 'I don't want to rush. It'll be my first time, you know that, and I want it to be special. Not a wham, bam, thank you ma'am.'

Clayton sighed and she could see the disappointment in his face. He'd have to lie again to his mates and tell them he was giving it her hard all the time. He had a reputation to live up to and it was what his mates expected. He smirked at her and whispered in her ear, 'I suppose a hand job or a blowie is out of the question?'

She playfully punched him in the arm. And she didn't want to admit she didn't have any experience of doing either of the things he'd requested. Candice had told her plenty, and she'd seen all the same videos that her mates laughed at, yet she cringed at the thought of putting a penis in her mouth. He was actually waiting on a reply as if he stood a chance. She licked her bottom lip and hoped she looked mysterious rather than clueless. She wasn't embarrassed to say she'd never slept with anyone, but to admit she was totally inexperienced – beyond a snog and a fumble – felt harder.

Oh my God, he was gorgeous though, and to whip her knickers off would have been so bloody easy. After all, she knew when she was on stage she was meant to be making the crowd dream of sleeping with her – and how could she convince them she was some kind of sex kitten when she hadn't even done it with her boyfriend? But she wasn't ready, not yet anyway. She decided to kiss him and remind him why he was waiting about for her. Her cherry-red lips softly connected with his and he seemed to melt into her arms. That should keep him quiet for a bit.

Elsa jumped up from the sofa when she heard somebody in the hallway, talking. She must have nodded off. She nudged Clayton. 'Somebody is here, quick, wake up,' she whispered. He rolled on his side and he wasn't in any rush to sit up.

'Relax, it will only be my mam.'

'Clayton, sit up, I don't want her to think I've been rolling about on the sofa with you.'

With effort, he pulled his tired body up from the sofa. The living room door opened and in walked Pam. Anyone could see she'd had a skinful. A man walked in behind her, his voice loud. He oozed confidence. Elsa blushed as he neared her.

'So, you're my son's girlfriend, then? I've heard loads about you and, may I say, Son, you've bagged a beauty here.' Jordan sat down next to Elsa. 'I'm Jordan.' He leant over and kissed her on the cheek.

'Don't get too comfy, Jordan – you promised me a takeaway' Pam shooed him towards the door.

Jordan looked at his son and raised his eyes. 'You know she won't shut up about it until we get it her, don't you? Shove your shoes on, and we'll go and get some scran.'

Once she heard the front door slam shut behind them, Pam smiled at Elsa. Her breath felt hot on Elsa's cheek. 'You're going to be the best dancer these clubs have seen in years. I've already been speaking to a few contacts about you and, when the time is right, I'm going to take you to meet them. Honest, you'll have money coming out of your arse. Enough cash to go wherever you want and to buy anything you see. How does that make you feel?'

Elsa shrugged, still finding it hard to imagine what it would feel like to dance for an audience, let alone get paid for it. 'It would be nice. I can treat my nana and take some of the strain from her, I suppose. But it still doesn't feel real – what if I get stage fright?'

'You're a natural – you were born to do this. But you need to make sure you never tell anybody about what I'm doing for you, because if anyone gets wind of it the game will be up and nothing will ever change – for you or me. You need to open your mind to change and the world I'm going to introduce you to. If we pull this off, nothing will ever be the same again. Trust me, I know.'

Elsa nodded and smiled. She hated listening to drunken talk; she'd heard it for years from her own mother. Pam stood up and staggered over to the drinks cabinet. She pulled out two glasses and filled them high with brandy. She slurred her words as she twisted her head back to Elsa.

'He's changed his tune. Have you seen him all over me now? That's because I told him it was over. He can't focus without me, you know. His world falls apart, no matter what he tells everyone else.'

'I was worried about you, Pam, honest, really worried.'

Pam held her head high and shrugged her shoulders. 'I'm a big girl, love. I've always been able to look after myself. I've done it all my life. I don't need nobody to look after me.' She passed Elsa a drink. 'It's always been me who's had to pick up the pieces, love. I watched my mother destroy herself with drink, and it was me who had to pick her up and try and help her. Do you know how hard that was for me? I was a young girl, and saw things no child should have to see at that age. She drank herself into an early grave, she just couldn't live without the bottle. It would be easy for me to follow in her footsteps, so bleeding easy.' She snivelled. 'But no answers are ever found at the bottom of a glass. The more you drink, the more the problems get a grip of you. If she was here now, I'd fling her in rehab and get her the help she needed,' she sighed. 'Because she did need help, she needed somebody to care about her, to tell her everything was going to be alright. But, nobody ever did. She entered this world alone, and she left it the same way.'

Elsa's heart melted for Pam as she reached over and touched her warm hands. 'But look at you now. You have done so well for yourself. Your mother would have been proud of you.'

Pam smiled through the tears. 'Too little, too late.'

Elsa knew there was nothing more to say, so she changed the subject. 'I've been practising dancing every spare minute I have. Some of the moves you showed me are on point now and the yoga has helped me so much, too. I think I'm ready. When can I show you the routine I've been working on?'

Pam's expression changed. 'Are you sure this is what you want, love? There's no going back once you're in this life.'

'You've given me a golden ticket to change my life, and for that I will be forever thankful.'

Pam looked like she had something to say, but the words seemed trapped in her mouth. Before the women could say another word, the boys were back with the food.

Elsa was quiet as she ate her food. Was she ready to do this? It was all or nothing. As she settled into the deep, plush cushions of the sofa and looked around at the luxury that surrounded her, she made up her mind. Sure there were risks, and she knew money didn't buy happiness – but it certainly bought a lot of other things.

Chapter Nineteen

M ary sat in the pub lounge. She seemed anxious; fidgeting, ripping a coaster up. Every time the door opened, she was on pins, head turning one way then the other. This was a nice enough bar, even in the daytime, deep-red painted walls edged with a vanilla-cream colour; but she knew the business she was mixed up in was far from nice. The door swung open and Mary swallowed hard as a large-framed man came marching towards her. He sat down facing her and stared at her for what seemed a life-time before he spoke.

'This is the last time, Mary. He said, next time you even think about asking for money for the kid, he will make sure it's the last. You understand what I'm saying, don't you?'

Mary gulped and pulled her shoulders back. Who did this dickhead think he was talking to? She'd never backed down to anyone in her life, and she wasn't starting now. Her nostrils flared and she sat cracking her fingers. 'Tell him, he'll pay for his mistakes for as long as she needs it. His child needs things, and if he doesn't cough up a few quid for her then I'll be knocking on his door and asking his wife for it. For years he's got away with bits of money here and bits of money there, so it's about time he put his hand in his pocket and paid for his daughter properly.'

The man reached over and gripped Mary's hand, squeezing it until her fingers turned white.

'I'm normally more in the business of debt collection – not being a fucking charity. Are you sure you want me passing your message up to the gaffer?'

She struggled and pulled her hand away.

'I'm not scared of you, or him, and make sure you tell him that. Why do you think he sends his cronies to come and see me, and doesn't face me himself?' She paused and smirked at him. 'Because he knows he will get a piece of my mind if I set eyes on him. He needs to man up and provide for his flesh and blood. He's a no-good bastard. And you can tell the cheeky cunt that I said that, too.'

The man looked unimpressed. 'But *is* she his flesh and blood? That's the big question. From what I've heard, her mother was a sperm bank. Everyone was making a deposit in her. Still are, from what I hear.'

Mary was tempted to spit in the guy's face. How dare he disrespect her daughter! 'You ever say anything like that again and I'll drag every bastard hair out of your scalp. He knows he is the father. Why do you think I get these little envelopes of silence money every couple of months? But that's pin money – now she's eighteen she needs setting up in life. A proper wedge so she can start a decent life. And if we get that, I won't come knocking again. But if he's saying he's not the father, we can soon set the record straight. We'll do a DNA test, and then what? Go on, tell me what he will do when his perfect little family life is turned upside down by a paternity test in black and white.'

The man sneered at her as he pushed the envelope across the table to her. 'Just listen to what I'm telling you. It's come straight from the horse's mouth, so tread carefully, very carefully. I'd hate for anything to happen to you or your family. The gaffer doesn't mess about. This is it – take this and shut up. Or you'll get silenced. Permanently.'

The look in his eyes told Mary he was serious. She watched him stand up and leave his seat. As soon as he was gone, she let out a laboured breath and took a few minutes to regain her composure. Her heart was racing, and the colour seemed to have drained from her skin: she was white as snow. Mary looked around the room and she was sure the couple sat across from her had heard her conversation. She eyeballed them and opened her eyes wide. If they had anything to say, then she was listening. Nothing, not a word. Mary slowly opened the brown envelope and checked the contents. She quickly folded it and shoved it in her pocket. It would do for now – but she wanted Elsa to have what she was due. And she'd get it for her – even if it was the last thing she'd do.

Karla stared into the mirror as she started to get ready. She tugged at the loose skin under her eyes. Dipping her finger into some clear gel, she patted it on the area to try and banish the big, dark circles that were forming there. Elsa walked into the bedroom with a white towel wrapped around her body. Karla looked at her through the mirror and spoke with a heavy heart. 'Well, it's official. Your mother is finally getting old. Look at the state of my skin. It's nothing like it used to be. All blotchy and greasy. Shoot me now and put me out of my misery.'

Elsa pottered about the bedroom and sniggered. 'You look good for your age, Mam. I hope I look like you when I get older. You're just having a bad day, that's all.' Elsa came to her side and perched on the bed. 'Come on, cheer up. It's not like you to be down in the dumps.'

As if somebody had pulled the plug on her emotions, Karla burst out crying, floods of tears rolling down her cheeks. This was so out of character, this woman never cried. Not even when the family dog had died. She was a tough cookie. Elsa stood up and placed her arms around her mother's neck. 'What's up? Tell me what's wrong?'

Karla was sobbing now. 'I've been thinking about things, love. I've made mistake after mistake in my life, and look at me now, a washed-up old wreck. I never bloody learn. I'll never see marriage or a happy family. I've always been the same. I'm always searching for the man who can change my life, when in fact it's only me who can change it. I'm sick of it all, sick of dating dickhead men who always let me down.'

Elsa readjusted her bath towel. 'If you want my advice, you should ditch this man you're seeing. Come on, Mam, it's been months now, and all you keep saying is that he's leaving his wife, and he never does. Don't you think it's about time to call it a day and move on? I'm sure you will find someone who isn't married who you can be happy with.'

'I've always been the same, Elsa, always wanting what I can't have. These men promise me the world when I first start seeing them, then it all turns to shit, a big pile of hot stinking shit.'

Elsa spoke up. 'So, change it, don't sit crying about it. This guy you're seeing doesn't seem like a nice person. Think about it, Mother, if he's cheating on his wife with you, he wouldn't think twice about cheating on you. It's not rocket science, is it?'

Karla wiped her nose with her sleeve. Her eyes were blood red, and her bottom lip was quivering. 'I know what you're saying is right, but I can't give up on him after this long. He said he's taking me on holiday soon, and I feel that, after a couple of weeks with me in the sunshine, he'll realise he can't live without me.'

Elsa rolled her eyes. 'Mam, are you for real? I've heard you shouting and screaming at this idiot down the phone nearly every other night, and you really think he's going to change at the click of a finger?'

'Yes, he loves me. I just need to give him time, that's all.'

'Then you'll always be sat in front of some mirror crying, won't you?'

Karla looked at her daughter. 'You've grown up so much, haven't you? I'm sorry I've not always been there for you, but I've always been mixed up with some tosser, trying to change our lives. Because that's what I've been doing, babes, trying to change our lives and make everything right. I hate sitting here without a pot to piss in and never having enough money to do the things a mother and daughter should be doing.'

Elsa nodded slowly. This was the truth. Karla had never spent any quality time with her daughter, and there was no way Elsa was making her feel any better about the decisions she'd made in the past.

She took a deep breath and her chest expanded as she prepared to speak. 'Mam, I will make some money and, when I have enough, you can sack this man off. You won't need him anymore. I've got stuff planned that will change our lives.'

Karla chuckled. 'And where do you plan getting your money from, eh? We need big money. We need a decent home, a car, all the things we see them women on TV with. We're not talking pennies, love, we need grands to have the life we're talking about.'

Elsa dipped her eyes to the floor. Her mother was a selfish cow. She hadn't been there for her daughter, but Elsa couldn't turn her back on her in her hour of need. 'We can have all that stuff, Mam. It just takes a bit of work. The grass isn't always greener on the other side – the grass is greener where you water it. That's what they say, isn't it?'

Karla burst out laughing and flicked her hair over her shoulder. 'Since when have you become all grown up? It should be me giving you the advice, not the other way around.'

'I *had* to grow up, Mother. There's a big world outside these four walls and I intend to see it. I've watched you and my nana struggle for years, and I don't want to be like that.'

Karla choked up. 'I'm so sorry, love.'

And this time, it actually sounded like she meant it.

Elsa and Karla were lying on the sofa together, watching a chick flick, when Mary came into the room. She smiled. 'What's going on here? Since when do you two cuddle up and watch a film together?'

Karla rolled on her side to reply. 'Where have *you* been, anyway?'

Mary pulled her coat off and walked to the bin to throw away an empty brown envelope. 'I've been at bingo. No bleeding luck, though.'

'Nana, have you won the lottery, or something? Because lately you're never out of the place. I thought you were skint.'

Mary pushed her shoulders back, and she never looked at her granddaughter once while she was speaking. 'I am skint, but I thought I would go and blow the gas money to see if I could earn any more money for us, but, nope, no such bleeding luck. I'm even worse off than I was before. Anyway, I thought you were starting work soon?'

Elsa kept her eyes on the TV. 'Yes, I will be soon, and then I can give you some money.'

Karla cleared her throat. 'And I've decided I'm looking for work, too. I'm sick of being down at the club. I want a proper job with proper hours.'

Mary nearly choked. 'Am I hearing things? Did you just say you are not going to the club anymore?'

'Correct, Mam. I've seen the light, thanks to Elsa. Things are changing around here, just you watch.'

Chapter Twenty

Pam stood staring at the silver pole, she seemed in a world of her own. Jenny waltzed into the room, dressed in her dancing outfit. A little black number that left nothing to the imagination: just smooth, unblemished, tanned skin and a sliver of fabric.

She smiled over at Pam. 'Did you have to hire this place?'

'Yes. It's quiet here, so we won't be bothered by anyone snooping about. I've got a new girl coming, too. I want you to watch her dance and tell me what you think.'

Jenny walked over to the long mirror and looked at her reflection. She slowly stroked her long talons down her thigh. 'I'll check her out, but you know I'm the best dancer in this neck of the woods, don't you?'

Pam smirked. 'I do, Jenny, but I'd still like your views on this one. I've taken her under my wing, and I'd like to think I've done a good job of training her.'

Jenny nodded and, as if the silver pole had magnetic powers, she made her way towards it. Her body oozed around it. Next, Jenny was upside down with her head nearly touching the floor, legs gripping the pole above her. She kicked her legs over her head and spun slowly down. This girl was flexible. Bloody hell, such control.

The doors behind Pam swung open and Elsa rushed in, looking flustered. Her hair was all over the place and her cheeks bright red. 'Sorry I'm late. The bus took ages to come.'

Jenny flicked her hair over her shoulder and stood studying the young girl. She slowly walked over to her, heels clipping across the shiny studio floor. 'So, you are the new dancer?'

Pam stood back and let Elsa fend for herself. After all, she'd have to get used to the way other girls in the dancing game spoke to her. There were some true friends to be made, but you had to prove yourself first. Suspicion was the name of the game, and there were plenty of girls who'd cut you as soon as look at you. That type were real bitches: sneaky, jealous bitches. It took a while to find your people – the ones who'd have your back, no matter what.

'Er, yes,' Elsa choked.

'So go and get your kit on, and let's see what you've got. When you're ready, I'll dance for you first and you can go after me. But, beware, to impress me you will need to bring something special to the table.'

Elsa swallowed hard. She was on the spot and, if she was being totally honest, she didn't like the sound of this cow; she was full of herself.

'Bang a tune on, Pam. Something with a good beat in it.'

Pam connected her Bluetooth to the speaker and scrolled through her phone. She had a decent playlist in her library.

'Work Bitch' by Britney Spears played at full volume and Jenny made her way to the pole. Elsa stood with her back against the wall, mesmerised. Jenny was in a league of her own. Every move she made, she was seductive. Her facial expression was sexy and, with every bend of her body, she had all eyes glued to her.

Pam nudged Elsa. 'You've got what it takes to be better than her. Believe in yourself and dance like you have been doing. I've been in this game a lot of years and I know class when I see it.'

Elsa's breathing changed, her chest rising rapidly. It was D-day. All her training, all the hours she'd been dancing were on show. She was vulnerable and Pam could see it. She gripped her arm and looked her directly in the eyes. There was no way she wanted her to mess this up. 'Take deep breaths and get your act together. You need to learn to switch off and get the job done. Remember, you want the punters eating out of your hand, throwing money at you, wanting more. Deep breaths.'

Jenny's body spun around the pole like a tornado now. As the beat kicked in, she showed off her toned, tanned body. Every inch, every crack, every crevice was on show; nothing was left to the imagination. Elsa peeled her black jogging bottoms down and there she was, for the first time, in an outfit Pam had given her. It was beautiful: red silk material, small silver diamonds. Pam nodded as she looked her up and down and smiled. All the training had paid off, and there was a lean strength to Elsa's frame now. The music finished and Elsa clapped. Pam joined in, too.

'Jenny, that was top-notch. The main reason I want you to dance at my club, when it opens, is to show the other girls how it's done.'

Elsa wasn't listening to what they were saying to each other. She stood stretching her body and moving from side to side.

Pam watched her apprentice make her way to the pole and found the track Elsa had been practising to. Just as she was about to press play, the door opened.

Pam turned and smiled as Lenny Jackson walked into the room. Jenny knew who he was straight away. Every dancer in town knew who Lenny was. Her eyes lit up, and already she was flirting with him. 'You've just missed my dance. I can do it again if you want. Elsa, wait up,' she yelled over to her.

Lenny sucked his teeth and his eyes never left Elsa as he spoke. 'Whoa, chill out. I'll watch you dance after this young lady. You look like you need to rest, anyway. Look at you sweating.'

Jenny stalked back to the corner. He could piss off if he thought this young girl was the main attraction here today. *She* was the dancer the men wanted to see, not this kid.

Pam called to Elsa. 'Give me a shout when you're ready. Lenny will be watching you, too, so make sure you make a good impression on him, because this man holds all the cards on your career.'

Elsa inhaled, deep breaths, one two three. She nodded over to Pam. Lenny found a chair and sat down facing the pole. Pam was watching him from the side of her eye, aware of the hunger in his eyes. The music started and Elsa took a few seconds to gain her composure. Then the beat dropped and Elsa's body was alive. All inhibitions left her once her hands touched the cold metal bar. Jenny looked at Pam, and then Lenny. What the fuck! This girl was on another level. She was putting moves into the mix that none of them had ever seen before. Lenny sat forward in his seat, his hands clasped tightly together. The tip of his tongue slowly slithered along his top lip and his brow glistened. Pam was on edge, and prayed she didn't mess it up. Elsa swung around the pole, her long hair sweeping along the floor and, as she reached the finale, everyone knew they'd just seen something very special indeed. Lenny's eyes never left Elsa. Even when the dance had finished, he sat in complete silence, eyes glued to her.

Pam hollered at the top of her voice. 'Amazing! Top class! Oh my God, you smashed it!' She cuddled Elsa, proud of how far she had come, excited about where she would go with a bit more experience.

Lenny finally stood up. 'That was one of the best dances I have ever witnessed and, trust me, sweetheart, I've been in this game for enough years to know when a dancer is above all the rest. You were born to do it, darling.'

Jenny was spitting feathers. Nobody was pissing on her parade. 'Lenny, I'll dance for you now. Then you can see why I'm the main attraction at *Passion* and why I could be the same at this new place.'

She quickly made her way to the pole, but she could tell Lenny had already chosen his favourite. Jenny danced again and she was good, but not a patch on the new kid on the block.

Lenny slowly clapped and sat forward in his seat. He waited until Jenny came to his side before he spoke. 'Good stuff. I can see you two really working it in the new gaff. Maybe you can even work together on a dance. The men will love that.'

Jenny squirmed. 'Lenny, are you being serious? I rake the cash in when I'm on that stage. I'm not sharing no money with some two-bit dancer who's just starting out.'

Pam could see this was getting heated, and diffused it straight away. 'Nobody is saying you're going to lose money, Jenny. Lenny is just throwing a few ideas out there. Relax and listen to what he has to say.'

Jenny leant against the wall to regain her breath. Lenny smiled at Elsa, stood up and moved closer to her. He slowly reached over and touched her hair. Pam moved in closer, too. 'I told you she was mint, didn't I?'

Elsa moved away from the man, with caution. He unsettled her and you could tell she wasn't used to anyone touching her.

'I'd like a private dance from Elsa. After all, I want to sample what the punters are going to be getting first-hand.'

Pam shook her head and pulled on Lenny's arm. 'There'll be plenty of time for that later, but for now I want to talk to you in private.' Pam led him away from the dancers through a door in the back.

Jenny waited for the door to close and edged closer to Elsa. 'Who are you, anyway? Where are you from? What's your story?'

Elsa swallowed hard; she didn't want any beef, she just

wanted a job and a chance to dance. She stuttered, hoping not to cause any more bad feelings between them both. 'I've not been doing this long. I just want to earn enough money to help my family.'

Jenny looked at her in disbelief. 'Everyone has a story, love, so don't play the innocent with me. Sooner or later, I'll find out what you're about. I only hope, for your sake, that you're ready for what lies ahead, because, trust me, darling, this world is not for the faint-hearted. I hope Pam has filled you in about the private parties, and the other shit that goes on behind closed doors.'

Elsa held her head high and nodded. She had to show this woman she had balls and she could stick up for herself. 'I can look after myself. You don't need to worry about me. I'm ready for whatever they throw at me.'

Jenny smirked. Hadn't every girl been that innocent once?

'I want Elsa to come to see me on her own after this, Pam. You promised I would be the one to break her in. Don't be fucking about with me.'

Pam leant back in her chair. 'You're still the same dirty old bastard you always were, Lenny, aren't you? What's changed since I caught you eye all those years back? So you've got a bit more cash – but you're still as greedy as ever. All comes to those who wait, remember that. We have a deal and, like I said, when the money swaps hands then you can do whatever you want with her.'

Lenny licked his gums. 'You're ruthless, Pam. It's always been about the money for you, hasn't it? I should have known when you left me for that prick of a husband of yours. But I thought motherhood had softened you – I thought you'd lost your edge these last few years. You've not been on the scene, and I thought you'd taken your eyes off the prize.'

'I learnt a long time ago, Lenny, that nobody gives a fuck about anyone else in this business. Only the strongest survive, as you know already. But sometimes you've got to play the long game. I've been biding my time, but it's my fucking time coming, you'd better believe it.'

'Well, if you've got the girls ready, I've got the gaff sorted. I'm thinking we can open next month. But we need a name. Once we have that agreed, I'll have the signs done and the flyers. I know the gossip mill is going like the clappers already about who bought the place. Let's put the name up in lights and give them something to talk about.'

'I was thinking we should call it *Tease*. It's all in the name, isn't it?'

Lenny sat thinking, stroking the end of his chin with his thumb and index finger. '*Tease*. I like it, yep. We'll go with that and get some promo done. Next month it is, then. Are we taking Jenny on, or leaving her where she is? She seems like she will give us a few problems if she doesn't get her own way, but she knows how to work a crowd. She's reliable, cocky, and she'd really turn up the heat if we got her on stage with your new girl.'

'Leave the girls to me, Lenny. I know how to make them feel special. Now, if we've agreed on *Tease*, I want everyone who's anyone to attend our opening night. Get the word out and make sure we look after all our VIPs. I'll find the rest of the girls who are going to be dancing and you concentrate on everything else. But keep my name out of it – if word gets back to Jordan that I'm in on it, then it all goes up in flames. Let him think it's all you. I'm happier waiting in the shadows … for now.' She held her hand out and waited for Lenny to shake it.

Slowly, the corners of his mouth rose before he shook her hand. 'No turning back now, Pam. Fasten your seat belt and enjoy the ride.'

Chapter Twenty-One

Karla sat in the car and waited until Jordan had finished on the phone, shouting and screaming at the top of his voice.

'Listen to me, will you? Find out who is behind that fucking nightclub. It's all anyone is talking about. Somebody is messing with me, opening a new club on my patch and, when I find out who it is, heads will roll. I'll fucking burn the gaff down. Nobody is taking the piss out of me. Gary, sort it, mate, before I lose the plot. Honest, my head is battered with it all.'

Jordan ended the call and hit the steering wheel in rage. 'Fucking wankers, I'll destroy them,' he muttered under his breath.

Karla sat looking at her fingernails and waited until he had calmed down. She had her own bombshell to drop. 'You need to calm down, Jordan. Why do you let people get to you like that? No club will ever beat *Passion*, so chill out and let the new owners crash and burn.'

He turned his head slowly towards her. His teeth were clenched tightly together. 'It's not the point, Karla. I wanted that club, but some cunt got in there first. I had plans for it, big plans.'

Karla knew she had to get this off her chest, before he sweet-talked or she caved. 'Listen, I've been thinking a lot lately, and we're not going anywhere fast. It's just promise after promise and, well,' she paused and sat up straight in her seat before she continued. 'I'm done. I've had enough. It's over.'

Jordan sucked hard on his gums and nodded his head slowly. He looked ahead and gripped the steering wheel tightly, his knuckles turning white.

'I'm looking after myself, that's all. You make me sad more than happy, lately, and I'm sick of feeling like second best all the time.'

'Fuck off, then. Get out of the car and do one. Go on, fucking jog on. Like I can be arsed with a dirty slapper like you anymore.'

Karla screwed her face up – there was no way she was taking this lying down. 'Fuck you, Jordan. You think you know it all, and you know fuck all. Go back to your wife. I actually feel sorry for her being stuck with a rat like you for the rest of her life.'

In an instant, his hands were gripping her throat, and he was squeezing her windpipe. Her eyes were wide open, and she was smacking his arm rapidly, trying to stop him choking her. She twisted and her mouth connected with his skin. She bit down as hard as she could. He screamed and, as his grip loosened, Karla wasted no time. She quickly opened the car door, and the cold wind from outside hit her face. She stumbled out of the car and scrambled along the cold pavement. She crawled to a nearby fence and used it to drag her body up from the ground. She was gagging for breath. Jordan started the engine. It roared at the side of her and she knew she had to make a quick getaway. The daft bastard was trying to reverse the car to get it on the pavement. He'd flatten her if she stayed here. Karla waited until the car screeched back, and sprinted across the road. She was running for her life and she never looked back. She ran and ran until she was safe.

At last, this toxic relationship was over, but she knew only too well what this man was capable of. She'd seen his rages when punters crossed the line, when a girl left the club for another gig, or simply when things got out of hand when he was high. She'd tried to look the other way, but she knew what happened when he ordered Max, the most lethal of his boys, to pay people a visit. Max Carter was a nutter. He was a snide bastard and the kind of guy who waited in the shadows of the night for you, if you'd rubbed him up the wrong way. No wonder Jordan used Max if he didn't want to do his own dirty work. To get to the top in clubland, you had to be tough. But Jordan, he was more than that: he was sick in the head, and she knew, from this day forward, she would have to watch her back. She wasn't safe anymore; she was on borrowed time.

Chapter Twenty-Two

Lenny Jackson sat gazing out of the large bay window. Lots of green hills, not another house in sight. He'd bought the farm house over ten years ago. This was his safe haven, the place he could act out all his fantasies with the girls he brought here. It was near enough to get to when he needed the peace and quiet, but far enough out of the city for him to be completely off the radar.

Lenny turned his head slowly as he heard somebody enter the room. His eyes met hers and his body turned to face her. The young girl came and stood at the side of him, wearing only her underwear. She only looked around sixteen years old, all skin and bones, dark circles under her eyes. Lenny stepped closer to get a better look at her. Slowly, he dipped his finger in his mouth, then he stroked it up her stomach.

'You're pretty, Scarlet – just what I need to take my mind from my problems, right now.'

Scarlet sniffed hard. There were traces of white powder on the edges of her nose. Lenny made sure all the girls who came here had a free supply of cocaine. He wanted them to relax, to give him everything he needed. Scarlet moved closer to him and sat on his lap, facing him. He held her thin waist and with two hands he pushed her body down off his lap and onto her knees. He opened his fly and his eyes closed. His wrinkled hands rested on top of the young girl's head and, every now and then, he pushed his cock deeper down her throat until she gagged. Lenny gripped the sides of the chair as he began to reach climax. He yanked her hair tightly and dragged it up and down as he shot his load. Groaning dirty words, filth came flying from his mouth. His body pushed back in the brown leather chair, his hands gripping the armrests, already creased with use. Each line in the leather held the story of another girl like this, another power game, another life tainted.

After a few minutes, he lifted Scarlet's head up with his two hands and smiled at her. 'That's a good girl. Go and have a rest, or something, and I'll be in to see you later.'

Scarlet got to her feet unsteadily. She was off her napper. Whatever had happened in this young girl's life that she'd landed in a world like this, right now none of it mattered. She was out of it all, the coke taking the edge off even this sordid scene. She should have been at home with her family, studying at college, or out having fun, not sucking off this crook for money.

Lenny tugged his pants back up and carried on looking out of the window. His mobile started ringing, and he smiled when he saw Pam's name flashing across the screen.

'Hello, gorgeous. I was just thinking about you.' He pressed the call onto speaker and rested the mobile on his lap.

'The girls are going to practise a dance together, Lenny. The punters will love them. Jenny knows what they want to see, and I'm sure she will sort Elsa out. It's going to be electric.'

'You were always a businesswoman, Pam. It's just a shame I wasn't at the side of you all these years. We could have ruled the world together, you and me. We would have had an empire by now.'

'Oh, stop it, Lenny, and change the record. You know as well as me that it wouldn't have worked.' There were a few seconds' silence before either of them spoke again. 'Jordan is rattled. All he's going on about is the new club. On my life, he's looking for traitors wherever he goes.'

'Fucking good,' Lenny barked. 'It's about time that prick got off his high horse. I'm going to have so much fun revealing that we're the new owners.'

They both laughed out loud.

'What are you up to, anyway? You seem relaxed for a change?'

'I'm at the farm, Pam. You know me: when I'm here it chills me out.'

'You mean you have some young girls parting their legs for you?'

He smirked and stroked his finger across his newly manicured nails. 'You know me well, Pam. Probably better than I know myself, love.'

'Yes, Lenny, I do.'

The call ended, and Lenny left the room to walk down the small corridor that led to the bedrooms. He gripped the gold handle and slowly opened the door. A stream of yellow light shone from the room. Without a word, he made his way to the bed and sat on the edge of it. His hand disappeared under the cover and he could hear mumbling from underneath the duvet. He smirked and started to strip off. Scarlet pulled the cover back and Lenny joined her in the bed.

Chapter Twenty-Three

Jenny was stretching as Elsa walked into the room. There was an atmosphere that could have been cut with a knife, and Elsa felt it as soon as she arrived.

'Afternoon, it's freezing out there, honest. Look at my hair. It took hours to style it this morning too, what a waste of time,' Elsa moaned.

Jenny shrugged. 'Just get ready. I've not got all pissing day. I don't know why we even have to dance with each other when it's obvious we are completely different dancers. I'm centre stage. I always have been. And, like I said before, I don't want any would-be dancer thinking they can steal the limelight from me. I've grafted and trained hard to reach the top. End of.'

Elsa edged forward and started to get ready. She didn't want to make an enemy of this woman, but she sensed, if she was going to make a friend of her, she needed to put her cards on the table. Her voice was soft. 'Jenny, you are hot stuff when you get on the stage. I'm nowhere as good as you, and hopefully you can help me improve. But I'm not going anywhere – if Pam thinks us two working together is the way to make the big bucks, I'm all in. I don't know about you, but I've never had nothing in my life, and this is a chance for me – a real chance. I'm that girl who has always been left in the shadows – but no more.'

Jenny turned around and looked at the girl in more detail. Maybe she'd been too hard on her. After all, she'd been in her boots before, and she knew how hard it was when life dealt you a bum deal and nothing was going right. She sat down and patted the space next to her. 'OK, you want a chance? If you're prepared to work – and I mean fucking hard work – I'll give you a chance. Maybe I was a bit tough on you when we first met, but I have my reasons. I need to protect what I've worked hard to get. Life for us dancing girls is hard and, trust me, Elsa, you have to save and save your money because, before you know it, another girl has stolen your thunder and you're slung out on your arse without a penny to your name. Or your looks fade and your body changes. I don't ever want to go as low as I've been in the past. It scares the living daylights out of me, honest. If I ever think of my life before, it gives me really bad anxiety. I have to take tablets for it when it gets out of control. It does my head in.'

Elsa was listening. She could see Jenny was getting upset, and patted her arm. Jenny jerked her body away and looked Elsa in the eye. 'I'm sorry, but I can't stand people touching me. I know when I dance I make it look like I'm dying to be touched, but I cannot bear physical contact.' She swallowed hard, and started to play with her fingers. Elsa remained still. She didn't move a muscle: she wanted Jenny to continue. 'I used to live on the streets, you know, I was homeless and skint. One night, I was asleep in a doorway when two men lifted me up and dragged me down some alleyway. Each of them had their way with me, horrible bastards they were. I couldn't do a thing. I shouted for help, but nobody came. I remember lying there, staring at the silver moon in the sky above me. It was the only thing that could see what I was going through. I never took my eyes from it until it was all over. The moon seemed to calm me. Ever since then, if things are going bad, I spend hours looking at. You should try it, it's therapeutic.' She looked away from her now as she continued. 'The men booted and kicked me. They left me for dead. When it was over, I finally scrambled back to the main road and sobbed my heart out. And do you know what? Not one person stopped to see if I was alright. I sat for hours and hours debating going to the police, but I never found the courage to report them for what they did to me. Who would have listened to me, a homeless girl who the coppers thought was turning tricks anyway?' She looked at Elsa and smiled softly. 'That's when this guy appeared and reached down and took my hand in his. He was there for me, a shoulder to cry on, the one who fixed me and gave me my life back.'

Elsa looked at her questioningly, wondering who her saviour had been.

'Jordan was the first person ever to offer me kindness without wanting something physical in return. He gave me a safe place to stay, and he made sure I had everything I needed. All I had to do was dance. I'll never forget what he done for me. But, if I look back now, he was looking after himself. He was the one coining it in. So, before you do this, are you sure you know what you're starting? Do your family know you're doing this?'

Elsa looked sheepish. 'I've told my nana and my mum I've got a job. I've been studying dance, and I said I've got some shifts at a club, but I've not told them exactly what kind of dancing I'll be doing. To be honest, I've let them think I'll be on the door, maybe behind the bar. I'm not sure my nana would understand what you do on stage, what I'm going to do. But honestly, I wish I could tell them how it feels when I'm out there, dancing. I feel alive.' Elsa smiled and her cheeks blushed. 'I've got a boyfriend, too, and he's lovely. I've not told him about the dancing, either, and I don't think I can. He's never wanted for anything in life, and he wouldn't understand what it's like to have nothing.'

Jenny rolled her eyes and shook her head. 'Good luck with that, love. Sooner or later, you will have to tell him the truth and, if I'm being honest, when he knows that all these guys are leering at you each night, he won't be able to handle it. It's too much pressure. You have to explain yourself all the time, and they're paranoid you're sleeping with someone else. The last relationship I had turned nasty at the end, and I had to get a few heavies to word him up, to keep away from me.' Jenny rubbed her arms and Elsa could see the small blonde hairs standing on end. 'And the private parties, are you going to be doing them? Because that's where the big money is, love. I can earn over two thousand pound in one night, if I go to a decent party.'

Elsa looked confused and Jenny could see she would have to explain herself further. 'It's for all these rich guys, the ones whose wives think they are out with the boys, having a drink or working away. They book a hotel room, or sometimes it's even their own gaff, and they book a few of the girls to go around. We dance for them and …' She paused and dropped her head low, as if the shame was weighing her down. 'We do whatever else they want.'

There were a few seconds when nobody spoke. Elsa looked one way then the other. Bloody hell, Jenny was a prostitute.

'It's a party, really. It's the same as going on a night out and having a one-night stand, isn't it? Come on, loads of women go out and get shagged at the weekend. The only difference is that we get paid for it.' Jenny was convincing herself that selling her body was a normal thing to do, and she smiled as she reached over and squeezed Elsa's knee. 'The sniff helps you blank it from your mind. A few lines of cocaine and you feel on top of the world. Have you ever had a bump?'

Elsa hunched her shoulders; she'd had a few blasts of a spliff from Candice in the past, but she'd never dabbled in Class As. She could feel her cheeks burning. Jenny was waiting on an answer. She stuttered. 'I'm not really into that. I've seen how they can destroy a person. There was a woman who lived on our street and she was addicted to heroin. It was such a shame to see how it robbed her of everything. You could see her searching the pavement for cig dimps and looking for money all the time. She was only forty-two when she died.'

Jenny blew a laboured breath. 'Yep, that's the hard stuff. Crack and smack are something I would never dabble in. Cocaine is a party drug, though; it keeps you awake and makes you feel so confident. Anyway, I'll have a word with Pam and ask her about taking you to a private party, because you're after making the big bucks, aren't you?'

Slowly, Elsa nodded her head. It seemed easier to go along with Jenny for now than make it sound like she was judging her. She'd have to tell Pam afterwards that the parties were not for her. Selling her body was not something she was willing to do, no matter how much money she would make.

Chapter Twenty-Four

Candice sat staring at Elsa, looking her up and down. Elsa was watching her from the corner of her eye, and she could sense she had a secret. Her friend seemed edgy, distant. Candice held her head in her hands, body bent slightly.

'So, cut the small talk. Has Clayton boned you, yet?'

Elsa playfully punched her leg. 'Has he 'eck. I'm making him wait.'

'Wait for what? You're mad, you are, just sleep with him and get it over with. You're like the last standing virgin. You don't get any medals for being a goody two shoes. Everyone is shagging. It's not a bad thing, you know.'

'Candice, I've always told you that, when I have sex for the first time, I want it to be special, not a quick knee-trembler somewhere.'

Candice licked her lips slowly. 'Well, lads like Clayton can get sex anywhere, so be mindful of that. Make sure he doesn't get sick of waiting.'

Elsa looked at Candice again. 'Why are you so interested in our sex life, anyway? You have your own fella. Leave mine alone.'

'Oh, don't even mention his name to me. The guy knocks me sick. I thought he was the one, but he's an arsehole. You should see him clocking all the girls when he's with me. He's a cheeky bastard, and he's lucky I've not bombed him.'

'I thought he was the love of your life?'

'Yeah, he was, but things change, and I've changed my mind. I'm single and ready to mingle again.'

They both chuckled, and Elsa nudged Candice. 'I've got a secret to tell you but, please, you have to swear down that you won't tell anyone.'

Candice rubbed her hands together in excitement. 'Come on, spill the beans. Oh, is it about Julie down the road? Because I already know about her sucking that older guy off. Everyone knows about her; she's not even denied it.'

'No. Eww!'

Elsa made her promise that this was their secret, and she would tell no one else. But before she blurted it out, Karla staggered into the bedroom, wobbled over to the bed and plonked down next to Candice. She stank of beer, and slurred her words. 'You two take my advice and enjoy your life. Don't get stuck with some man who fills your head with shit, like me. I'm single now, and I'm never, ever, getting involved with any bloke that has a ring on their finger.'

Candice sniggered under her hand as she held it to her mouth.

'Mam, wow, it's not even six o'clock and you're steaming drunk. What's up with you now? Don't tell me, men problems again. I thought, the last time we spoke, you were ending it and starting to look after yourself?' Elsa was used to her mum being embarrassing, but this was another level.

Karla inhaled deeply and dipped her head as if it was too heavy to hold up. 'I've told him. I said I would, and I did. The bastard tried to run me down. You should see all the text messages he's been sending me. Apparently, I'm going in a body bag when he gets his hands on me.'

Candice's jaw dropped. 'Ring the dibble on him. You can get one of them things to make sure he doesn't come near you. My Auntie Sam got one for her ex. He was a nutter, a screw loose, honest. He would turn up at her house nearly every night shouting abuse at her for everyone to hear. He ended up getting nicked. I think it's called an injunction. In fact I'm sure it is.'

Elsa shot a look at Candice and rolled her eyes. 'Mam, stop waffling, and go and get in bed.'

'I thought you were bringing this new boyfriend of yours to meet me? What happened to that? Are you ashamed of me or something?'

Elsa stood in front of her with hands on hips. 'Well, it's a good job he's not here tonight, isn't it, because look at the state of you. Go and get in bed before my nana comes in from bingo. She'll shit a brick if she sees you like this.' Elsa was losing patience now. She grabbed her mother's arm and yanked her up from the bed. 'Get out of my bedroom. I need to finish getting ready.'

Karla stood up and wobbled. 'And where do you think

you're going? You're never in this house anymore. Are you up to something? Because you've gone from never going out, to never being in.'

'Oh my God, are you still here? I've got a life, too, you know, and now I've started working, I'm busy. I told you about this, but you've had your head so far up your own arse you must have forgot.'

Karla bit down on her bottom lip as she gripped the doorframe to steady herself. 'Lose the attitude, darling, it doesn't suit you. You might have told me, but I've had that much shit going on in my head lately that I must have forgot. I've had terrible anxiety, honest. My head's been bursting for days, weeks.'

Candice spoke up, as she could see her best friend was getting fed up. 'Aw, you will love Clayton, Karla, he's really cute. Fit, he is. She needs to be careful nobody nicks him from her.'

Elsa shot a concerned look over at Candice. Why on earth was she singing her boyfriend's praises all the time?

'He's a great catch and your daughter is lucky to have him. I would jump through hoops for him if he was my man, let me tell you.'

Karla left the room. If the conversation wasn't about her and her problems, she wasn't interested. Elsa stood fuming. She paced the room, running her fingers through her hair. 'And this is why I need to get out of this place. If I stay here any longer than I need to, I will end up messed up like her.'

Candice rubbed her hands together again, half-heartedly this time. 'Enough of that. Secret: come on, tell me.'

The moment seemed to have gone and there was no

excitement in her voice anymore. Elsa decided to put her big secret on the back-burner. 'Oh, it was only about my new job. I might be serving behind the bar, even though I told my nana I was collecting glasses and that.'

Candice looked deflated and held her hands out in front of her. 'Is that it? The big secret?'

Elsa carried on brushing her hair, and looked at her through the mirror. 'It *is* a secret. If my nana got wind of it, she would kick off. Anyway, you, what's this big fascination with Clayton? You've not shut up about him lately.'

Candice went beetroot and started biting her fingernails. 'I'm just saying, that's all. God, wind your neck in and relax. I'm only saying.'

Elsa grabbed her coat from the bed and looked sternly at Candice. 'Ready when you are.'

———

Elsa and Candice were headed into Manchester town centre. The Arndale was busy today, and crowds of people were hustling and bustling around the streets, talking, shouting and singing. As they walked down Market Street, Elsa squirmed as she debated telling her friend about her new job. Either that, or she needed to invent a reason for shopping for skimpy new underwear.

'I've been thinking more about what you said earlier, about me and Clayton sleeping together. I think I need to build my confidence …' Elsa began.

'Doing the deed is easy once you get used to it,' grinned Candice. 'Climb on top and, if you spell coconut with your hips when you're riding him, that usually works. So when are you and Clayton finally going to do it?' she asked, keenly.

'We've been close a few times, but I don't know, something happens and I freeze and the moment passes. He's drop-dead gorgeous, and I know he's been waiting for me for a long time, but I just don't feel ready. Maybe I need some new underwear to get me in the mood. Where do you think is the best place?'

'I thought you wasn't ready to have sex?'

'I guess it doesn't hurt to be prepared,' Elsa said, as they dived into a raunchy shop that had always made her blush before.

Candice was already giggling at the vibrators she'd spotted at the back of the shop. 'Elsa, check this one out. How on earth can someone fit that in their motty?'

Elsa went bright red. 'Oh my God, is that how big they are?' She swallowed hard and started to look at a set of underwear instead. It was lovely: bright red, lacy, sexy. She quickly looked over her shoulder and made sure she wasn't being judged by anyone. Jenny had told her to buy sexy, raunchy underwear and that was exactly what she was doing. Without hesitation, she grabbed another two sets of underwear and made her way to the checkout. Candice seemed enthralled with the conversation she was having with the assistant, and didn't even realise her best friend had made a purchase.

Jenny was taking Elsa to her first private party tonight to show her the ropes. When Elsa had tried to tell Pam she didn't want to do the parties, Pam had insisted it would be a good experience for her to learn about the world she was entering. But, Pam had stressed, she was not to have sex under any circumstances. Elsa felt awkward, but Pam stuck to her guns and told her she would tell the organiser that she would be there on a strictly look but don't touch basis. She insisted it would be the perfect way to get used to dancing for an audience without getting stage fright. Elsa didn't want to upset Pam. The dancing had been going well with Jenny, and the routine they had worked on was going to be a hit, she could tell. Raunchy, sexy and forbidden. Everything Jenny had told her the punters loved.

Candice watched her friend spending as they went into different shops. 'So, how much does this job pay? Because you are rolling in money all the time, these days, even though you've only done a few shifts. And is Clayton treating you? He must bung you a few quid too.'

Elsa shrugged, puzzled. 'I know his family's wadded, but he doesn't even have a job.'

'Wow, Elsa, you're thick, you are, if you believe that. Clayton is a grafter. He sells drugs, steroids mainly. He has a few of the lads from the estate working for him, too. Don't tell me you didn't know?'

'Since when has he been doing that?'

'Since like forever. Have you ever wondered why his phone is ringing all the time?'

Elsa was confused. 'He's always at the gym. And, yes, sometimes he's had to nip out when I have been at his house, but I never thought for one second that he was a dealer.' She stood thinking. It all made sense now. Why hadn't she seen what was right in front of her? She acted cool in front of her friend, and carried on talking. 'Oh, yeah, when I think about it, he did mention that he does a few bits now and then to earn some money.'

Candice was no idiot; she was streetwise and knew her friend was lying. But Elsa didn't have time to fight with her today. They parted company and Elsa made her way to the bus stop. Tonight was her first night of work. Two dances, Jenny had told her, and that was it. She could do it. She could dance and bring some money home, how simple was that? Sure, her nana would not be pleased if she found out, but Elsa felt free. She was a grown woman, earning money how she chose. If Clayton could break a few rules, why not her? She was fed up of the men round here earning all the money. Tonight, she'd be stepping up.

Chapter Twenty-Five

Jenny stood in front of the mirror and smiled. She was dressed in a red and gold all-in-one that left nothing to the imagination. She dragged a cream fur coat from the bed and draped it over her shoulders. Elsa was liked a scared animal when she passed her a long black fur coat to put on over her underwear.

'Is this all that I'm wearing?' Elsa asked in a timid voice.

Jenny chuckled. 'That's all you need, love. Once we get to the house, you'll be parading around in your underwear. A few punters will ask you for dances, and that's it, basically. If you dance good, you'll earn some money. A few of the girls will be having sex with the guys, but Pam said you won't be doing anything like that. Not yet, anyway ...'

Elsa was alarmed. 'I know I won't. There is no way in this world that I could sleep with a random guy.'

Jenny faced her, and quickly checked the clock on the wall. 'You need to change your outlook on this world. And don't let any of the other girls hear you talking like that, or they'll scratch your eyes out. They're just girls who want to change their lives, love. We all have to make a living, so don't judge girls you know nothing about. They all have a story, Elsa, some that would make your toes curl.'

That was her told.

'I'm just saying it's not for me. I'm not judging anyone.'

A car honked its horn outside, and Jenny walked to the door. 'Bear in mind what I've said. Tonight will be an eye-opener for you and you'll see what this game is about. Play it by ear and stick close to me. Don't be moving out of my sight, because those horny fuckers will take advantage of you, given the chance.'

Elsa fastened every button up on her coat. Her confidence from earlier had vanished like smoke. What on earth had she got herself into?

The driver looked into his rear-view mirror and smiled at Jenny. She smiled back. 'Jake, isn't it? Can you make sure you pick us up on time? I don't want to be there any longer than I need to be tonight.' She squeezed Elsa's hand, sitting next to her, and surveyed the tank of a guy driving. A handsome guy he was; big, solid build.

'Stop worrying, woman. If Jake says he'll be here at a certain time, then he will be. I don't know what they were like at your old club, but anyone who works for Lenny, we know how to look after the merchandise. I hear Jordan has been spitting feathers since you've left *Passion*. You'd better watch your back with that one, as he's not a happy chappy, so I've been told.'

Jenny thought back to the conversation she'd had with Jordan the day before. She'd expected him to smash stuff up, shout – even threaten her. But it had been worse: he'd been silent, calm, with only one question. 'Is it Lenny you're going to work for? This new joint? Because you're dead to me now, Jenny. Don't think you can come crawling back.'

And she'd heard Jordan's boys had been to *Lush Laps* last night, probably to check if she was dancing there. She shivered, but glanced at the driver in the rear-view – she was under Lenny's protection now.

'Jordan can fuck off, Jake. I worked my arse off for him and made him plenty of money. How can he blame a dancer for wanting to do better for themselves? I gave him the option a week ago of paying me more money, and he told me straight to do one, so it's his loss, isn't it?'

'The club will go downhill now. I've heard some of the girls are thinking about leaving, too. He left a few of his girls at a party, didn't he, and they were raped?'

Jenny could see Elsa looking scared to death and ready to jump out of the moving car. She gripped her hand tighter as she replied, 'No, that's all been blown up. Some guys got hands-on with one of the girls, and she didn't know how to handle it, that's all. But you're right. Jordan should have protected them, and he didn't, so he deserves everything he gets. The dancers are his bread and butter, and he should make sure they're safe, always.'

As Jake messed with his sat-nav, Jenny turned to Elsa. 'Are you alright? You've not said a word since we got in the car.'

'I'm scared, Jenny. I'm not sure this is for me. I'm thinking of phoning Pam and telling her I can't go through with it.'

'Don't be bleeding daft, girl. You've got the jitters, that's all. Once you get in and start dancing, you'll be fine. On my life, I was exactly like you when I started out and, once I got the first dance over with, it was easy. Taking money from the punters is like taking candy from a baby. Once you've danced at a party, you won't have any nerves when you get on stage at the new joint. Now, pull yourself together and sort your head out. Focus on the main guys, keep the big players happy and you'll be quids in. When we go into this party, we're looking out for a bloke called Tommy. He's the one with all the moolah. I've danced for him before. Money is no object to him and, if he takes a shine to you, expect to come home with a grand in your back pocket.'

Elsa swallowed hard. Her heart was thumping inside her chest and her windpipe seemed to be closing up. She was hot and clammy, and her mouth was dry. The thought of men's eyes all over her body was getting real now. But the thought of that much cash was enough to get her back on track. Bloody hell, a thousand pounds for one night of dancing; that was more money than she could ever imagine. She could do so much with it: help her nana, pay bills, go and get a big shop without looking for yellow labels or special offers. And with that kind of cash, she could definitely get something special for herself, too. Something to remember this moment by ... She wanted some of the perfume Pam wore. To Elsa, that was the smell of money, sophistication and power. Yes, she could do with the readies, alright. She turned her head and gazed out of the window. It was a full moon tonight, and the silver glow in the night sky looked magical. Elsa stared at it and snuggled down into the warm black fur. She could do this. She had to get her head together and start to relax, deep breaths.

The car came to a halt and Jake looked back at the girls. 'Any substances tonight, ladies? Something to ease the nerves, perhaps?'

Jenny nodded and took two bags of white powder from his hand. 'I'll sort you out with the money on the way back.'

Jake looked at Elsa. 'What about you, Baby-face? I think you're going to need something to calm yourself down.'

Elsa shook her head slowly and Jenny answered for her. 'She's alright, Jake, I'll sort her out. Just make sure you're back here on time, tonight.'

Jake turned back to the road and nodded. 'I'll be here, stop flapping.'

The two ladies left the vehicle and walked down the long path that led to the house. It looked like an old Victorian house. Lots of windows, with dim yellow lights shining from inside. The gravel crunched under their heels. Jenny found a small wall to their left and halted. She reached inside her coat and pulled out the white powder.

Elsa's eyes were wide, her heart still beating like a speeding train.

Jenny said, 'I need to get sorted before I go in there. This stuff makes the job a lot more bearable.' She dug a silver key deep into the powder and lifted it up to her nose. Then she covered one nostril with her finger and snorted the powder.

Elsa didn't know where to look. A few of her friends had tried coke, but she was always scared she'd be the one who would die after taking it. She knew the kind of shit the dealers round this way cut into it. And she knew what her nana would have thought about her little girl getting high.

Jenny dug the key deep into the bag again and this time she passed it to Elsa. 'Here, call this my treat. You'll feel on top of the world once you've had a bit.'

Elsa hesitated. She needed something to stop her from turning back, she knew that much. Maybe just once? Just tonight to get her through her first party, her first dance? It must be OK stuff, if Jenny was taking it – and surely she wouldn't get hooked after one night? She'd come this far – why not break a few more rules? Elsa hesitantly took the stuff from her and copied what she'd seen Jenny do. She held her head back, and closed her eyes. Bloody hell, what was she doing? This was so out of character for her and against everything she believed in. Drugs ruined people, changed them, split families up, and here she was, about to shove cocaine up her nose. But she'd never imagined she'd be standing in a bikini and fur coat outside some unknown bloke's house, either. Coke whore, she thought, that's what her nana would say. But she needed to be a different girl to go through the door ahead of her – not the old innocent Elsa. She leant in.

Jenny was right: the drug did give her confidence. Right then, she felt on top of the world. As she walked into the party, she tossed her fur coat onto a chair and looked around the room, oozing confidence. This place smelt of money. Gold-framed pictures hung from the walls and the carpet was thicker than she'd ever seen.

Jenny was by her side, whispering in her ear. 'Right, there's Tommy. Don't go over straight away. Let him see you first and invite you over. Remember it's all about the game. Tempt them, let them think they're the one choosing you and, most of all, give them fuck all for nothing. Every bend you make, every beat you dance, you want paying. Give nothing away for free. These cunts have money. Let them spend it.'

Elsa listened to the music and the baseline was entering her body. Her foot started to tap on the floor as she swung her hair over her shoulder. A man's large hands touched her shoulder and she quickly turned to face him. The man was old enough to be her grandad: white hair, wrinkled and spotted hands. She didn't flinch. Instead, she raised a smile and looked directly at Jenny, who gave her the nod. This was it; this was what she had trained for. She had one thing on her mind. Money was the only reason she was here tonight. She had to keep her head in the game and make sure she gave them all something to talk about.

Jenny was the one who started the conversation with the old codger. 'Would you like her to dance for you?'

His voice was low, seedy. 'Yes, bring her over here where I can get a better look at her. She's a real beauty. I'll put my glasses on for this one.'

Elsa started to follow them to a corner of the room. But on the way she was grabbed by Tommy. 'Oi, you're staying here with me, new girl.' He nodded to Jenny. 'Take that old fucker to one of the other girls, love. This one is mine.'

Jenny smiled and grabbed the old man's hand. 'Come with me, you dirty devil, I'll make sure you get your money's worth. Go and sit over there, and I'll get one of the girls to come and take care of you.' She chuckled, but she was eager to get back over to Tommy. He was the don, and she wanted to make sure Elsa didn't mess up. Plus there was no way she was letting Elsa dance all night for him on her own.

Elsa was pulled down onto Tommy's lap. His sweet aftershave tickled her nostrils. He was an overweight man, but he had an attractive face – bright-blue eyes and the whitest teeth she'd seen in a long time. His hands were like bunches of bananas and, once he locked them around her body, she was unable to move. His warm breath flowed over her exposed skin as he leant in. He closed his eyes for a moment, his chest rising as if he was breathing her in.

'I've not seen you before. Where have you been hiding?'

Elsa tried to steady her breathing and not shiver as she felt his touch. She knew she had to pretend she was confident but innocent. 'This is my first private party.'

'You are gorgeous. You can stay by my side all night. I want to look after you.'

Elsa took a breath. It was now or never. She ran her long finger down the side of his face. 'Would you like me to dance for you?'

His fat fingers dug deep into her waist as his warm, wet tongue licked up her arm. She prised his fingers from her body and stood tall looking at him, gritting her teeth so she didn't shudder at his slavering. This was it – all her practice, all the YouTube videos she'd watched, all the routines she'd learnt – it was all about now. She had to make this dance count. This was the man with the money, and she had to leave him gagging for more. She tuned into the music the speakers in the corner of the room were playing, and the rest of the world slipped away. Oh, she was in the zone now, oozing self-belief. She kicked his legs open with the side of her foot and started to tease him with her perfect body, every bend, every twist, letting this man think she was the only man she could see. Her eyes stared deep into his soul, she never flinched.

Elsa stood with her back to Tommy now and slowly bent her body down so she could see him through her legs. He was excited alright; she could see a big bulge in his crotch. She watched him peel notes from the wad of money he was holding in his hand, and she could feel it being stuffed into the side of her knickers. This was going like clockwork. This idiot had more money than sense. Her body rocked up and down his. She could feel his throbbing member as she sat on his lap. All she could hear now was the music and nothing else seemed to matter. The money kept coming and, looking at Tommy's expression, he was ready to burst. The music finished just before he did. Before Elsa could work out what to do next, Jenny barged in and pushed her aside. She never said a word, just started dancing for him as the next track began.

Elsa backed off and searched for a cold drink. She pulled the money from her G-string and her eyes lit up. This was more cash than she'd seen in a long time. The cold water rushed down her throat and quenched her thirst. She was eager now to earn more money and there was no time for rest: time was money. She circulated the room. She didn't need a babysitter anymore, she could handle herself. There were girls dancing everywhere, strutting their stuff. Elsa was looking for the toilet when she opened the wrong door. Inside were two girls sprawled over a man's body on a bed. She covered her mouth with her hands as she watched one of the girls straddle the older man and grind all over him. She quickly closed the door and made her way to the toilet.

Elsa flushed and stood behind the toilet door for a few seconds, thinking. The music was booming and she could feel the drugs were wearing off now. She captured a glimpse of herself in the mirror and stood looking at her reflection. If Mary could have seen her, she would be so disappointed. Where had her morals gone? Where was her self-respect? She was out of her comfort zone, certainly, and she had a sense that there was no going back. Tears brimmed in her eyes, but she blinked them away and thought of the cash. As she straightened her hair and got ready to get back out there, she saw the silver door handle moving up and down, someone trying hard to get in. Elsa hesitated before she opened the door.

It all happened so fast. Tommy pushed her back inside the toilet and gripped her by the hair. He folded her body over and pushed her head down onto the toilet seat. There was nothing she could do, he was so strong. She was helpless.

'Come on, you dirty bitch, it's what you've been gagging for all night. Come to Daddy, you dirty girl,' he sneered.

Elsa screamed at the top of her voice and wriggled frantically to try and break free. What a fool she was. She had been told not to leave Jenny's side and here she was, like a sitting duck, ready for the taking. This man was like a lead weight on her body, his hands dragging at her smooth flesh, eager to get inside her.

'Please, I'm not here for that, Tommy. The other girls might be, but not me. I'm only a dancer, I have a boyfriend,' she pleaded.

'Fuck off, you're just like all the other dirty slags out there. Filthy, cock-loving sluts, the fucking lot of you.'

'I'm not like that, ask Jenny, please let me go, please, I want to go home.' Her words fell on deaf ears. This tank of a man was trying to unfasten his large black leather belt, and she knew she only had seconds to get out of this situation. She twisted her head back and smiled at him. 'Let's go back in the other room, Tommy. I'll dance for you again and who knows where it might lead? We could do this properly – not a quickie in a toilet. You're a handsome man, someone I'd like to get to know better, don't go and rush it.'

He smiled and licked his fat red lips. He really thought he stood a chance. He rolled from her body, sweat glistening on his forehead. 'I can do that. Maybe you're right, I should get to know you a bit better. We could have a good thing, me and you.'

Her heart was racing. He was off her now and she hurried to the door. As he moved out of her way, she yanked the door open and gasped the cold air from the hallway. She hurried out, rushed into the front room and found Jenny. She felt hysterical, but fought the panic down. 'Jenny, get me out of here. Tommy grabbed me in the toilet, he tried raping me. Ring the police, get the prick locked up. How dare he think he can touch me like that! And it can't be the first time he's tried that.'

Jenny dug her fingers into Elsa's arm and moved her away from the man she was dancing for. 'Listen, you silly bastard, what the fuck did you think was going to happen here? Take your head out of your arse and smell the coffee beans. That's what happens at these kind of parties, and it's up to each girl to make sure they keep safe. I'm not your babysitter, love, despite what Pam says. I'm here to make money, not look after a smacked-arse kid who thinks she can dance. Man up and deal with it. And what do you think the dibble would say if we called them? You think they're going to believe a girl like you?'

These strong words knocked Elsa for six. She had thought Jenny was her friend, her guardian angel. How wrong could she be? She was only another money-grabbing bitch who cared about nothing but lining her pocket. Elsa could hear Tommy's voice behind her, groaning, shouting her name. She bit down hard on her bottom lip and closed her eyes. Jenny was right, she had to own her choices and fend for herself. Her fists curled into two rounded balls at her side and she growled before she turned to face Tommy. She walked towards him slowly. If this was the game, she was ready to play it. She was here to earn money. She had to get her head sorted out, and fast. She flicked her hair over her shoulder and smiled at him. This was all staged and she had better give the performance of a lifetime. She had to string him along until Jake came to fetch them, but to do that she had to show Tommy she was worth waiting for. She bent her body down until she could look Tommy in his eyes, and licked her lips slowly. Her voice was soft as she whispered, 'You want this, then pay for it. The more you pay, the more you can see.'

Tommy howled out and rubbed his hands together. 'I've got more money than sense, love, so dance, fucking dance for me.'

Elsa kicked one leg over his head, her razor-sharp heel just missing the side of his face. If he wanted pussy shots, then that's what he was getting. Tommy's hands were all over her, grubby, dirty, fat fingers, stroking and mauling her thighs. Elsa let him get close – close enough to make him think she wanted him – but, at the last minute, she'd grind her hips away. This was the tease Pam had told her about. She'd always thought it was a game – but now she realised the stakes were much higher than that.

The night finally came to an end and Elsa stopped as the cold air hit her. She leant against the house wall, hardly believing she'd survived her first night. She'd kept Tommy on the brink, making him wait, and eventually he'd drunk so much he'd fallen asleep in his chair and she could stop her gyrating and grinding. She had more money in her coat than she could have ever imagined. Jenny came to her side and dropped her head onto her shoulder. She was twisted still, high as kite. Elsa hadn't gone back for more coke. She missed the high of that first hit but, after dealing with Tommy, she realised she needed her senses sharpened, not dulled.

'And there you go. Your first night is over with. It wasn't as bad as you thought, was it?'

'It was the worst thing I've ever experienced in my life. When Tommy had me in the toilet, I saw my life flash before my eyes. But hey, I survived.'

'Tommy is a rich fucker, but he's a harmless prick really

and, if the truth be known, he can't stay hard long enough to do any real damage anyway.'

Elsa wasn't so sure, remembering the fear she'd felt at his mercy. But tonight was a lesson learnt. A very big lesson indeed. Survival wasn't about who was strongest, it was about who was smartest, and she realised she'd have to play guys like Tommy if she was going to make a killing in this life. The girls left the house together and headed to the waiting car.

Chapter Twenty-Six

Mary sat bathing her swollen lip with a cold flannel. It was black and blue, and a small trickle of red blood dribbled down the side of her head. Her arms were bruised and very sore to touch. Slowly, she stood up and the pain was etched in her face as she made her way to the mirror. She cringed as she stroked her finger along her bottom lip. 'Bastard.' She squirmed when she checked the damage in the mirror. She was in a bad way.

There was a shout from the hallway. Mary licked her lips frantically and tried to straighten her hair as Karla walked into the living room. She kept her head low and tried to hide her injuries away.

'I'm sick of it, Mam. I went for two jobs today and not one of them offered me anything. They liked the younger girls, the tits-and-teeth ones.' Karla made her way to the sofa, plonked herself down and took her red high-heeled shoes off. She looked pretty today. She'd made an effort; nicely fitted black skinny jeans and a white t-shirt. 'Mam, I might go working in a shop, or something. I need normality in my life, don't I?'

'Are you asking me or telling me, Karla? Because, for as long as I can remember, you have always wanted the nightlife.'

'I know, but things change and maybe I am changing. Honest to God, I've never felt as low as I have been these last few weeks,' Karla replied.

Mary covered her mouth. 'Welcome to my world.'

Karla looked puzzled as she flung her shoes to the side of the sofa and twisted her head around so she could see her mother better. She stared at her for a few seconds and clocked the red marks on her arm. 'Mam, what's up?'

Mary fidgeted about, but it was too late, her swollen lip could not be hidden away any longer.

Karla gasped and jumped up from her seat. 'For crying out loud, what the hell has happened?'

'Nothing. I fell on some wet leaves when I was on the way back from the shop. You know what I'm like, I fall over fresh air.'

Karla examined her mother's lip in more detail. 'This is a bloody mess. It will swell more than that, Mam. You need to put some ice on it.'

'Yeah, I will. Stop fussing, I'm fine.'

Karla backed off and sat down again. 'Where's Elsa? Has she been home yet?'

'Nope. I've been in for over an hour and she wasn't home when I got in.'

'We never see her now she's loved up, do we? I wonder when we'll get to meet him?' Karla sat chewing on the corner of her fingernail. She coughed to clear her throat and looked over at Mary. 'Mam, I'm going to say something, and I don't want you to bite my head off. I've been thinking about it for a while now, so don't be going sick when I tell you.'

Mary held her head to the side, still dabbing her mouth with the wet flannel. 'I'm all ears.'

'Right, we're skint, aren't we, and nothing looks like it's going to change anytime soon.' Mary nodded, still listening. Her daughter was right: they were on the bones of their arses. 'I'm thinking of going to see Elsa's dad and asking him for some money. He's never given us nothing, not a penny, and I think it's about time he started to provide for her.'

Mary bolted up from her seat like boiling water had been poured over her. 'Are you fucking right in the head? We've never needed anything from that man, so why do you want to start raking up the past now? Is that what you want, eh? Elsa meeting a man like that? You have a short memory, you do. For fuck's sake, have you forgotten all the tears you cried over that no-good bastard?'

'No, I haven't, but he should pay for his child,' she retaliated. 'I would have sorted this out years ago, but it was you, Mother, who told me that we would never have anything to do with him. In fact, you were the only one who spoke to him after Elsa was born, and you were the one who said to ask him for nothing and that we could manage without him. Elsa is my child, and it should have been up to me to talk to her father, not you.'

'Oh, piss off, Karla. The man wanted you gone from his life. He was married, or are you forgetting that part of it?

You were his dirty little secret that he didn't want anyone to know about. I should have had the cheating bastard done in for the way he left you barefoot and pregnant – barely more than a kid, you were. Please, don't ever ask him for anything. Elsa doesn't even know who he is. Are you ready to sit her down and tell her about him, to tell her that he likes young girls?'

Karla swallowed hard and sat twisting her fingers. 'I was only going to ask him for money, nothing more.'

'And you think that wanker will not want to see his daughter if he's giving you money? Think about it, you plonker. Do you want him pouring his filth into Elsa's ears?'

'Mother, why do you always have to put the dampeners on everything? Forget that I said anything, I can't be arsed with you anymore. I'll get a job.'

Mary was still going on, frustrated words pouring out of her. 'That's more like it. Never depend on a man for fuck all. You need to stand on your own two feet and fend for yourself. I can't even believe you have said that to me. You know even the mention of him makes my blood boil.'

Karla turned the television up and lay flat on the sofa. She was in a mood. Mary left the room. She stood in the hallway with one hand pressed firmly on her chest, her breathing laboured and the colour drained from her skin.

Elsa rushed into the front room carrying shopping bags. Karla rolled onto her side and looked at her. 'Bleeding hell, have you robbed a bank or something?'

Elsa dropped her bags to the floor and took her jacket off. 'I won fifty quid on a scratch card, and Clayton treated me, too.'

Elsa ran upstairs with her shopping. She placed her new clothes on hangers in her wardrobe, and stood back to admire them. This was the first time she'd ever had anything decent hung up in there. Her mobile started ringing and she dug deep in her new handbag to find it.

'Hi, Clayton, I was just going to ring you. I'm going to get changed, and then I'll head over to your house.' She listened to him and her face dropped. 'But I thought you were staying in tonight with me and having a date night?' After a few more minutes of angry words, she ended the call. She flung her phone on the bed and stood looking at it for a few seconds. Then she grabbed it and quickly dialled a number.

'Hi, Candice, do you fancy a girly night? Clayton's got something to do down at the gym, he said, and he's binned me off for tonight.' Elsa lay down on the bed with the phone held to her ear, not hiding her disappointment with her friend's answer. She couldn't wait to end the call. 'No worries. I better book in here then for my tea. I'll probably watch a film with my mam, if you're busy too.' She hung up, stripped off and got her pyjamas on. A night in with the family was on the cards. She could do with the rest if she was being honest: she was knackered.

Karla sat up when she saw her daughter walk back into the room. 'I thought you was going out for tea with lover-boy?'

'Nope, change of plan. Clayton's got something on, and Candice is babysitting for her neighbour. It looks like you've copped for me tonight.'

Karla shouted into the kitchen. 'Mam, Elsa will have

some tea after all. She's like us, lonely and miserable,' she sniggered.

Mary came into the front room and Elsa gasped. 'Nana, what on earth has happened to your face? You look like you've done three rounds with Tyson Fury!'

'Oh, it's nothing. You know what I'm like, I'm a dopey bleeder. Tripping over, I should have been more careful.'

But Elsa was worried. She knew there were plenty of loan-sharks around – guys who wouldn't hesitate to send a warning if you were late paying back what you owed. And she knew her nana would be too proud to tell her. Looking at the state of this woman who'd given her everything, Elsa knew she would do whatever it took to get more money – and soon. This wasn't only about a new life for her, it was about protecting the people she loved. She had hopes and dreams now, and nobody was going to stop her making the money she needed for a better life. Nobody.

Chapter Twenty-Seven

Lenny stood in the main space at *Tease* and watched Elsa and Jenny practising their dance for opening night. Pam was by his side and she kept looking over at him, watching his beady eyes, his arousal. Elsa had upped her game and these two girls were on the stage fighting for the top girl position. Jenny's leg spun around the silver pole and narrowly missed Elsa's face, but the new girl was wising up and didn't even flinch.

This was a job well done, and the deal Lenny and Pam had made together was nearly signed and sealed. Pam placed her hand on his broad shoulder. She whispered into his ear, her breath tickling his neck, 'We did it, Lenny, we really did it. Tonight's opening is all that everyone is talking about. We're going to smash it.'

Lenny nodded, watching the dancers. 'Just one last thing needed, Pam.'

She stared at him and hunched her shoulders, as if to

brace herself. She'd stuck to everything on her side of the bargain, all but one.

His voice was low, and he made sure nobody was listening. 'The girl, I want her first. Once I've had her, that's your last payment made. This place is yours.'

Pam swallowed hard; she was hoping he might have changed his mind. Elsa had been the lure to tempt him, but she'd thought she'd be able to talk her way out of it later. She looked at Elsa. She was a world away from the girl she'd first met – so confident on the stage now – but there was still a purity to her, a life in her eyes that Pam didn't want to see deadened. But business was business.

'Oh, Lenny, you can have any girl you want. Leave Elsa alone. She's still a kid. You'll have plenty of time to break her in, in the future.'

His face changed and his nose was nearly touching hers. 'Listen, I want the girl, like we agreed. Don't fucking mess me about, Pam. Like we said, untouched.'

Pam felt defeated for a moment, then the steely look returned to her eyes. 'Relax, Lenny, if you're that bloody keen, after tonight's show you can take her. I will tell her she's going with you to a private party. The rest is up to you, but please look after her.'

'Fuck me, you actually care about her, don't you? I never thought I would see the day,' he chuckled.

Pam looked over at Elsa as she finished the routine. Lenny started clapping, and he shouted over to the girls. 'Great guns, the punters will be gagging for it. Go and relax for a bit. Tonight's probably going to be the biggest night of your life.' He looked over his shoulder, and Pam was gone.

The door was still swinging open and a cold draught seeped in from outside.

Pam sat in her car with her head resting on the steering wheel, and sobbed her heart out. She lifted her head up and streams of black tears ran down from her eyes. Maybe she did have a conscience, after all. But a deal was a deal and there was no way she could risk everything now: she'd come too far.

Chapter Twenty-Eight

'I want that club fucked up tonight. Make sure it never opens again, do you hear me, boys? Destroy the place.'

Clayton stood at his father's side like a general and gritted his teeth. He and his boys had been called in as foot soldiers. Their jobs were to smash windows, smash cars up, mess the place up from the outside. But Max and the heavy mob were the real muscle here today. The shit was going to hit the fan when they smashed through the new club's doors with all guns blazing on opening night. Max Carter was a nutter. He spoke with an accent that made him fit in everywhere and nowhere, Mancunian and Romanian mixed. His hard features looked daunting, and he was not the kind of man you would like to meet on a dark night. Max had carried out a few special jobs for Jordan in the past, and if him and his boys were on the scene, it was serious.

Clayton bounced about, fizzing with nervous energy. He had a name to live up to here today, and he was set on showing his old man that he had what it took to rule his empire alongside him. 'This cheeky bastard needs showing that he can't mess with us, Dad. You should have taken him down years ago. The man is a fucking pensioner, for crying out loud, a fucking fossil.' There was mumbling amongst the younger lads: they were ready to rumble.

Jordan had bankrolled his son when he first started out selling drugs. 'Sporting supplements' seemed like a fancy way of saying steroids, but it had been a nice little start in business for Clayton. He was his boy and he had taught him from an early age that money was what he needed to survive in this world. And now his son had his own crew of boys ready to take orders and not ask questions. After all, Jordan had taught his son another life lesson: silence. The boy's mother knew nothing of the world he was involved in. She was oblivious. She thought he simply liked the gym. But Clayton had earned his own name on the estate, and if anyone crossed his path and stepped on his turf, they got fucked up. Oh yes, this blue-eyed boy wasn't as innocent as he looked. The knife he carried wasn't just for show. It was a dog-eat-dog world and you stood up to anyone who crossed your path. That's the way it was in this part of Manchester. You had to fight to the end to protect your turf.

But Jordan could see Clayton was getting above his station and Max was sneering at him. Max stepped forward and nodded his head at Clayton. His voice was chilling, and he held a look in his eye that sent shivers down your spine. 'You stick to the simple stuff outside and let the big boys sort this out. This is no place for kids.'

Jordan could see his son getting ready to confront Max, and jumped into the conversation before any trouble started.

Max would jaw Clayton and think nothing about it, if the kid tried to challenge him about the way he was handling things.

'Max, you're the one calling the shots. Clayton and his boys are just there as back-up. They're smashing a few windows, smoking a few cars. You're the one who'll be doing the real damage. I want Lenny Jackson out of business as soon as. Make sure the job is a good one, and give that old twat a good kicking if you come across him.'

'I'll snap his jaw, mate. I've never let you down before, have I?'

Jordan walked over to Max and draped his arm around his shoulder. 'Correct. You always get the job done; don't let me down on this one and there will be a good wage waiting for you when you get back.'

Clayton watched Max walk off to take a phone call. He was fuming he had belittled him in front of his boys. If this prick carried on, he'd show him what he was all about. He'd smash a mallet right over his head tonight when things kicked off and show him who was boss.

For now, Clayton had heard enough; he patted his old man on the arm as he walked past him with his boys. 'Dad, consider it done. I'll bell you later to fill you in. We're team-handed, and those dickheads won't know what's hit them when we come flying through the doors.'

'Be careful, Son. Leave the messy stuff to Max. If your mother gets wind of this, she'll go berserk. I want you in and out as soon as possible. Don't be trophy hunting. Do you hear me?'

Clayton sniggered. 'Like I said, stop worrying.'

He left the room with a trail of five youths with him. Kids, really; young lads who would do anything to earn some street cred.

Jordan held his head back and inhaled deeply. His ears pinned back, and his eyes closed for a few seconds. Max returned, sank down on the chair opposite and held his hands in front of him. 'And what's the other problem you want sorting, pal?'

Jordan looked at him straight. He was unsure of what he was about to say. He sat cracking his knuckles. 'There's a woman I want visiting. Let's just say she's become a problem to me, and I don't want her calling round to speak to my wife, like she's been threatening.'

Max chuckled and shook his head. 'That cock of yours always gets you in trouble. How many times have I told you that you don't shit on your own front doorstep. Fucking women have loose tongues, and you know more than anyone how they can upset the apple cart. You're making life harder for yourself. Keep it in your pants in future.'

Jordan rolled his eyes. He wouldn't let anyone else speak to him like that, but Max had earned the right. He'd kept enough secrets for Jordan, got him out of enough corners. Jordan smiled now. 'You know me, mate, any hole's a goal.'

Max hunched his shoulders, waiting on instructions. Jordan licked his lips slowly and looked around the room, eyes concentrating on the wall clock. 'Karla Bradshaw is the name. I'll text you her address later. Just give her a warning, a few slaps here and there, just enough to keep her big trap shut.'

Max stood up and stretched his arms above his head. 'Trust me, I'll make sure the slapper is silenced.'

There was a noise from outside and they both looked at the door, but there was nothing to see.

Max grabbed his car keys from the table and nodded his head over at Jordan. 'Catch you later,' and he left the room.

Jordan sat alone with his thoughts. The door behind him opened slowly.

'What's up?' Angela edged into the room and approached Jordan slowly. She stroked her long finger across his stubble. 'I hear Karla has carted you. I could have written what was going to happen. She was a gold-digger and out for what she could get from you.'

'Like you were, then,' he hissed.

She slammed her flat palm down on the table. 'Fuck off, Jordan. I loved you and you binned me as soon as another bit of fluff came along.'

He wasn't listening. He looked out of the window. 'Whatever, what's done is done, isn't it?'

'It doesn't have to be. We can pick up where we left off. I would show you what it is to have a *real* woman by your side, supporting you, loving you, working together.'

Jordan threw his head back and chuckled. 'What, me and you? Are you having a laugh or what? Been there and worn the t-shirt, love. Give your head a shake, woman. Sort the girls out for tonight, and do the job I pay you to do.'

Angela stood, frozen. He was humiliating her; if looks could kill, he would have been a dead man. Her words were slow, and she meant every one of them. 'Be careful who you meet on the way up, Jordan, because you'll meet them again on the way back down.'

Chapter Twenty-Nine

It was early doors and Candice lay on the end of Elsa's bed, kicking her legs. Elsa seemed nervous. Something was playing on her mind. Candice's mobile phone was near her and she kept staring at it. Suddenly, Elsa reached over and gripped the phone. 'Let's have a look at your photos.' She held her friend's phone tightly, and Candice went white as she jumped up from the bed, wrestling to get the phone back. Elsa ran out of the bedroom, laughing, and locked herself in the bathroom. She shouted from behind the door. 'Wow, what's wrong with you? Have you been sending filthy snaps, or something? I'm your friend. We don't have secrets, remember?'

'Give me my phone back, Elsa, I'm not joking. Open the door.'

Silence.

More silence.

Then the lock on the bathroom door slid open slowly, and Elsa stood there looking at her best friend. Her nostrils flared and her teeth clenched tightly together. She swallowed before she spoke. 'You dirty slag. Get the hell out of my house. I thought you was my friend. You're a lying, cheating slut.' She launched the mobile phone at Candice's chest.

Candice quickly picked up her phone, and turned to face her friend. 'You don't want him; you've not even slept with him. He likes me, and I like him. What can I do if you're frigid?'

Elsa lost the plot and ran at her, gripping her hair in her fingers and ragging her about the landing. They both screamed and shouted. The house was in uproar.

Karla came sprinting up the stairs and dragged her daughter off Candice, who was hysterical by this point.

'What on earth is going on here?' Karla screeched at the top of her voice.

'Ask that slut there. Go on, ask her, because she's a snake, a dirty bitch who's been seeing Clayton behind my back. I've read the text messages too, so don't even try denying it to me. She's been sending dirty photos to him. Oh my God, you're disgusting.'

Karla didn't hesitate. 'Candice, get the fuck out of this house before I show you what a good arse-kicking is.'

The sound of feet pounded down the stairs. The front door slammed shut.

Karla ran back to her daughter and placed her arms around her. 'Come on, love. Come and sit down. You need to calm down.'

'I knew it, Mam. I had a gut feeling something was wrong, but I never thought for one second it was my boyfriend that she was seeing. Oh my God, they've both been laughing at me behind my back. I'm a joke.' She searched through her contact numbers, found Clayton's name and hit dial. As soon as she heard his voice, she never let him get a word in edgeways. Her hurt and anger poured out of her, never stopping for breath. 'We're done. If I never set eyes on you again, it'll be too soon.' She ended the call and sobbed to her mum, 'I'll show him. You wait until I'm rolling in the cash and the men are all over me. I'll show him, I'll show them all.'

Karla was confused as she listened to her daughter. 'Love, come and sit down now, and calm down. Like you said, at least you never slept with him. Candice is lower than a snake's belly for doing what she's done, and it only goes to show she's desperate. Why would she ever do that to you, after all you've done for her?'

'Exactly, Mam. Why would she do something like that? Well, it's my own fault for being so nice. Lesson learnt, eh?' Elsa checked the clock and grabbed the large bath towel from her bed. 'I need to get ready; I'm working tonight.'

Half an hour later, and only minutes after Elsa left, loud, hard knocks started on the front door. Mary got up to answer it and, as she did so, two hefty men flung her away from the door. One of the guys secured her so she couldn't move and the other ran into the front room. Karla jumped to her feet and, before she could say a word, the man had his hand wrapped tight around her throat.

'This is a warning to keep away. You know what I'm on about. I don't need to explain it, do I?'

Karla couldn't breathe, let alone answer.

Mary screamed from the hallway as she clocked her daughter getting manhandled. 'It's me you want, not her. Tell Lenny I won't ask for any more money, so get your bleeding hands off her. She knows nothing about it. Look at the state of my face that those bastards done to me last time. Get your hands from her now.'

Max turned his head like a barn owl. What on earth was this crank going on about? 'I'm here for Jordan: stay away from his wife and his club.' He released Karla, but his hand swung back and he slapped her twice in the face. She sank to the floor like a lead weight.

Mary ran to her side now and cradled her in her arms as she looked up at the heavy mob. 'Get the fuck out of my house now before I ring the police. Go on, piss off and leave us alone.'

Max bent his knees and came down to the same level as Karla. He spat in her face and sneered at her. 'Keep away, do you hear me? Otherwise the next time you see me, it will be your last.'

Karla was sobbing as she watched them leave. The two women were shaking like leaves, and it wasn't until they heard the front door slam shut that either of them spoke.

'What the fuck?' gasped Karla.

Mary ran to the front door and slid the top and bottom locks on with shaking hands. When she returned, Karla sat looking up at her.

'How could Jordan do that to me, Mam? Send his boys round as if I'm some kind of scumbag he can threaten to make me go away. And why ...' she trailed off and looked at her mother. 'Mam, you said you didn't want any more money from Lenny. What did you mean by that?'

Mary walked around in a circle, hands ragging through her hair. 'I got my wires crossed. It was Jordan who sent those boys, not Lenny. Forget it, I got mixed up, you know what I'm like. I'm a bag of nerves, lately.'

'But you said Lenny's name. You thought they were here to do his bidding. Don't hide anything from me, Mother, because I'll go and see him myself, if you don't tell me what's been going on. You've been in touch with him, haven't you? How long has this been going on?'

Mary was on the spot. Her bottom lip trembled. She couldn't hold eye contact. 'When Elsa was small, you know we had no money, and we were in a bad way. If it wasn't for the payments I got from him, we would have lost the house years ago.'

Karla threw her head back against the wall, banging it with force as if she was trying to knock the thoughts out of her head. 'Tell me I am hearing this right? Was it only after she was born or have you been back to him? Please, tell me you have not been getting money from Lenny all this time?'

'Did you really think I've been supporting the three of us and this house on my cleaning jobs? He's Elsa's father, and he might be the lowest of low, but we have hid in the shadows for years with his secret lovechild. Why should he sit there rich as a king and without a care in the world? We could have got him sent down for what he did to you – you were underage. So I decided we'd make him pay in other ways. Yes, I have been getting a few quid from him for years. I never told you because I knew you would have wanted more. You'd have pushed our luck and he'd have you shut up – permanently. I had to put food on the table for his daughter, but I knew I had to play by his rules to do it. So don't bleeding judge me.'

Karla wobbled as she stood up, one hand flat against the wall. 'I can't believe this. All these years, whenever I said I would ask Lenny for some money, you were set against it. No bleeding wonder when you've been creaming it in for years. I only mentioned it the other day and you went ballistic.'

'Lenny told me to keep my mouth shut because he didn't want you knowing. You'd have been at his front door every bleeding week if you knew that any money was flying about, and don't say you wouldn't, because you would without a shadow of doubt. And this wasn't guilt money, because the bastard has no shame – it was hush money to stop us talking, and we both know you'd have told every-one from here to Trafford if you thought there was cash in it.'

'This is unbelievable. I'm going to see Lenny myself and he can deal with me in the future. Elsa is my daughter, not yours, so keep your nose out.'

'You're too late. He said he's not paying any more money for Elsa now she's eighteen, so don't waste your breath. Look at the state of me. He sent his mob to do this to me as a warning to back off.'

'Is he forgetting that I was barely more than a child when I got pregnant? He might know I won't tell the pigs, but I'll tell his wife. I'll tell everyone who knows him, the wanker. I've kept my mouth shut for too long now. The truth is going to come out. I'm telling Elsa who her father is the moment she gets home.'

'Are you for real? She doesn't need to know who her father is. He will only bring her misery and tears. He'll never admit she's his blood, so don't put her through that pain, I'm begging you.' Mary tugged at her daughter's arm, looking deep into her eyes.

Karla shook her body free and moved away from Mary. 'The time has come, Mother. No more secrets. Lenny Jackson will step up as Elsa's father, otherwise I'll make sure his world falls apart.' Karla examined her face in the mirror, red welts clearly visible around her neck. 'And as for Jordan? If those men want war, then they'd better be prepared. I'm going to ruin them both, the bastards. And I'm going to enjoy doing it.'

Chapter Thirty

Karla was dressed to the nines in a black tight-fitted dress. Her make-up was spot on and you could smell her perfume before you could see her. She stood looking at herself in the long mirror in her bedroom and nodded her head at her reflection. She whispered under her breath, 'Payback time, boys. I won't take this lying down, no way.'

Mary was waiting for her daughter at the bottom of the stairs. 'Be careful. You know both of these men and what they can do. Don't be putting yourself in any danger.'

Karla grabbed her black leather jacket from the chair and swung it over her shoulder. 'Don't wait up, it's going to be a long night for me.' She yanked the door open and she was gone.

The night was cold, pitch black. Clouds hung low in the night sky. The wind was howling eerily. The sound of Karla's black heels clipped along the pavement and, with each step she took, she looked one way then the other. She finally reached her destination and stood in the shadows across the road from *Passion*. It seemed quiet tonight, not as many clubbers as usual. They must all be at the opening of that new club Jordan was so bothered about, Karla thought. Taking a deep breath, she rushed across the main road and into the club. She was a woman on a mission.

She kept her head down and headed straight for Jordan's office. Sooner or later he would turn up there. She would wait all night if that's what she had to do to see him. She closed the door behind her and stood breathing heavily. With haste she ran over to the desk and opened the drawer. She rummaged until she found the silver key. She grabbed it and rushed over to the wall safe that was hidden behind a small set of drawers. Her heart was pounding, and small beads of sweat sprang up on her forehead. Breathe girl, get a grip and calm down, she told herself. She found what she was looking for and stashed it in her jacket pocket. Then she reached for a glass and poured herself a large glass of vodka from the drinks cabinet. She necked the first shot in one and quickly filled the glass up again. She needed to steady her nerves, to be ready for when she faced him.

———

Only a few streets away, Pam stood next to Lenny and smiled. The glowing neon signs had brought their club to life. *Tease* looked like the real deal, and the place was packed for opening night. Elsa and Jenny were backstage, waiting to go on. There were a few dancers before them, getting the punters ready for the main attraction. Pam sipped her champagne and smiled. 'This has been a long time coming and I'm so thankful for it, Lenny.'

'After all these years, I think we have worked well together. I've enjoyed it. But I'll enjoy it more when Jordan finds out,' he chuckled.

'He'll know soon enough. Everyone's seen me here. Come tomorrow, he'll be gone, out of my life for ever.'

Lenny shook his head. 'Be careful, Pam, he's not going to let you go that easy. I don't even know what you've got planned – and I don't want to know – but men like him will take a lot of shaking off. You won't be able to hide, trust me. He'll never give up.'

'Don't you think I know that? I've been planning this. I'm not leaving him – I'm taking him down.'

———

The music boomed throughout the room, the base kicking in. It was nearly time for Elsa to make her debut.

Clayton sat outside the club with his boys. Music on low, heads nodding to the beat. They were sat in a black series one BMW with John, his wingman, as driver. Clayton sat forward in his seat, making sure he could see everything he needed – one eye on the main entrance, the other keeping his exit clear. John was hyped as well and they both knew that anytime soon this place would be in uproar. Gunshots would be fired, windows would be smashed, people would be screaming and running onto the streets. The dibble would be swarming the area. Arrests would be made, but he'd make sure he was well clear by then. For now, they had to sit tight and be patient. Clayton looked down at his phone then looked over at John and shook his head.

'Fuck me, mate, Elsa found out earlier that I've been banging Candice. She went sick on the phone before.' He was smirking and making out he wasn't bothered, but it was written all over his face that losing Elsa had gutted him. He was wounded. 'I'll go and see her once she's calmed down. A bunch of flowers, a few gifts should sort her out. It always works for my dad.'

Elsa sat in the dressing room. She was a bag of nerves. Jenny had offered her some sniff but she refused. There was no way she was getting off her head again; it wasn't right, she didn't like it. And besides, she was still reeling from finding out about Clayton; she had enough to deal with.

Pam popped her head in the room, then walked inside. With one look at Elsa, she could see something was wrong. She approached her with caution. 'What's up, love?'

Elsa dipped her head and her bottom lip trembled. 'It's Clayton, he's been cheating on me with my best friend.'

Pam's jaw dropped. 'No! He idolises you, he'd never risk losing you.'

'Well, he has, Pam. I know he's your son and you want to see the best in him, but I saw messages on her phone and dirty photos they'd been sending to each other. The pair of them are welcome to each other.'

Pam had to smooth this over, get the girl ready to go on stage. 'Wait until you see him. I'm sure he can explain.'

Elsa inhaled deeply and closed her eyes for a few seconds. Then she bent to take her high-heeled shoes off. 'I can't do this, Pam. Earlier I was so fired up to dance – to show him what he was missing – but I don't want to go on stage for revenge. I want to dance because I love it, because I know I'm good at it. But my heart's not in it after today. Jenny can do it solo.'

Pam went white, flustering, 'Don't be silly, you're just nervous and not thinking straight. Why don't you have a few slugs of vodka and calm down? This is your big chance; you will never get the chance again to earn money like this. I've put time and effort into you. Lenny would go mental if you let him down.'

Elsa shrugged. 'I'll speak to him myself; make him understand. I can't do it.'

Pam looked around the room and quickly moved next to Elsa. She gripped her arm and sank her long fingernails deep into her skin. 'Listen, you smacked arse, get those shoes back on and get on that stage. I've got plans and I'm not letting some moody bitch mess them up over teenage heartbreak. Do you hear me? Get ready and sort yourself out.'

Elsa's eyes were wide. This woman was supposed to be her friend. Pam shouted over to Jenny. 'Get this one a few drinks, and get them down her neck. Stay with her and make sure she gets on that stage.' Pam shot a look at Elsa and snarled, 'Do *not* let me down. A lot depends on this for me.'

Pam stormed out of the room and Jenny marched over to Elsa. There was no time for drama. 'Fuck me, sort your shit out. This is a big night for us both, so don't be fucking this up for me too. What's up with you, anyway?'

Elsa's eyes clouded over, and a fat, salty tear streamed down her cheek. 'My boyfriend has been cheating on me with my best friend.'

Jenny howled laughing. 'Is that all? Soon you won't even look at another useless lad your age. After tonight you'll realise you can have any man you want: rich men, guys who want to take you on holiday, buy you expensive gifts. But, for now, get a smile on your face and let's get ready to earn some money. You can go home and cry over him – or you can go out there and be fucking queen of the world.'

Elsa listened, and felt the fire inside her spark again. She'd been wrong thinking dancing was all about the money. There was power in it, too – and she was taking control.

Chapter Thirty-One

Karla could hear footsteps coming down the corridor. She jumped up from the edge of the desk and hid behind the cupboard. It was Jordan, she could hear him shouting back to somebody. The door swung open and he went straight over to the small table at the back of the room and started snorting cocaine, at least two lines of the stuff. She was used to his routine. Every night he spent at the club, once the punters were in and the evening underway, he always did a couple of lines to carry him through the night.

She never moved a muscle; even covered her mouth with one hand to silence her heavy breathing. He still hadn't spotted her. Karla could almost see the drug rush through his body. His head fell back, and his chest expanded as if someone was pumping it up. Now. Now was her moment. Slowly, she moved out from the shadows. Jordan sat up in his chair and clenched his teeth as he spotted her, fist curling instinctively.

His tone was aggressive, and she knew this wasn't going to end well. 'What the fuck are you doing here? I thought you'd been told not to come near me again. Are you thick, or something?'

It took a few seconds for her to reply. She swallowed hard, aware he could strike at any second.

'Did you think you could get rid of me just like that?'

He leant forward and held his head in his hands. He sighed. 'You fucked it up. It was all sweet and then you wanted more. You were never happy with being a bit on the side, you had to come gunning for Pam.'

'You promised me more, that's why, you tosser. You filled my head with shit and then, when you'd got what you wanted from me, you thought you could walk away.' She sucked in a large mouthful of air. 'But it doesn't work like that. No, I will never let you treat me like that. I'll ruin you like you've ruined me. As soon as I can, I'll be telling your wife all about us. Don't think your heavies scared me. Sure, they beat me – but I'm not broken.'

Jordan sprang up from his chair. He was ready to attack her when he froze. Karla stood with shaking hands pointing a silver pistol right at him. She was sweating, eyelids blinking rapidly. She knew he'd recognise it as the one from the safe, knew he'd know it was loaded.

'I'll do it, Jordan, so sit back down before I pull the trigger. I will, you know. Trust me, I'll make sure you never breath again.'

Jordan couldn't take the chance; she held a look in her eye that unsettled him. He backed off slowly, never taking his eyes from her.

'Whoa, calm the fuck down, woman. Are you right in the head? You'll go to jail if you do me in. Think about it, can you handle being locked up?'

She stood tall. She was the one in control now, not him. 'I'm stronger than you think. Who's even going to miss you?'

Jordan sensed a hesitation in her. He chuckled and stretched his arms above his head. He sneered at her. 'Look at you, you're steaming drunk. Washed up, you are. You probably couldn't aim straight, even if you had the guts. What's this going to achieve? Your daughter will have a convict for a mum – not that you've been winning Mother of the Year awards before now.'

'Fuck off, Jordan. This isn't just revenge. This is about my future – mine and my girl's. If I do you in, there's a long line of people who'll consider it a massive fucking favour. And do you know who'll be right at the front of that queue? Lenny Jackson. I think he'd be very interested to know who'd taken his biggest rival out of the game.' Karla pointed the pistol closer – no one could miss from this range.

But Jordan laughed. 'You think Lenny's going to look at a woman like you for a moment? An old woman who has more mileage on her than a vintage car? Everyone knows he likes them young … really young.'

She was trying to find the words to make a comeback when suddenly he dived up from the desk and pounced on her, bringing her to the ground. He covered her mouth with his hand and pounded her arm up and down against the floor. Finally he smashed the gun out of her hand. It landed near the door. This was not how she planned it. She should have thought this through more. Even though he had the advantage now, Jordan didn't let up. He pressed both her hands over her head and head-butted her. Karla was fighting for consciousness now, legs kicking, body rolling one way then another. Her teeth connected with his shoulder, and she bit down as hard as she could. But he never flinched, kept on punching her. Just as she felt she was going under, a loud bang split the air.

Jordan looked down at Karla, his eyes bulging from the sockets. A stillness filled his body. Like a block of flats being demolished, his body fell down onto hers with a thud. Karla squirmed underneath him. He wasn't moving. Deep-red blood dribbled down his neck from the back of his head. Karla used all her strength and wriggled free from under him. What the hell had happened? She was fighting for every breath she took, and nothing was making any sense, anymore. She looked round at the door – the pistol still lay on the floor, but the position had changed. A cold wind blew in from outside the door and she saw the fire exit was open. Karla scrambled over the body and waved her hand in front of his face. Jordan had breathed his last. She covered her mouth with her hands and held in her screams. She'd never wanted to end him, only to scare him, but someone had beaten her to it. She panicked. She needed to get away from this place as quickly as she could, before she was framed for the murder of Jordan Maylett.

Chapter Thirty-Two

E lsa stood up and stretched her body one way then the other. She could hear the punters outside shouting at the dancers already on stage. They sounded horny tonight, eager for the new girls. Elsa tuned out the shouts and heckles, and felt the base line like a heartbeat.

Next to her, Jenny looked at herself in the mirror. Confident, in control and ready to make herself rich, she looked unstoppable.

'Elsa, this is it. Remember what I told you, it's all about the …' she let the novice finish the sentence.

'I know, Jenny. It's all about the tease.'

Jenny nodded. 'It's a big crowd out there. We have two dances together tonight, so let's make them count.'

Deep in the middle of the crowd, Clayton and his boys were scanning the punters. Max would lose the plot if he knew he'd not followed his orders, but the place was heaving, the lights were low – hiding was easy. Clayton sat down in the corner of the club, drinking a bottle of beer with his head dipped low. Then, from the corner of his eye, he spotted someone. He bolted up from his seat. This wasn't good, she needed to be out of here. It was going to kick-off any time now.

Barging past the drunken groups of men, he rushed to his mother's side. He dragged her by the arm to the corner of the bar. 'What the fuck are you doing here? This is Lenny fucking Jackson's joint, Mam, you must know that. You need to leave. Get your coat on, and get home. It's not safe for you, shit's going down. Mam, look at me, I'm being serious, you need to leave.'

She pulled away, shocked to see him. 'Has your dad sent you to find me? Because this isn't Lenny Jackson territory, it's–'

Before she could say another word, the music changed, the spotlights shone, and Pamela was like a rabbit in the headlights. Her son followed her eyes to the stage and did a double-take as he spotted Elsa. He looked at his mother and then at the stage. Nothing was making sense anymore.

'What the fuck is she playing at? Mam, why is she dancing?' His voice got louder. 'Did you know about this?'

'Listen, the girl wanted to earn some money, so I showed her how to dance. Come on, Clayton, it's not like she has many other options.'

The words stuck to his teeth. 'You're a prize piece of work, Mother. Here's me thinking you were bonding with her, and really you were having me over. Fuck me, I'm your son, and that girl could have been my wife.'

Pam narrowed her eyes and went nose to nose with her son. 'Get a grip, you idiot. You didn't want her, otherwise you wouldn't have been sticking it up her best friend. Things are changing for us. After tonight, I'm binning your father once and for all. You can stay with your dad or come with me. But I'm never, ever taking any shit from your father again. I want peace, I deserve it. And this? This club is half mine, and soon it will be fully mine, so don't you think you can mess things up in here.'

Clayton had his head in his hands. 'Mam, what are you saying? This is Lenny Jackson's joint, I told you. Dad has sent the boys here to destroy it. And I don't mean just me and the lads. Look over there ...' He gestured to where Max stood waiting for the right moment.

Pam knew she had to alert Lenny. She turned on her heels and cut through the crowds.

Clayton was left standing on his own. He glared at the stage and, without thinking, he sprinted towards Elsa. He vaulted over the barriers but, before he could get onto the stage, two bouncers gripped him and dragged him away. To them, he was just another pissed-up, handsy punter. As they hauled him off, he screamed and shouted, 'Elsa! How could you? Think about it, Elsa, think about what you're doing ...'

On stage, Elsa didn't bat an eyelid as Clayton was manhandled out of sight. The adrenaline was surging and all eyes were on her as the music built. There was a raw energy coming from her, a heat the crowd could almost drink in. As she began to move, Jenny could tell Elsa was the only girl anyone cared about, and a dark look shone in her eyes. Before Elsa could get into her stride, Jenny grabbed the pole at full stretch and flicked her legs. Her high heel sliced Elsa's cheek as she passed her on the pole. Bright-red claret sprayed from her face. The young girl's expression changed as she felt the warm blood gushing. Jenny was still dancing and, as she leant in, she hissed through clenched teeth, 'Get off the fucking stage.' This was Jenny's show now, she had no time for any drama.

But Max and his boys had other ideas. Seizing the moment as the audience watched the drama onstage, he pushed over the table he stood next to – a signal to all his cronies. Suddenly shots were fired into the ceiling, and the sounds of glass smashing, screaming and shouting drowned out the music. Punters scrambled for the exits as Max jumped behind the bar and started smashing the optics. Max watched members of the public scramble past him and nodded his head slowly. This club would not be open for a long time after this. But better safe than sorry. He pulled a lighter out from his pocket, and some lighter fuel, and let out a menacing laugh.

Backstage, Elsa examined at her face in the mirror. She could hear the shouting from outside the room. Suddenly, the door swung open and Lenny ran to her, dragging at her, pulling her.

'Come on, we need to get out of here. Follow me, hurry the fuck up.' Lenny dug his large fingers into her shoulder and made sure she understood every word he was saying. 'Move it, I said. Now!'

They ran down the small corridor at the back of the club. Lenny was gasping for breath, and his hands shook as he tried to get his long silver key into the lock. Finally, the door opened and the car park was visible. There wasn't a second to spare.

'Follow me,' he screamed. Elsa followed him into the night. Once outside, the cold wind stung her body and she felt more exposed than ever. Lenny ran for his life, and didn't stop until he got to the car. 'Get in and keep your head down,' he shouted. Elsa didn't know what was going on, but the tone of his voice was enough to convince her to follow. She jumped into the passenger seat and sank her body low. She could hear shouting, police sirens in the distance. She looked up at Lenny and she could see the fear in his eyes as he searched in his coat for his car keys. 'Maylett, I'll fucking do you in myself after this. How dare you cross me again,' he muttered as he found the key and rammed it in the ignition. The car screeched out of the car park, wheels spinning in the gravel.

———

Clayton saw Lenny's car leave with Elsa, but it was too late to follow, he'd smoked him. The car sped out from the car park and hit the main road.

Clayton sank to his knees and held his head up to the night sky as he let out a roar from the pit of his stomach. Blood trickled down the side of his eye. Pam ran to her son's side and cradled him in her arms. 'Leave her, Son. We need to get away from here before the police come.'

They both looked as they heard a woman, shouting loudly as she ran to them. Karla was out of breath, and her body crumpled as she reached them. Her hands gripped her knees as she tried to regain her breath. She looked a mess, hair all over, clothes ripped.

'Was that Lenny who just left?'

Pam recognised Karla from the club and didn't hide her sour expression. 'What do you want with Lenny?'

Karla looked at the woman and stopped as soon as she saw it was Pam. A brief look of something like sympathy crossed her face. 'I've gone over and over what this moment would be like. Telling you what your no-good lying bastard of a husband has been doing behind your back. But do you know what? None of that matters anymore.' Karla swallowed hard and her nostrils flared as she got ready to deliver her killer blow.

But before she could speak again, Pam said, 'You're welcome to him, sweetheart. Do you actually think I didn't know he was sleeping with some tart? You're not the first slapper he's slept with and, trust me, you won't be the last. My marriage was over a long time ago, love, after I found out he was shagging some dancer in the club, but he begged me to forgive him and told me he'd never do it again. Have you heard this, Son? This is another one of your father's whores. Tell her. Tell her how much he tells me he loves me and needs me.'

Clayton stared at Karla and swallowed hard. Candice had pointed this woman out to him, and he was sure it was

Elsa's mother. Pam was waiting on his reply. He knew they couldn't stay here much longer. The police would be swarming the car park any second now. 'Are you Elsa's mam?'

Karla looked flustered; how did this Maylett toerag know her daughter?

'Yes, why? What has she got to do with this?'

Clayton paced one way, then the other. 'Did you know she has been dancing at the club?'

Karla let out a sarcastic laugh. 'The club has only just opened. She might be collecting glasses here, but she's definitely not dancing. My Elsa is a good girl.'

'Are you thick or something, woman? I came in the club tonight and she was on the stage, dancing. I'm Clayton. Come on, she must have mentioned me?'

Karla nearly collapsed, her breathing ragged, as she started to put two and two together.

It was Pam's turn now the tide had turned. 'If you'd kept your knickers on and not been on your back all the time with my husband, you would have known where and what your daughter was doing. I trained her to be a pole-dancer and, I'll give her that, she was top-notch. Just a shame Lenny has taken her, because I'd have liked her to hear what is being said here tonight.'

Karla's expression froze. 'Lenny's taken Elsa?'

Pam smirked as she replied, 'Yes, he's just left with her. He's probably taken her to his farmhouse for a few private dances.'

Karla lost the plot. 'Lenny Jackson is Elsa's father, you fucking idiots! I need to find her, and quick, before he gets his hands on her.'

'What the hell are you talking about?' Pamela gasped. 'I used to be one of Lenny's girls twenty years back – til Jordan got me clear – I'd have known your face if you were on the scene then.'

'Fuck.' A slow realisation hit Karla. 'Lenny was always going on about one of his best girls stolen by a rival. That was you, wasn't it? I was a young girl when Lenny got his hands on me. Fifteen. I guess I was meant to be a replacement. Until he got me pregnant and then carted me. He told me if I ever told anyone about Elsa he would put me and my family in a body bag.'

The penny had dropped with Pam, too: this was Lenny through and through.

Clayton saw police cars pulling up at the front of the club but, even though they'd be round the back in moments, he was in shock, trying to piece together what he'd heard about his parents. Bright red flames pushed through the roof of *Tease*, and fire-engines were already trying to put the blaze out.

Clayton finally jolted into action. 'We need to go. And we need to find Elsa. Do any of you two know where this farm is?'

Of course they knew. Any woman who'd worked the Manchester clubs knew where it was, if only to keep away. Pam was distraught, realising now what she'd done to Elsa, all in the name of business. And now the club she'd traded Elsa for was burning. 'Quick, I'll drive. Get in the car.'

The three of them dashed towards Pam's car. As soon as they reached it, Clayton snatched the keys from his mother's hand. 'I'll drive. You've been drinking.'

Karla jumped into the back and slammed the door shut behind her. Clayton kept the headlights low until they were out of the car park. The nightclub was ablaze. There was no way any part of it would be saved. Pam watched it burn as they drove past. This was her savings gone for ever. Her dream of starting a new life out of Manchester had gone up in smoke. She had been a fool to think she could leave this life.

Chapter Thirty-Three

*P*assion had been closed for over an hour, and Angela was locking the club up now the last few punters had left. She walked down the dimly lit corridor, wrapped in an unnerving silence. The atmosphere seemed to change as she placed her hand on the office door handle. She walked into the room and saw Jordan's lifeless body in a pool of congealing blood. Barely reacting, she sat down on the leather chair. She popped a cigarette into the side of her mouth and looked over at the body. Sucking in a large mouthful of smoke, she closed her eyes for a few seconds, and blew the smoke out slowly.

'Not so big now, are you, Jordan?' She stood up and walked to the body, then bent her knees slowly and spoke directly to him. 'I loved you with all my heart and you promised me the world. How do you think it felt to watch you with all those women, day in, day out, telling them the same story you told me? When I pulled that trigger to end your life, I pulled it knowing it would end my addiction to you. I always thought you would come back to me and we could be happy, like we were when we first met. I helped you run this club and dealt with all the shit for you. I was by your side no matter what, and you never once thanked me for anything. You deserved to lose everything, the club, your wife, your family, your life. Good riddance, you bastard.'

She went to the window and looked out into the night sky. Her suffering was finally over.

Chapter Thirty-Four

Clayton sped up along the country lanes. Pam cringed as they took a corner. It was pitch black and visibility was poor. He was driving like the police were chasing him, braking at the last minute, taking chances. Rossendale was around thirty-five minutes away from the club and they still had fifteen minutes left of the journey.

The two women in the car had hardly said a word to each other. Pam sat in silence with her head pressed against the cold window. Her world had fallen apart. Karla kept switching between two awful images: the thought of Lenny with her daughter made her sick but, when she tried to banish that mental picture, all she saw instead was Jordan, bleeding out. She longed to tell Pam, but knew she'd be prime suspect if she said a word. And even though she had no time for Clayton, right now he was the one getting her to Elsa. If she told him his dad had been shot, she'd lose any chance of getting to her daughter before it was too late. She sat forward and held the sides of the passenger seat in front with a tight grip.

'How long now? You need to put your foot down. My daughter's in danger and I need to get there before that pervert gets his hands on her.'

She made the sign of the cross on her body, and prayed in silence. When she'd finished speaking to the big man in the sky she crossed herself again.

Pam pulled her mobile out and tried to ring Lenny's phone again, but it kept going to voicemail. Every time they heard his voice message, their hearts sank farther, both women knowing from experience exactly what Lenny might be doing right now.

Lenny parked the car up and led Elsa to the front door. All the way there, she'd been sobbing her heart out. She wanted to go home, to be with her family. Blood was still trickling down the side of her face, and the club she thought was going to change her life would probably be smouldering ash by now.

Lenny reached into his pocket and pulled out his phone. Shit: the battery had died. Opening the large doors at the front of his house, he barged inside. 'This is fucking war! Who does that cunt Maylett think he's dealing with? I'll destroy him. I'll take everything he owns.'

Elsa trudged inside the house; it was freezing. She spoke in a soft voice. 'Can I use your phone? My family will be worried if I'm not home soon. My nana will be climbing the walls and walking the streets if she doesn't know where I am.'

He brushed her comment off. 'My phone has died, sweetheart. Let's get settled and I'll charge it up. You can go in that bedroom, there.' He pointed his finger behind him, as he drew a large bolt across the front door. 'And get into something more comfortable to wear. You can't be comfy in that outfit?'

Elsa was apprehensive. She barely knew this man, and she had a gut feeling all was not what it was made out to be. Slowly, she made her way to the bedroom, always looking over her shoulder, aware that his eyes were following her. Once she got inside the bedroom, she stood with her back pressed firmly against the door. Her chest was rising and falling frantically, and she was realising that she was now more vulnerable than ever. Echoes of the night of her first private party flooded her mind. She'd only just escaped Tommy. Lenny was her boss, she supposed. He was only protecting his staff, she tried to tell herself. Yes, he'd saved her from the chaos of the attack on *Tease*, but what if what lay ahead was even worse …?

Lenny found another mobile phone in a desk nearby and searched the contacts. He held the phone to his ear and listened to the ringing tone. 'I want the team around at that bastard's home, his club, his family's house. I want them all suffering. How dare that prick step on my toes. I should have been ready. I took my eye off the ball for a few seconds and look what's happened. There's a price on that cunt's head and I want him ended.' His voice rose: he was livid. 'I won't be happy until that prick is six feet under.'

Lenny ended the call and placed his flat palm on his chest. He froze, then staggered over to the table to steady himself. He started to take deep breaths, long, hard breaths. Dipping his hand into his pocket, he pulled out a small tablet bottle and shook a white tablet into the middle of his hand. Once he'd shoved it under his tongue, he stood still and never moved a muscle until finally his breathing steadied. He walked over to the bedroom door and pressed his ear against it. He slid his tongue across his bottom lip, and his nostrils flared. Curling his knuckles, he knocked on the door. 'Are you alright in there? I'm having a tipple; do you want one?'

'I'll be out in a minute,' Elsa said softly. Lenny smirked and walked over to the drinks cabinet. His hands gripped the brandy bottle as he poured two measures.

Elsa found a pair of tracksuit bottoms and a white t-shirt in the drawers. Maybe Lenny had relations who stayed here, because they were definitely women's clothes. As she peeled off her skimpy dancing outfit, she felt better to be covering up, especially around Lenny. After she cleaned her face up, she was ready to go back into the front room. Lenny watched her from the corner of his eye as she crept to a chair to sit down. Lenny sat in the red leather chesterfield armchair facing her. He'd taken his black jacket off and loosened his tie.

'Come and sit near the fire, darling. It takes a while to warm up in this place,' he rasped.

Elsa stood up and edged closer to the open fire. The wood crackled as the flames started to dance about in ribbons of orange and yellow. Elsa sat on the floor and drew her legs up to her chest.

'Your face looks better now it's been cleaned up. It'll heal in no time, and you'll be back on a stage before you know it.'

'I don't think I will be dancing again, Lenny. I got myself mixed up in this world and, before I knew it, it was too late. I only wanted to earn some money, nothing more.'

Lenny lit a cigarette and grey smoke seeped out from the corner of his mouth as he replied, 'I can help you with money. There is no need to dance anymore, if you don't want. You scratch my back and I'll scratch yours, so to speak.'

She looked puzzled and hunched her shoulders. It was obvious he would have to explain. 'I can look after you, and make sure you never go without. This could be our secret; nobody ever has to know.'

She gulped and shook her head. No words would come.

Lenny's nostrils flared, his hands gripped the edge of the sofa, his knuckles turning white. He wasn't used to getting a knockback. 'I don't think you fully understand how this works. I'll explain, shall I?'

Elsa backed away, as the truth of what he was suggesting dawned on her. Suddenly she was scared he was going to attack her, to take what he wanted right now if she wasn't prepared to accept his offer.

'Pam and I had a deal, and you were part of it. Don't tell me she didn't tell you?'

'She's told me nothing, and I'm having no part of whatever you have planned,' she hissed.

Lenny stood up and started to undo his thick leather belt. Elsa's body shook from head to toe as reality hit home.

She sprang to her feet, and backed against the wall. 'You lay one finger on me, old man, and I'll have you charged. Go on, touch me, and watch what happens.'

Lenny unbuttoned his crisp white shirt and placed it neatly on the arm of the chair behind him. He turned slowly to his victim again. 'You can do this the easy way, or the hard way. I'm not arsed either way, but one thing for sure is that I'm having you first. You're still a virgin, right?'

Elsa squirmed. He was knocking her sick. He made her skin crawl. She reached over and picked up a brass ornament from the small table to her left. This wasn't a business deal, it was a battle, she knew that now. The difference in strength was clear. Elsa realised she'd have to keep him talking as long as she could. She growled over at him, 'If you lay one finger on me, I won't be held responsible for what happens next. Leave me alone. I want to go home.'

Her words fell on deaf ears. There was only one thing on this man's mind and, judging by the look in his eye, he was going to make sure he had sex with her tonight, no matter what. He smirked as he neared her, aroused that he had a fight on his hands. Maybe this was his kink, maybe he liked her playing hard to get. Elsa felt another wave of revulsion.

Lenny pounced on her before she had a chance to do anything. Despite his age, he was strong, and threw her to the floor like a rag doll. He was biting her body, ripping at her clothes. This man was an animal. The more flesh he could see, the more he grunted and groaned. Elsa screamed, kicking and jerking her body up and down, but he was too heavy. He squeezed her hands together over her head and dropped his head to her neck. She could feel his hot breath rushing down her spine, the smell of him rubbing against her skin.

Clayton could hear the commotion coming from inside. He smashed the window. There wasn't a moment to spare. He scrambled through the gap as a sharp piece of jagged glass dug deep into his thigh. Pain in his eyes, he carried on through. As if his life depended on it, he motored through the house until he found Elsa.

Clayton dived onto Lenny and pulled his head back, nearly snapping his neck. The older man was heavier, but Clayton's anger gave him strength beyond his years. Elsa crawled to the corner of the room and watched as Clayton booted and punched Lenny. Pam and Karla appeared in the room now and rushed over to Elsa. They stood in front of her, guarding her from this man who had marked all their lives.

Lenny was gagging for breath now, turning a grey colour, and his eyes were straining from their sockets. 'My tablets, get me my tablets,' he gasped.

Pam didn't move a muscle. Karla made sure Lenny could see her face, then screamed at him, 'You pervert! Elsa is your daughter. You know, the child you never saw, the one you wanted hidden away? Well, here she is. Hello, Daddy ...'

Lenny gasped for breath. He was mumbling, but none of them could hear what he was saying. His hand banged against the floor as his lungs flooded.

Elsa got up and slowly walked to Lenny's side. She looked back at her mother and shook her head. 'Are you serious? This kiddy-fiddler is my father? Mum, *please* tell me you're lying. I can't handle this.'

The tears pouring from Karla's eyes told her daughter all she needed to know. 'This isn't how I wanted to tell you, love. I never wanted this filthy animal anywhere near you.'

Elsa held her head high and sneered down at her father, struggling to breathe at her feet. She sobbed as she said to him, 'Do you know what? I've always wanted a father. I created this lovely picture in my mind of how you must look, and that's what kept me sane each and every day of my life. But, look at you, you're a monster. Nothing like I ever dreamt you would be. Turns out, I don't need a father, especially not one like you. Take your last breath knowing you will never ever be part of my life. Rot in hell.'

Lenny's palm banged on the floor rapidly. Desperate, he looked at each of them to help him. None of them did. Karla ran to her daughter's side and cradled her in her arms. The four of them stood by and watched Lenny Jackson take his final breath. His body shuddered and his mouth opened as his fight for air was lost.

Clayton hobbled over to Elsa. 'I just got here in time. A few more minutes and who knows what would have happened?'

Elsa pulled away from her mother's arms and looked him directly in the eye. 'Aren't *you* the hero of the hour?' she said sarcastically.

Pam snapped, 'He put his neck on the line for you. A thank-you would be nice.'

Elsa turned to Pam now. 'Tell your son that you sold me to Lenny. Go on, tell him that was part of the deal that you brought him a virgin.' She faced her ex-boyfriend again. 'Clayton, did you know she trained me? Showed me all her old moves? Told me this life would set me free? Go on, Pam, tell your son exactly what you tried to do.'

Clayton was distraught. When he looked at his mother, he didn't need an answer: the truth was written all over her face. Karla brought her hand back and swung it hard onto Pam's cheek.

Pam retaliated and slapped her back. 'Touché, baby. I deserve a slap for what I've done, but, come on, you are no better than me. You were sleeping with my husband.'

Elsa span round to face her mother. 'Clayton's dad was the married rat you were seeing? Fucking unbelievable, you are!' She looked at Clayton, and then at her mother, and then at Pam. She had heard enough. 'You know what, you three deserve each other. I'm getting my stuff together and I'm going. You're all messed up in the head, the lot of you. I'm going home.'

She stormed into the bedroom and started to pick her clothes up from the floor. She spotted a black leather bag hanging on the wardrobe door handle, and shoved her belongings inside. She needed to get out of this place as soon as possible. Her head was all over the place and, if she stayed here a minute longer, she would lose the plot. This was so messed up, too much for her to get a grip on.

But by the time she was packed, the others were waiting for her, quiet now as the events of the night sank in. They all left the farmhouse together. Lenny Jackson was left slumped against the wall where he took his final breath. Not one of them looked back as they drove down the gravel path towards the road. Elsa sat in the back of the car and looked out of the window. She wanted her nana. She wanted to go home.

Chapter Thirty-Five

Clayton pulled up outside his house. They'd barely got inside when the bell rang.

Pamela answered the door and saw two police officers standing there. No one ever called the police round here unless it was serious. She braced herself.

'Mrs Pamela Maylett, can we come in? I'm afraid we've got some bad news about your husband.'

The next twenty-four hours were a blur. Pamela was hysterical when she got the news, while Clayton's fury burned white hot – until they were both taken in for questioning, only to be released without charge the next day.

Karla took Elsa home, and waited for the police to come calling. But as the hours stretched on, she wondered if she was in the clear. Maybe it hadn't been a set-up – maybe she had a guardian angel out there, after all.

Jordan's funeral was a quiet affair. Pamela always thought the police had turned a blind eye to some of what went on at *Passion*, and she suspected the kickbacks her husband had given them in life now took the heat off him, even in death. A few of the club's dancers came along to the short service, a whirl of black netting veiling their faces, their heels clicking across the cemetery path. No one looked twice at Angela, dabbing her eyes and dropping a rose on top of the coffin.

Lenny Jackson was laid to rest three weeks later. It was a big funeral and anyone who was anyone was there showing their respect to the man who had ruled this side of Manchester for as long as they could remember. Lenny's son stood tall at his graveside and held a stiff upper lip. Clayton stood watching them from a distance. This war was far from over, but he knew he needed to retreat and lick his wounds. *Tease* was gone – but the rivalry between *Passion* and *Lush Laps* would soon be as fierce ever. Already the girls were back on stage at each club under the heat of the lights. The feud between Jordan and Lenny would live on through their sons – blood was thicker than water, after all – and with every passing day Clayton was planning his revenge. He would be the next big man in Manchester, he'd make sure of it.

Mary was worried about her granddaughter. Elsa was quiet, and on her phone a lot. Karla had already moved on to her latest man; the one who she was sure this time would change her life, the one who would treat her like a princess. Mary knew her daughter would always fall on her feet. But Elsa was different. She talked less and went out more. Mary didn't know exactly what had happened at the farmhouse that night, but she knew something had changed in her granddaughter.

Elsa knew exactly what had changed. When she'd got back from Lenny's, she'd not wanted to unpack, to look at the tiny rhinestone costume she'd worn that night. But she knew she had to face her demons at some point, and she pulled out the large black leather bag. Slowly, she dragged the zip across the bag to open it. She blinked as she stared and stared at its contents. Dropping her hand inside, she pulled out wads of money, big bundles of it. She held it up to her nose and inhaled the smell from it. A smirk appeared across her face as she quickly rammed the money back inside the bag. She held her head high. This was her father's last and only gift to her.

I'll show them all when I open my own club, she thought. Just wait. One day soon, I'll be the biggest name Manchester has ever seen. Nobody will ever forget me. Trust me, I'm no tease. It's just a matter of time.

Acknowledgements

I would like to thank my husband James as well as my children: Ashley, Blake, Declan and Darcy for always supporting me.

My mother Margaret who is the strongest woman I know for her continuous support.

A big massive thank you to all at HarperNorth who believed in my stories and made my dream a reality. Genevieve, Megan and Alice you are all amazing.

A big thanks to John Ireland and Ashley Shaw from Empire Publications who published my earlier 20 novels.

And finally a huge thank you to all my readers, your support has been amazing and I'm forever thankful.

Harper North

Book Credits

HarperNorth would like to thank the following staff and contributors for their involvement in making this book a reality:

Hannah Avery
Fionnuala Barrett
Claire Boal
Charlotte Brown
Sarah Burke
Alan Cracknell
Jonathan de Peyer
Anna Derkacz
Tom Dunstan
Kate Elton
Mick Fawcett
Simon Gerratt
Monica Green
CJ Harter

Paige Henderson
Graham Holmes
Megan Jones
Jean-Marie Kelly
Nicky Lovick
Oliver Malcolm
Alice Murphy-Pyle
Adam Murray
Genevieve Pegg
Agnes Rigou
Florence Shepherd
Emma Sullivan
Katrina Troy
Sarah Whittaker

For more unmissable reads,
sign up to the HarperNorth newsletter at
www.harpernorth.co.uk

or find us on Twitter at
@HarperNorthUK

**Harper
North**